A PLUME BOOK

FIFTEEN MINUTES OF SHAME

LISA DAILY is a real-life TV relationships expert and the author of *Stop Getting Dumped! All You Need to Know to Make Men Fall Madly in Love with You and Marry "The One" in 3 Years or Less*. She's a syndicated relationships columnist who's been seen everywhere from *iVillage Live* to MTV to *Entertainment Tonight,* and quoted everywhere from *Cosmopolitan* and *US Weekly* to the *New York Times*. Women from sixteen to sixty flock to Lisa's Dreamgirl Academy classes across the country. Lisa lives in Florida with her husband and two children; this is her first novel. For more, visit www.lisadaily.com.

Praise for *Fifteen Minutes of Shame*

"What happens when the queen of dating is cheated on, dumped, and humiliated? *Fifteen Minutes of Shame* is a great story teeming with all the dishy voyeuristic detail we love about behind-the-scenes, is-it-true-or-isn't-it novels, coupled with the hilarious and practical real-life dating tips Lisa Daily is famous for."

—Lisa Earle McLeod, syndicated columnist, *Buffalo News*

"This book is going to be a bestseller. I loved *Fifteen Minutes of Shame*, and I don't know a woman who wouldn't."

—Michael Alvear,
syndicated columnist and star of HBO's *Sex Inspectors*

"Lisa Daily puts the 'pop' back into pop culture."

—Marci Wise, WFLA Tampa

Praise for *Stop Getting Dumped!*

"What makes this book different from the bestselling *Rules* is that it's written in a more uplifting, less sanctimonious tone . . ."

—*New York Daily News*

"Packed with tips on how to get—and keep—the man of your dreams."

—*New Woman*

"Lisa Daily writes like she's your best girlfriend or big sister offering logical, witty advice that will have you feeling smarter, stronger, and in control of your own destiny."

—Brenda Ross, About.com Guide to Dating

"Even if your guy did try to sneak a peek at the secrets in *Stop Getting Dumped!* all he would find would be a recipe for a confident, well-balanced woman who takes the time for pedicure pampering, knows how to be a best friend, and, as the title of chapter 12 suggests, 'doesn't take any crap.'" —*Tampa Tribune*

"Stand back and watch the men come running."

—*Milwaukee Journal-Sentinel*

"A runaway success . . . America's latest authority on dating."

—*64 Magazine*

"Forget Bridget Jones's Chardonnay and cigarettes—the latest solution to romantic predicaments is *Stop Getting Dumped!*"

—*London Daily Telegraph*

"If all your love affairs end in tears, a brilliant new book could change your life." —*Sunday Express* (London)

Fifteen Minutes of Shame

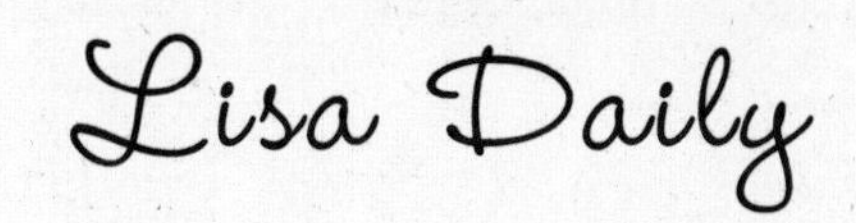

A PLUME BOOK

PLUME
Published by Penguin Group
Penguin Group (USA) Inc., 375 Hudson Street, New York, New York 10014, U.S.A.
Penguin Group (Canada), 90 Eglinton Avenue East, Suite 700, Toronto, Ontario, Canada M4P 2Y3
(a division of Pearson Penguin Canada Inc.)
Penguin Books Ltd., 80 Strand, London WC2R 0RL, England
Penguin Ireland, 25 St Stephen's Green, Dublin 2, Ireland (a division of Penguin Books Ltd.)
Penguin Group (Australia), 250 Camberwell Road, Camberwell, Victoria 3124, Australia (a division of Pearson Australia Group Pty. Ltd.)
Penguin Books India Pvt. Ltd., 11 Community Centre, Panchsheel Park, New Delhi – 110 017, India
Penguin Books (NZ), 67 Apollo Drive, Rosedale, North Shore 0632, New Zealand
(a division of Pearson New Zealand Ltd.)
Penguin Books (South Africa) (Pty.) Ltd., 24 Sturdee Avenue, Rosebank, Johannesburg 2196, South Africa

Penguin Books Ltd., Registered Offices: 80 Strand, London WC2R 0RL, England

First published by Plume, a member of Penguin Group (USA) Inc.

First Printing, April 2008
10 9 8 7 6 5 4 3 2 1

LIBRARY OF CONGRESS CATALOGING-IN-PUBLICATION DATA
Daily, Lisa.
Fifteen minutes of shame / Lisa Daily.
p. cm.
ISBN 978-0-452-28913-0
1. Reality television programs—Fiction. 2. Dating (Social customs)—Fiction.
3. Divorce—Fiction. 4. Women—Fiction. I. Title.
PS3604.A347F54 2008
813'.6—dc22 2007035413

Printed in the United States of America
Set in Bembo with display set in Wendy Medium
Designed by Leonard Telesca

PUBLISHER'S NOTE
This is a work of fiction. Names, characters, places, and incidents are either the product of the author's imagination or are used fictitiously, and any resemblance to actual persons, living or dead, business establishments, events, or locales is entirely coincidental.

To Elle, Quinn, and Tom,
for giving me a million minutes of bliss.

To Mom,
for giving me a million minutes of inspiration.

To Lisa Earle McLeod,
for giving me a million minutes of laughter.
And entirely too much to think about.

Fifteen Minutes of Shame

You'll Never Meet Prince Charming Unless You're Ready to Go to the Ball

Refresh your lipstick throughout the day. Run a brush through your hair before you hit the street. Check your shoes for toilet paper before you leave a public restroom. Be prepared. That way, if you do end up meeting Mr. Right while you're out walking the dog, you won't have to strategically veil your face with your hand because you've got that little Fu Manchu thing growing on your chin.

—*The Dreamgirl Academy*

Chapter 1

"I'm utterly humiliated."

I hiss this to my best friend Jules as I squat behind the smelly dumpster of a Gas-N-Go, trying to sneak a glimpse of my husband without getting caught.

"Damn."

He glances in the general direction of the dumpster and I panic. I nearly fall over backward and accidentally drop my cell phone into a murky puddle. It hasn't rained in weeks, and I fear toxic waste, or worse, old convenience store hot-dog water, as I fish out my phone and wipe it off on my sweatpants. It leaves a sort of greenish smear, and I don't even want to imagine what it could be.

Last week I was on national television, wearing a cute little non-mommy outfit and my favorite pair of Christian Louboutins, talking about how every woman deserves a fabulous life, and how they too can snag the man of their dreams. This week I'm crouching in filth, looking a lot like a homeless person because I forgot it was my turn to drive carpool this morning and I rushed out of the house wearing dirty sweatpants, the WHO'S YOUR DADDY? T-shirt I slept in, and a pair of sparkly pink flip-flops. I can't remember brushing my hair. Or my teeth.

"Are you there?" I whisper to Jules. "Sorry, I dropped the phone."

"What on this earth are you doin'?" she asks, in that honey-dipped drawl all men melt for. Jules is a flesh-and-blood, eighth-generation Southern belle. She hasn't left the house without earrings since puberty. Any two-hour car ride with her includes a picnic basket fully stocked with ham biscuits. She's always polite, and she's always enviable. Jules would never be caught squatting behind a dumpster, spying on her husband in her pajamas.

The truth is, I have no idea what I'm doing.

"He's supposed to be in Atlanta." I can feel myself rambling, "I packed his suitcase myself."

"Are you absolutely sure it's him?" Jules responds gently. "Maybe it's just someone who looks a lot like him."

"You mean like an evil twin?" I crack. "No, I saw him straight on. It's Will."

Something is definitely up. Will exits the store carrying a small paper bag. He looks both ways before stepping off the curb and then opens the door of his silver SUV and slides into the driver's seat. What's in the bag? I wonder. Condoms? A microwave burrito?

"Maybe he's taking a later flight," Jules offered.

"Maybe." I don't think so. We live in Sarasota, a small city with a small airport. Usually the first flight is the last flight. Plus, Will does this Atlanta trip at least once a week for a liquor client based in Georgia. His flight leaves at 8:37 in the morning and he usually makes it home the next morning around the same time.

"Damn." I can't decide if I should hop back into my car and follow him to see where he's going, or throw myself in front of his car so he knows he's been busted. I panic and the moment passes. He drives off, and I stand, frozen in my puddle of muck until his car passes the intersection. My big opportunity to catch him in the act of whatever's keeping him from Atlanta has vanished. I feel like a jerk, but I don't know if I could stomach whatever I might learn.

Normally, Will is not the kind of husband you worry about. He's a blue-suit-wearing/sex-on-Friday/baseball-on-Saturday kind of guy. But my imagination starts churning and I envision all sorts of sinister possibilities: He's having an affair. He's an undercover agent for the CIA. He's lost his biggest client and he's too chickenshit to tell me. I feel the early tinglings of panic.

"Or," says Jules, "maybe his trip just got canceled." Leave it to Jules to be rational. "Why don't you call him?"

Why don't I call him? Genius! Jules is a genius! I'll just call him and he'll explain everything and we'll laugh about the whole thing. I hang up with Jules and speed-dial Will. No answer. Crap.

His phone clicks over to voicemail immediately, which means the damned thing isn't even turned on.

I get back into my car, which is parked high-speed-chase-style behind the dumpster. (Okay, so I wasn't exactly focused on my parallel parking skills this morning when I swerved into the Gas-N-Go.) I was driving home after dropping off our carpool kids at school and almost drove over the median when I saw Will's car pull into the parking lot.

As I head home, I try to clear my mind and think rationally. I take a deep breath and try to figure out how I've gone from "happily ever after" to panicking that my husband is an international terrorist/philanderer/pathological liar within the space of a few minutes.

It's probably nothing. Crap, it's definitely something.

I pull in to our gated community, slowing down so that the scanner can read the bar code on the side of my gas-guzzling mommymobile. I inch forward until the nose of my car is just inches from the flimsy stick otherwise known as the "gate" designed to keep all manner of undesirables out of my neighborhood. What's funny is that where I live in Florida, nearly all of the communities are gated communities. I'm not sure that we even have "undesirables." If we do, knowing my neighbors, they're special-ordered from Barney's. If you travel down any semi-main road here you'll see guard shacks and electric gates every few miles. The parking lots at Whole Foods, Nuovo, and Siesta Beach are all populated with cars bearing a telltale bar-code sticker on the rear passenger window.

Sometimes, I can hardly believe I live here. Overnight, I went from a single-girl shoe box of an apartment (apropos, I think, since my most prized possessions were primarily shoes), where I felt like I'd hit the jackpot if I was lucky enough to get an up-close parking space or an open lounge chair at the pool, straight to suburbia (Do Not Pass Go), where my wedding ring and bar-code sticker grant me an all-access pass to the gated kingdom of Botox moms.

And although I never had trouble fitting in, even after three years, I still kind of feel like I don't really belong here.

I hit REDIAL on my phone. Will's voicemail clicks on. Again. The gate is stuck. Again. The guard is busy with the line of cars in the visitor's lane and doesn't look up from his clipboard. He waves three cars through, barely glancing up. Apparently, all you need is a pizza or a lawn mower to gain entrance to this gated haven in suburbia. The front of my car is now practically touching the gate. It's not moving. I roll down the window and wait patiently because I don't want to be one of "those" women—the ones who wave their manicured nails out the window for the backhanded salute, while they lean on the horn with their elbows, demanding priority service.

I try to catch the guard's eye, hoping a little smile and a wave will do the trick.

"That lane is for residents only," he shouts to me over the sound of a muffler-deficient station wagon filled with mops and Brazilian housekeepers.

"I am a resident." I shout back, smiling purposefully. "The gate is not working today." He rolls his eyes at me. Will and I have lived here for the entire three years we've been married. I go through this gate about six times a day. I call the guard shack about twice a day to add our friends, the bug man, the pool guy to "the list." The man with the clipboard is Frank. He has two kids and works the day shift at the north gate. He looks at me as though he has never seen me before.

"You need a sticker," he says authoritatively.

"I have a sticker. Can you please just raise the gate? I'm really in a hurry," I plead. All of a sudden, I'm flashing back to the scene from that old movie *Trading Places,* where Dan Aykroyd has just gotten out of jail, and when he gets to his house, not only will his key not work in the lock, but his butler pretends he's never seen him before. *Ohmygod, I'm going to have to move in with a hooker.*

"You need a sticker," he says again, pressing the magic button inside the guard shack.

Access at last. I peel through the gate, squealing the tires as I turn onto my street, popping my car into the garage like a pinball going down the chute for the last time. A wave of dread and denial washes over me like sewage.

Crap. Crap. Crap. Get it together. Get it together. Get it together.

Let's review, okay? What did I really see?

Generally, I try not to be the overreacting type. I am, in fact, a quite rational, thirty-one-year-old author and stepmother of two kids, Lilly and Aidan. Obviously, the Prince Charming I'd envisioned from the time I was eight years old was not exactly a divorced guy with two kids. But the kids I once thought would be a burden have turned out to be the center of my life.

Will is thirty-six, was formerly married to a formerly sane beauty queen (Miss Arkansas, if you must know), and we, the two of us, have custody of his kids, children I consider to be the most amazing six- and eight-year-old on the planet. (Of course, I'm crazy about them, so I may be a little biased.)

Will and I have been married three years. We met when I was on tour for my first book, *Secrets to Make the Guys Go Gaga,* and he was the PR guy who landed me a spot on *Soap Talk.* (Don't laugh, it's a real show.) After years of writing toothpaste jingles and doling out dating advice to my girlfriends over margaritas, I figured that a dating book was a good start to the dream I'd always had about becoming a "real" writer, not just someone who made a living spinning canned meat and golf spikes to the American public.

So, by sole virtue of my ability to turn a phrase and peg a loser at five hundred feet, I've now become a dating guru.

To be honest, I've spent my whole life trying to make sense of men. Both of my parents died in an accident when I was just a baby, and I was raised by my Grandma Vernie and her four sisters in an estrogen bubble. They were a wild, strong, loving, tight knot of Southern women; all of them had been married at one time to men they adored. Unfortunately, they were all widowed long before I hit kindergarten—husbands had a habit of croaking at very early ages in our family. Great Uncle Joe was a legend; he'd lived to the ripe old age of forty-three. Until junior high, my only personal experience with how the male sex was supposed to operate came from secondhand stories the aunties told me under the influence of bundt cake during our seven-hour Yahtzee marathons, late-night reruns of Gene Kelly movies, and old clippings they'd saved from 1950s issues of *Good Housekeeping* on how to keep your husband happy. The first of my beloved aunties, Ila Mae, passed away when I entered high school. My grandmother died the next year. By the time I was nineteen, they were all gone. And I found myself orphaned for the second time.

I thought that once I wrote the book, Oprah would call and I'd be instantly catapulted to fame and riches. (Which, I've since learned, is a common fantasy among clueless first-time authors.) Instead, it brought me to Will, who told me, "Unless you're a celebrity or a celebrity's personal trainer, nobody cares whether you wrote a book or not." When he booked me on *Soap Talk*, he told me, "I had to beg, borrow, and steal to get you this one."

I was grateful and horribly disappointed at the same time. Like finding out you've won a $5.7 million lottery, and then learning you'll be getting a nickel a week for 324 years.

Eventually, after a few years of dismal sales, the book took off and became a bestseller, surprising everyone including me. I was catapulted to the dating expert hall of fame. Producers and agents started calling, and suddenly I had a weekly guest spot on a big national TV show, my own radio call-in program, and even my own perfume. Two years after my book hit the shelves, I was recognizable to every woman in America under the age of sixty. Darby Vaughn: the Dr. Phil of Dating.

I dial Will's phone again, and this time he picks up on the first ring.

"Hey!" I say quickly, attempting to sound like my usual perky self, rather than the dumpster-diving maniac I've become in the last seventeen minutes or so.

"Hi, sweetheart," he answers offhandedly, "I can only talk for a second, my flight was delayed and I'm already late for the meeting."

"What do you mean? You're still here?" God, I'm an idiot. Talk about freaking out over nothing. A sensation of reprieve rushes over me, and I feel the sickly sweet relief of someone who's just stepped off the human centrifuge ride at the carnival.

"Did you miss your Starbucks this morning or something?" he teases, "I'm in Atlanta, remember?"

My heart drops. "Wait, you mean right now?"

"Jesus, Darby. I've only been making this same exact trip for two years. What's up with you today?"

"N-nothing," I choke out, and my brain starts spinning again. My mind goes from zero to divorce court in 3.6 seconds.

"Um, when will you be back in town?" I ask cautiously.

"Tomorrow morning, same as always," he snaps, and then softens. "Sorry, Darby, I don't mean to be so cranky. I had a bad flight and it's just sort of put a damper on my morning."

"It's okay . . ." I say numbly, unable to think of anything else at the moment.

"Hey babe, I've gotta run. Love you, love the kids." His phone snaps off before I have a chance to respond. Instead, I throw up.

I scramble to aim for my open car window. Bad aim or bad luck, I miss the mark and vomit oozes down the inside of my door and into the window crack.

I am *not* going to have a breakdown in my three-car garage.

Are You Crazy, or Is He Cheating?

by Darby Vaughn

The weird hang-up calls. The erratic work hours. The stories that just don't quite add up.

You have the gnawing, sickly feeling that your man is cheating on you. But how do you know for sure? Finding signs of cheating is like pulling a stray piece of yarn in a pair of socks. It only takes one good yank, and the whole thing starts to unravel.

Telephone Tyrant: Watch out for the prepaid cell phone or pager (no bill, no evidence), and odd phone numbers found in his pockets, written on receipts or scraps of paper. Does he call at all hours? Hang up on you when he's mad? Both are signs of a lack of impulse control.

Blaming Boy: His girlfriend is too jealous, his boss is too stupid, and the rest of the planet just doesn't get it. Does your guy think he can do no wrong? When the Blaming Boy breaks the rules, it's the rule that was wrong, not him. He may have cheated, but it's your fault.

Fashionista Flame: Has your guy starting working out after six years of bliss on the couch? Does he have a sudden interest in Armani when nacho-cheese-covered chinos have always been just fine? Whether it's a new gym membership or a new cologne, big appearance changes can mean big trouble.

Workaholic Wooer: He works late all the time, or the big boss needs him to come in on Saturday *again*. Seventy percent of affairs happen on the job—even if he's not fooling around at work, he may be using it as a cover.

What should you do if you suspect your guy is cheating? Throw his clothes out on the lawn? Quit your job and trail him like a cop on *Law & Order*? Never confront your guy until you've got solid proof; otherwise he'll just deny it. Collect as much evidence as you can, and then make him face facts. The only way to move forward is to get it all on the table.

Better still, go ahead and throw his clothes on the lawn. If you stay with a cheater, you've taught him that he can sleep around and you'll take him back. Find somebody faithful. Otherwise you're just cheating yourself.

Chapter 2

I sit obsessing in my car for an indeterminate period of time, unable to move. I will not let myself cry. Eventually the stench of car-heated vomit becomes stronger than my inertia, and I drag my nervous breakdown into the house.

I drop my purse on my desk and numbly sit down in front of my computer. As I weed through Viagra spam and PTA notices in my e-mail it hits me: *What am I doing? My husband is probably cheating on me—why the hell am I checking my e-mail?*

I have five hours before the kids get home from school to pull myself together. My initial thought is to climb into bed and sob myself dry for the rest of the day, but I won't let myself. Terror is one hell of a motivator. I need to figure out what's going on. Why would he lie?

I call Jules and ask her to pick up the kids after school and bring them to her house until after dinnertime.

"What happened?" she asks quietly, feeling the despair in my voice.

"He lied about being in Atlanta. I can't talk about it right now. I need to get to the bottom of this," I sputter.

"Take all the time you need," she soothes. "Let me know if you want the kids to spend the night."

"Thanks," I say. "I really want to be with them tonight. I just need to pull myself together before I bring them home."

"Whatever you need, darlin'," she says gently, "whatever you need."

"You're a good friend," I choke out over the lump in my throat. I've now bought myself nine hours to figure out why Will lied about being in Atlanta.

Option One: He's planning a big trip to Bora Bora, or a surprise luau or some other sweet, husbandly thing to celebrate the end of my book tour in two weeks.

Option Two: He's having an affair. (Hey, it's not pretty, but I'm a realist.)

Option Three: Something not horrible, to be named later.

Obviously, I'm rooting for Option One, an all-expenses-paid trip to somewhere romantic and relaxing, the kind of place where no one looks at you like you're the lost cast member of *WKRP in Cincinnati* if you happen to order a banana daiquiri. Or two.

I start in Will's home office, which seems the most obvious place for him to hide something. He always bitches if the cleaning lady tries to straighten his desk, or if the kids rummage through it for colored pens. It's the one place in the house where I never go. So, naturally, it's the first place I think to look.

I'm feeling a little like sleuth-babe Bailey Weggins as I ransack desk drawers and file cabinets, not exactly sure of what I'm looking for. Receipts seem an obvious choice, and I rummage around, trying to figure out which drawer Will keeps the credit card bills in. I hate paying bills, always have, the never-ending process of writing checks and balancing accounts is just so tedious. It felt like I'd hit the matrimonial jackpot early in our marriage when

Will started taking care of those things: He takes out the trash. He fixes the disposal when it gets clogged. He pays the bills. Good-bye plumber, hello married life. Usually I just stack the mail on the hall table, and Will whisks it all away when he comes home each night: the Bill Fairy. Now, I'm wishing I'd paid a little more attention. Fabulous. I'm a cliché.

After riffling through four file drawers of old press releases and a stash of dirty magazines tucked into a folder marked SPAM ACCOUNT, I finally hit pay dirt. The bottom drawer is locked.

I hunt around his desk drawer for the key and find it easily, floating around with the ballpoint pens and paper clips. Why do people lock their filing cabinets and then put the key in the most obvious place in the room?

The key fits easily into the lock, and I slide the heavy drawer out gingerly. Our bills and bank statements are all filed neatly and categorized in color-coded file folders.

I carefully sift through each file, looking for anything suspicious. The Visa bill contains lots of flower orders, but that's nothing unusual. As a publicist, Will routinely sends flowers to clients, potential clients, TV producers, and anybody else he's trying to schmooze. When Will and I first started dating, he sent me a bouquet of pink tulips every week, and even now that we've been married for three years, there's always a big VIP bouquet waiting for me each time I check in to a hotel. All of my friends think Will is the most romantic guy on the planet.

And now, I'm digging through a locked file cabinet.

Next come the phone bills. Our home phone bill is nothing surprising except for a few hour-long calls to Will's ex-wife, Gigi. His cell phone is more of the same, the calls evenly divided between me, Will's assistant, Kendall, and again, Gigi. Nothing odd there. Gigi regularly requires a great deal of attention, and since

Will has built his life's work around his ability to soothe needy authors and Hollywood types, he takes her drama of the month in stride.

Their divorce settlement stipulates that Will must continue to act as Gigi's publicist until such time as she no longer requires his services. Welcome to the modern divorce: half the assets, all the shrimp forks, and free publicity in perpetuity.

Gigi and Will—despite the fact that they had a nasty divorce, and the lovely Gigi is just the tiniest bit off her rocker—have a reasonably serviceable relationship. Thankfully, they're both pretty focused on what's best for Lilly and Aidan. Will's biggest fear when the marriage fell apart was that he'd be relegated to being one of those "summer dads" who only see their kids at Christmas and summer breaks, especially since Gigi's first order of business was to move away from Florida to Los Angeles, where she could pursue her acting career.

As luck would have it, Gigi immediately snagged a part on a reality show where she went to live on an island with a bunch of weird strangers and had to eat bugs and bark to earn an extended stay. Score one for Will, a successful, business-owning member of the community who convinced a judge that it would be better for the kids if they stayed in Sarasota with him, in light of the fact that Gigi's reality-show tent wasn't exactly kid-friendly. Will was granted full custody. We met one year to the day after his divorce was final.

Next, I search the file marked FREQUENT FLYER and scrutinize the stack of statements, which is nearly an inch thick. Because we live in Florida, it is practically impossible to leave the state without boarding a Delta aircraft. And because Will travels so much on business, his frequent flyer points generally number in the hundreds of thousands. I check this month's statement against last month's and the month before. Will should have made about twelve trips to Atlanta in the last three months, but his account is credited for only four. Eight trips short. My heart starts pounding faster. I check the three months before that. Again, he should have made around twelve or thirteen trips, but his frequent flyer account is credited for only five. Seven, or maybe eight trips missing. Which means my husband has spent the night away from home *fifteen times* in the last six months and I have no idea where he's been sleeping.

Crap.

I run back to my desk, yank my pink Daytimer out of my bag, and sprint back to Will's office, where the paper trail is scattered around the room. I yank a legal pad off Will's huge mahogany desk and flip open the calendar page to check for the missing trips. I start comparing dates from my calendar to those on the Delta statement and scribbling them down on the pad. I go back through another six months of statements, but those seem to be in order. When I finish compiling the list of dates when Will was MIA (Missing in Atlanta) I have a total of sixteen dates. I pull the file containing our credit card statements and look up the dates for the trips Will didn't make.

On the first three dates, there are no charges at all on his card. (And even if there was some glitch on the airline miles, or if he flew a different airline, he'd still need to rent a car, right?) On the next date, there is one charge, for $182 at the Vernona restaurant at the Ritz-Carlton, right here in Sarasota. I start to freak a little when I see the Ritz-Carlton, but clarity returns when I realize that a) it's a restaurant charge and b) you can't *get* a room at the Ritz-Carlton for $182. Plus, it's not exactly the type of place that rents by the hour.

I scan his credit card bills for the other missing dates and gasp to find *seven* more restaurant charges from the Ritz-Carlton, one of which totals $783. What sort of happy surprise could possibly require thousands of dollars' worth of stealth dinners?

I suddenly feel sick again.

I scramble to get to the bathroom and sit on the floor staring into the water in the toilet bowl for twenty minutes. When the churning in my stomach passes, I lay exhausted, too spent to cry, on the bathroom tiles. The faint scent of Fabuloso stings my nostrils, and I start to feel nauseated again.

I love Will as much as I ever thought possible, and I can't fathom the idea that he could deceive me. My life with Will and the kids feels more like family to me than anything I've experienced since my grandmother died. Sure, it took me a few months (okay, years) to manage the whole stepmom gig. The kids were three and five when we got married, and Will has always traveled frequently for work, so I was on my own with Lilly and Aidan quite a lot. Before I came along, Will had a full-time nanny, but I was really happy to jump right into the role of mother. Lilly and Aidan are such great kids, and the poor things had already been through so much: First they were abandoned by their globetrotting reality-show mom, followed by six days a week with a nanny. I felt like I was the answer to their prayers, and they were the answer to mine. Frankly, I was happy to step in.

After a couple of years, most moms are beginning to figure things out and hit their stride, but there I was, starting from scratch, completely unaware of the consequences of mixing Kate Spade and juice boxes, without that helpful "ramping up to motherhood" period right after the baby is born, when a real mom learns to function well without sleep or showers. I always feel much less together than the moms who have had their babies from the very start, but I'm so crazy about the kids that I can't imagine how I ever lived without them.

Will's charms were hard to resist. Handsome, charismatic, romantic. He has a dazzling smile, and he makes me laugh in a way no one else can. I love how his eyes sparkle when he's made one of his wry little observations, and that he always looks pulled together, as though he just popped out of a photo shoot for Banana Republic or Ralph Lauren. When he spoons up against me at night, I finally feel like I belong somewhere. He knows most of my stories, he's fond of my weirdnesses—like the fact that I'm always freezing, even when it's eighty degrees outside, or that I can't stand it if anyone happens to touch my skin with their toenails (a method of torture for me that both Will and the kids find hilariously amusing for hours on end). He loves to talk. He's a great father. And he has as much fun at the ballet as he does at a Devil Rays game. Men admire him, women drool over him. Ask any woman in my neighborhood—hell, on the planet—and they'd say Will is the perfect husband.

When I was single, I looked forward to married life with great expectations. I imagined that married bliss looked a lot like a Pottery Barn catalog, complete with shed-free chocolate labs, beach barbecues with a handsome, adoring husband who rakes in $200K and still makes it home in plenty of time for every family event, and two charming, mannerly children who wipe their feet in the mudroom and play together for hours without conflict in the $900 lemonade stand.

I thought I'd finally stepped into that life.

Now, I'm having a hard time visualizing the lovely blonde mom from the catalog, down on her hands and knees on the smart Sisal Rug ($349), digging through the Bedford Desk ($899) for evidence of infidelity, while the family dog naps nearby (Cabana Stripe Dog Bed, $89).

I'm teetering but not quite ready to accept the possibility that Will might be having an affair. A dreadful feeling has begun to seep in: My charmed life may be circling the drain.

Usually, I'm not prone to jump to conclusions, but after four years of working as a dating expert, I've heard every story and seen every sign of impending relationship disaster. In my profession, I'd have to be some kind of idiot not to pay attention to clues this obvious.

Men generally only lie to their wives about two subjects: money and sex. Although I'm not ready to rule anything out, I'm guessing that if money were the problem, Will wouldn't be drowning his sorrows in Veuve at the Ritz-Carlton. Which leaves sex.

I pull myself up on the sink, splash some cool water on my face, and scrub the inside of my mouth with a toothbrush. I need to think this through. Numbly, I change out of my carpool-wear, throw on a pretty sundress, and run a brush through my hair. (I know, it probably seems weird to fuss with my hair at a time like this, but I come from a long line of Southern women who trained me from birth to believe that any crisis is best handled with fresh lipstick and a nice hairdo.) For a minute, I consider calling Jules to report what I've found out and get her forgiving, rational take on the matter, but a part of me is embarrassed to admit what I've learned, and I'm completely mortified to admit I've sunk to snooping on my husband. I stare at my ruddy-eyed reflection, dabbing concealer at the mess, and suddenly I realize what I need to do.

I have to get to Will's office.

To Snoop or Not to Snoop?

By Darby Vaughn

Okay, let's get past the fact that in our greatest moments of weakness or weirdness most of us *may* have *inadvertently* looked through our guy's bedside table (for hand lotion!) while he was otherwise occupied, or casually inventoried the dry-cleaning receipts, straw wrappers, and lint in his jacket pocket. But here's the bottom line: Snooping is bad. Why do we snoop? Rampant insecurity and female intuition.

Insecurity: Things are going great, but that voice in your head tells you this guy can't possibly be as good as he seems. He must be hiding something. So you glance, casually at first, at the stack of mail on his countertop, or poke your fingers in between the cushions of his couch while he's pouring the wine. Then, while he runs out to pick up your pizza with extra cheese, you conduct an intensive, all-out search mission that could rival the CIA.

This will always get you into trouble. First, it's not very nice. Second, you could get caught, which would be both horribly embarrassing and difficult to explain. Last, if you do find something out of the ordinary, even if it's nothing, it will gnaw away at you like a flesh-eating bacteria. Eventually you'll crack and interrogate your guy on how he came to be in possession of a diamond-studded nipple ring or a ticket stub to *Music & Lyrics*. And then you'll be forced to explain exactly how you know what you know. He will likely have a completely logical explanation for whatever it is you managed to find, and you will have humiliated and tormented yourself for nothing.

Female Intuition: There is one good reason to snoop: to confirm what you already know. As in, you're pretty damned sure he's cheating and you need solid proof. Give some serious thought to why you feel this way. Do you always feel this way? Or is it just this guy that's causing you to fret? Do you have actual evidence of infidelity, or a creeping "something's not right" feeling lingering in your gut? Trust your instinct and figure out what's bugging you. In the end (or in the darkness of the closet), only you can answer the question of whether you should snoop. Whatever you decide, the first place you should look is in the mirror.

Chapter 3

It's one-thirty in the afternoon and I'm doing 75 in the vomit-mobile.

Clearly, my quickie-clean in the garage with the carpet shampooer did not do the trick. Even with the windows down, the stench, now ripe from baking for four hours at 87 degrees, is completely overpowering.

Since Will is pretending to be out of town, I know the coast is clear for me to poke around in his office. I consider a brief stopover at the auto detailer to get rid of the sick smell, or at least mask it with some synthetic alternative like Essence of Pine Tree or Lemon Meringue Pie, but I can't withstand the escalating suspense at what I might find in Will's office, and I figure I'll suffer the rest of the ten-minute drive hanging my head out the window like a dog.

I try to distract myself from the stench by formulating a plan of attack. I arrive at Will's offices a few minutes later, park in his spot, and hurry through the front door.

"Hey, Darby!" says Kendall, Will's adorably enthusiastic assistant. "How's my favorite relationship expert today?"

Oh, the shame.

I like Kendall, I always have. She has been Will's assistant for almost six years, and despite the fact that many women would feel uncomfortable with their husbands spending ten hours a day with a pretty, smart, younger, wickedly funny blonde, I don't mind at all. I'm not a jealous person, and I don't believe that mere proximity automatically begets infidelity. Kendall worked for Will two whole years before I met him, and I figure if the two of them were going to hit it off romantically, it would have happened long before I showed up. Kendall knows Will better than almost anyone, she's fabulously competent, and she's just all-around nice. When Will and I first started dating, she'd leave covert messages on my cell phone about some sweet thing or other that Will had said about me that day. The two of us became fast friends; we chat on the phone regularly and get together for lunch and shopping.

She also makes all of Will's flight arrangements, so I know she knows exactly where he's been going. Or not.

She is sitting at her desk, and I'm standing a few feet away from her. I look her directly in the eye and ask firmly, "Kendall, what's going on? Where is Will?"

Her hand wobbles a bit, and she begins fumbling with papers on her desk, unwilling to meet my eyes. "Um . . . Atlanta, right?" Looking back at me awkwardly, she forces a weak smile. She shuffles through her desk drawer again, primarily, I think, so she doesn't have to look directly at me.

I don't blink, but move my face lower so that I meet her eyes.

"I know he's not in Atlanta today," I state firmly. She seems confused, even bewildered. "Kendall," I say very slowly, "what do you know?"

She looks stricken, and her eyes dart around the room for a few seconds as though she might try to run away. Finally she looks back at me, meets my gaze, as big tears begin to form in her pale blue eyes.

"Darby," she sobs, "I'm so sorry."

Oh. My. God.

I feel as though the air is being squashed out of my lungs. My mind starts whirling, with horrible, panicky thoughts spewing out like Lotto balls.

I sink into the chair across from her, steadying myself on her desk. Biting my lower lip to distract myself from the growing lump in my chest, I force myself to ask the question I dread the answer to: "Kendall, what are you sorry about?"

She starts to cry, big rackety sobs punctuated by desperate, sucking draws of breath, unable to speak. I watch her cry, bouncing uncontrollably between feeling sympathy for my friend, who is so clearly distressed, and utter panic about whatever could be causing her plight.

I sit there for what feels like forever, watching her sob, waiting for her answer. I reach out to touch her shoulder, and we sit like that for a few minutes until she is able to compose herself enough to speak.

"Darby, I didn't know what to do. I was afraid he'd fire me if I told you."

"Told me what?"

"He's been meeting with Sol Weinstein for three months." She exhales, as if lightened to have finally said the words out loud.

A wave of much-needed relief bubbles over me, and I finally take a full breath. Will told me months ago that Sol had become a publicity client, but it was no wonder she was so troubled. Sol Weinstein is the most prominent divorce attorney in south

Florida. In Sarasota, a city populated with wealthy businessmen on the MILF-of-the-Month plan, marriage here was more likely to resemble a two-year lease than a lifetime commitment. Divorce attorneys are plenty and popular, and whichever attorney snags the most TV time usually pulls in the grandest fees. Sol is the king. He represents all the high-profile cases, and he's notoriously known all along the coast as the Nup Buster because he can always find a way to crack a prenuptial agreement if it means a bigger settlement for his client. Many of the society girls keep Sol on permanent retainer even when they are between husbands, just in case. Better to be out a couple thousand a month in fees than scramble at the first sign of trouble and have your outgoing spouse sign him first. And, although he is a bit of a slick character, he'd be a profitable client for Will. If nothing else, Sol knows how to work the media. He is a publicist's dream.

"Oh, sweetie! You poor thing!" I put my arm around Kendall to console her. "That's what you're worried about? It's nothing! Sol's a client."

She shudders and looks up at me gravely. "That's what Will told me, too, but I keep the firm's books. If Sol is our client, why is he billing *us*?"

I sit stunned for about two minutes in shock and disappointment before my brain clicks into action.

"Show me the bills."

Kendall riffles through a filing cabinet and pulls out a small stack of invoices from Weinstein, Cabbott & Ringling totaling around $4,000 for legal services over the last few months. Reaching for the phone on her desk, I dial the number on Sol's letterhead.

"Excuse me," I say politely to the receptionist at Sol's massive law firm, "would you mind giving me the name of Mr. Weinstein's publicist? Who would I speak with to schedule an interview with him?"

Kendall leans forward inquisitively as I thank the receptionist and hang up, waiting for me to relay the answer. "Sol does his own publicity."

No Atlanta. No Sol. The worst of it is that I'm starting to feel like we're just scratching the surface. Kendall says she knew something was up, but she wasn't sure what. She was afraid to tell me that she suspected Will had lied about why he was meeting with Sol because she feared for her job, nor did she want to pry into something so private as possible trouble in our marriage if I knew about it but wasn't ready to talk about it.

Then, Kendall assuages some of the guilt she's felt over the last three months by helping me ransack Will's office to look for more clues about what the hell he's been up to.

When I ask her if she knows anything about the dinners at the Ritz-Carlton on the dates Will was supposed to be in Atlanta, the blood drains from her face.

"What do you mean?" she asks, tentatively. "He's been staying at the Ritz-Carlton on the nights he's supposed to be in Atlanta?"

"No, he's been eating there." I tell her about the restaurant charges on his credit card bill, but that there don't seem to be any room charges.

"We have a corporate account with the Ritz," she says. "If he were staying at the hotel, the bills would come through the office." She double-checks the dates on the Ritz-Carlton ledger. No charges for the dates in question.

"What about his trips to Atlanta?" I ask.

"I don't understand. What makes you think he's not going to Atlanta?"

"I saw him in town this morning, when he should have been on his flight. Thirty minutes later, on the phone, he claimed to be in Atlanta. Plus, according to his frequent-flyer account, he's missed sixteen trips in the last six months."

"That's so weird," says Kendall, with a puzzled look on her face, "because we've bought airline tickets for his trip every week."

After three hours, we've found nothing.

I need a plan, and I need one fast. I have to leave the day after tomorrow to do the final leg of my book tour, so if I don't find out in the next day and a half what's going on, I'm going to have to suffer with the knowledge that my husband is lying to me for two whole weeks before I get back home. The last seven hours have been excruciating. I don't think I can stand two more weeks of this.

On the other hand, if I confront him tomorrow and he tells me he's having an affair or some other horrible thing, I would have to live with that nightmare while I figure out what to do next, pretending that everything is just grand, while I travel around the country being interviewed on television and radio about the joys of love. Me, Darby Vaughn, the poster child for successful relationships. My stomach does a flip-flop at the thought.

Kendall and I talk it over, and agree that I should just put my head down and make it through the end of the book tour.

"You've got to keep focused on this tour," says Kendall. "This is a gigantic opportunity for you. There's a lot at stake."

"I know," I say, "you're right."

I'm completely stoked about this trip because I'm actually booked on the *Today* show, which is one third of the Literary Holy Trinity that every author aspires to: *Oprah, Today,* the *New York Times* bestseller list.

Getting booked on *Today* is huge. I feel completely validated as a writer, as a dating expert, as a human being. It's a big deal. It means I'm finally at the top: Millions of fans crowding into bookstores. A serious bump up to the A-list parties. John Grisham's home number in my Rolodex. (Okay, I'm not sure about that one, but hey, a girl can dream.)

Maybe I'm overreacting about this situation with Will. Maybe there's a perfectly reasonable explanation for all of this. I love Will, and I should trust him. Kendall has known Will for a long time, and we both know him to be a basically good guy. I have never had a reason before not to trust him. Or . . . maybe he's a lying, cheating pig.

Rule number one when dealing with a cheater is to get irrefutable proof before you confront them. If you confront them with your suspicions without proof, they'll deny everything and work harder to cover their tracks. The best strategy is to collect all the evidence you can and back them into a corner. You can't move forward until you know for sure.

I take a deep breath and try to regroup. The only thing I'm certain of now is that my husband is apparently very fond of eating dinner at the Ritz. And that I still have no idea exactly where he's been sleeping. But, basically, I know nothing.

Kendall agrees the Atlanta thing is weird, but she feels pretty sure he's not having an affair, because there have been no strange women regularly calling the office. She handles most of the day-to-day client calls, so she'd likely notice anything out of the ordinary. She wonders out loud if the airline miles might just be an error of some type, maybe the travel agent forgot to key in his frequent-flyer number. She promises to call the agency the next morning and check it out.

I need some time to cool off. Maybe I've gotten a little

carried away with the whole amateur investigator thing. I'm sure I saw Will this morning, but I'm not sure of anything else. If I give it some time, and whatever is happening doesn't make any more sense than it does now, I'll figure out a way to find out what's really going on. In the meantime, the tour will be stressful enough, I don't really know enough to confront Will about anything, and the last thing I want to do is start something before my trip that would upset the kids.

The kids!

I check my watch, almost six. Thank God for Jules, who will be feeding them dinner about now. I hug Kendall, thank her for her help, and we agree that neither one of us will ever mention this little escapade to Will.

Kendall wants to keep her job as much as I want to keep my husband. Who can blame either of us?

I leave the office, jump into the car, and swing through the car wash on the way home. The attendant opens my door, shuddering at the odor, takes one knowing look at the two booster seats in the back of my SUV, sighs, and tells me he'll have the car cleaned in twenty minutes. I debate for a half second whether to confess to the mess, deciding instead to keep my mouth shut and drive on through. A half hour later, I drive away in a freshly sanitized automobile with a cardboard orange swinging from my rearview mirror, working its magic.

By the time I get to Jules's house, it's almost seven. I pop through the front door and Lilly and Aidan run into my arms smelling of macaroni and chocolate cake. I breathe deeply, inhaling their sweetness. I love these little monkeys.

Jules and I have a quiet conversation in the corner of the kitchen while the kids gather their shoes and school backpacks.

"Everything all right?" she asks cautiously. I relay the day's events to her in a way that makes me seem slightly more sane and less pathetic than I actually feel, but that covers the low points all the same.

Jules agrees that taking a few weeks to assess the situation is the best plan. "Don't you worry, darlin'," she drawls. "It'll all work out."

The kids and I head home for an hour-long story marathon and snugglefest on the couch before bed. I've missed them all day, so I give them an extra thirty minutes at bedtime even though I know we'll all be paying for it tomorrow when it's time to wake them up. I tuck them in to their beds with kisses and hugs, wish them sweet dreams, and tell them I love them.

"Dar-mama," asks Lilly, "will you read me one more story?"

"We'll read more tomorrow," I say. "It's late now, sweetie, and you need to go to sleep."

Dar-mama is the name that Lilly and Aidan gave me a few months after Will and I were married. Aidan was only five when he simply announced one afternoon after school that neither Mommy nor Darby were exactly right, and that he had decided what I should be called. Lilly, like any adoring baby sister, thought Aidan's idea was genius. I was awestruck by how quickly they'd opened up their little hearts to me. The name stuck, and I felt honored by it.

Lilly throws her little arms around my neck and pulls my face close to her cheek. "I love you so much, Dar-mama."

I kiss her silky, sweet little face again and whisper in her ear, "Dar-mama loves you too, Lilly Bean."

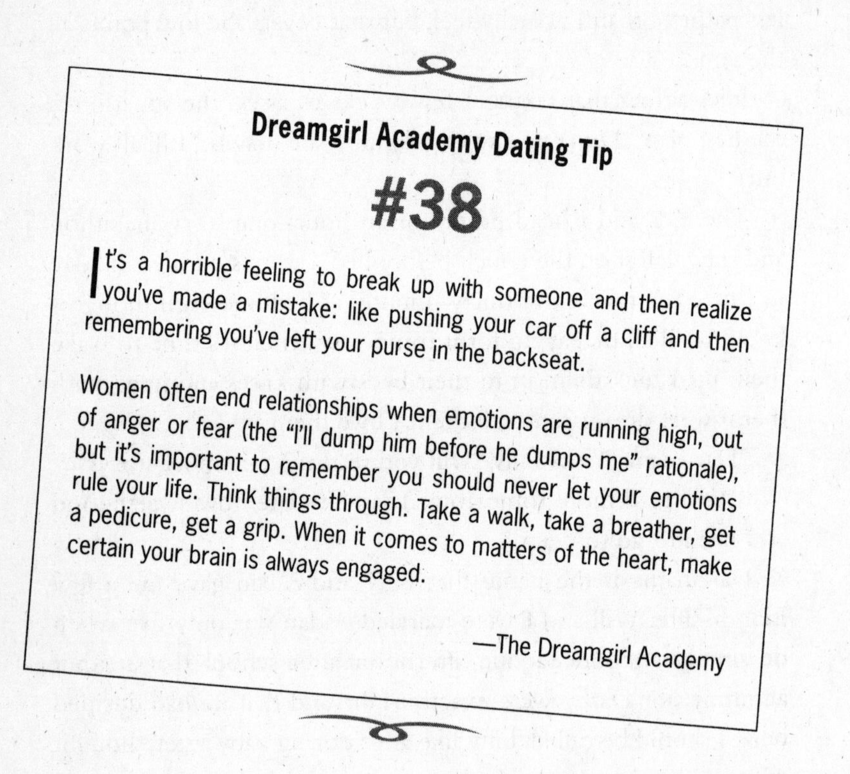

Dreamgirl Academy Dating Tip

#38

It's a horrible feeling to break up with someone and then realize you've made a mistake: like pushing your car off a cliff and then remembering you've left your purse in the backseat.

Women often end relationships when emotions are running high, out of anger or fear (the "I'll dump him before he dumps me" rationale), but it's important to remember you should never let your emotions rule your life. Think things through. Take a walk, take a breather, get a pedicure, get a grip. When it comes to matters of the heart, make certain your brain is always engaged.

—The Dreamgirl Academy

Chapter 4

The problem with snooping is that once you've found something suspicious, it's nearly impossible not to bring it up.

As much as I want to put all of the questions about what Will's been up to out of my mind, I just can't seem to let it go.

I get up early, hide all the evidence that I've been ransacking Will's office, and relock the cabinet. Then I get dressed, make Lilly and Aidan a fabulous breakfast of French toast with powdered sugar, and drop them and the rest of my carpool kids off at Montessori school. As I watch them greet their friends and bound into their classrooms, a little pang of sadness hits me. As much as I love my work, I dread being away from them for two whole weeks. The best part of my job for the last three years has been the luxury of being a mostly stay-at-home mom, hardly missing a moment, ballet recital, or karate match of their amazing little lives. I don't even have to leave home to do my radio show—Will had our guest house equipped as a studio, and I can do the show in my pajamas if I want to (which I frequently do, on the days I don't have to drive carpool). Even taping my segments on the TV show works pretty seamlessly into our family life: I tape my segments every three weeks, which I have strategically managed to coincide with Gigi's time with the kids. I get to be there for Lilly and Aidan. And that really matters to me.

With Will traveling so much, I think the stability of normal, everyday family life has been good for all of us.

I head for the airport to meet the flight that would normally bring Will home from Atlanta. I know, I know. I promised myself that I would let this craziness go until after the tour, but I just can't.

Apparently, I'm a glutton for torture.

I pull in to the last spot in hourly parking ten minutes before the flight arrives, sprint through the airport, and park myself on a bench next to the security checkpoint by the giant fishtank.

The monitor indicates that the flight is scheduled to land on time, and I sit, tense in anticipation, scanning the waves of travelers walking up the concourse for Will's familiar form. It seems the minutes are ticking by in slow motion, and the wait is agony.

Twenty-five minutes later, I can feel my heart breaking wide open, as the recent arrivals begin to thin out. And then, I see him. Tall and elegant, with his overnight bag slung casually over his shoulder. I squint to make sure it's really him, and there he is, dressed in my favorite gray Armani suit and a pink shirt that only Will or a movie star could pull off. When he sees my face, he looks surprised for a second and then breaks into a wide grin.

I have never been so happy to see anyone in my entire life.

He hurries up the ramp and pulls me into his arms, then kisses me sweetly on the lips. "Hey, I didn't know you were coming to meet me today! I've got my car here."

"Oh, well," I stammer, "I just decided to surprise you."

"Nice surprise," he says, smiling.

As we walk out together to the parking lot, I can't stop touching his arms, his back, his face; I'm so happy to see him. So happy he was right where he was supposed to be. Maybe I was mistaken yesterday. Maybe I've worked myself up over nothing. The only thought that keeps nagging me is why Will has been meeting with Sol, splintering my feeling that there's a reasonable explanation for everything I've been doubting.

Since the best defense is always a good offense, I go for the surprise attack, "Will, darling, I was just wondering exactly why you've hired Sol Weinstein."

"I thought I told you," he says, matter-of-factly. "I met with him to talk about revising the settlement for my divorce from Gigi."

Of course! It makes perfect sense. I can't believe I've been driving myself crazy. Will's been trying to get out of his mandatory requirement of acting as Gigi's publicist since before we even met. And frankly, if anyone can set him free, it's Sol.

"Is he still a client?" I ask, fake-casually.

"Not sure about that. He was pretty hot to trot at first. We signed a contract to do PR work for him, but every time I try to set up a meeting to go over the publicity plan he blows me off and tells me he's prepping for a big trial. Whatever. I'm sure he'll call when he needs something."

Mystery solved. No work done, no reason to bill him. I feel like a jerk for distrusting him. I drop the subject and give Will a big, passionate kiss. He smiles at me, his eyes twinkling, and asks, "What's that all about?"

"I just really missed you," I say, slipping my arm around him.

I'm so glad my husband is back.

"Hey," he says, "what do you think about taking the day off? I'd love to spend time with you before you hit the road for two weeks."

"Sounds like a plan to me," I say.

We head home first in our separate cars, slather on a little sunscreen, and change into our swimsuits and shorts. As I gather up the towels and beach chairs, Will spends a solid twenty minutes with his BlackBerry glued to his head, making calls to rearrange his day. We drive over to Lido Key with the windows down and Jimmy Buffett blaring on the CD player. We play together in the gulf, stroll along the sugary beach, picking up seashells. It is one of those perfect, sunny days, the very reason I love living in Florida. We hold hands from our beach chairs, giggling and talking like honeymooners, and chow down on cheeseburgers and cold beer at our favorite little beach bar.

Then, I stay with the beach chairs, catching up on community gossip with the bikini-clad octogenarian seated next to us, while Will takes the car to pick up Lilly and Aidan from school and swing by the house to drop off backpacks and change clothes. Twenty minutes later he's back with the kids, I lather them up with a generous coating of sunscreen, and the four of us spend the rest of the afternoon building sand castles and working on our skimboarding technique.

We load up the car and head home when the sun sinks low, our happy family sticky with sand and seawater. After a round of showers and dinner, I finish packing and tuck Lilly and Aidan in to bed.

Will opens up a bottle of wine and puts on some music: Louis Armstrong, one of my favorites. This is one of Will's surefire seduction techniques, a spin and a dip in the tango of desires between married couples. Plus, it's practically an unwritten law that you give your husband a little going-away action the night before you leave on a trip. We sway together in the kitchen, as he whispers the words to "Dream a Little Dream of Me" in my ear. I feel foolish for overreacting yesterday. Will is a great husband. We love each other, and we have a wonderful family. He nuzzles my neck and pulls me close to him while we dance, and then leads me into the bedroom, pulling my hand to his lips. He kisses me just inside the bedroom door, his hands moving over me. I can feel my body responding, even though my dating expert mind is ever watchful of possible clues to infidelity: Decrease in desire? Apparently not. New bedroom skills? Well, if he *has* learned any new tricks, he's not using them on me. Will and I make love as we always do, with sweetness and ease. When we've finished, I lie in Will's arms, allowing peace to creep over me, listening to his breathing until I start to fall asleep.

It's the nicest day I can remember. So nice, in fact, that I can almost put Atlanta out of my mind.

How to Date Your Husband

by Darby Vaughn

After a few years of marriage, a lot of people find they don't have anything to talk about but who left their toenails under the couch and what happened on *Grey's Anatomy*. If you're in a long-term relationship that's lost its sizzle, now's the time to figure out how to get that sizzle back.

The key to revving up romance is to bring one new element to date night:

Change the Place
Go to tango class rather than spending another Saturday night at Outback, or get freaky in the guest room (or even the backyard) instead of the usual romp in your own bed.

Change the Subject
Instead of talking about the kids, what's for dinner, or what happened on the Beula's Bratwurst account, ask questions like you did when you were dating: What was your college essay about? What's the most embarrassing thing that ever happened to you as a kid? Where's the weirdest place you ever had sex?

Change What You Wear
Forget jeans and dump the tracksuit. Get all dressed up for a big night out, even if you just hit the local Denny's. The act of spending time on your appearance in anticipation of your date will make you feel more romantic before you even get your pantyhose on.

Change Your Color
Dye your hair or slink out in something scarlet. Wearing red increases your heart rate (and his) and mimics attraction—just enough to kick-start a slow night.

Chapter 5

My flight leaves at seven A.M., which means that the taxi driver will be outside my house at five-thirty, which is just too damned early.

I double-check the seven pages of instructions and notes on the kids' schedules that I've written out for Miss Vivian, our babysitter extraordinaire/surrogate grandmother who will be watching the kids while I'm gone and Will's at work. She's wonderful, and Lilly and Aidan adore her.

Planting silent kisses on the foreheads of Will, Aidan, and Lilly as they lay sleeping, I sneak love notes under their pillows.

Will stirs, groggy from sleep, and says, "Darby, good luck on the *Today* show. I know you're going to be great. This is a big moment for you. I'm really proud of you sweetheart—go get 'em."

I kiss him softly on the forehead one last time before I go, before rolling my red monster suitcase down the driveway to the waiting cab.

When I say I'm going "on tour" most people get this really glamorous idea of five-star hotels and limousines, formal wear, a ready-made entourage, and noninvasive paparazzi hanging around to take photos from your best angle outside your hotel, while a handler whisks you from party to interview to party to every author's fantasy, a book signing with throngs of your adoring fans lined up around the block.

The truth is that most authors don't even get to go on a book tour. I was lucky enough to get fifteen cities, because my agent, Holland, is a shark. A sweet-smiling, smartly outfitted shark dressed to kill in dramatic African jewelry.

The reality of a glamorous book tour is that you either a) take a flight at the crack of dawn or b) show up in an airport the night before, and take a cab to a Ramada or some other similarly ornamented halfway house for business travelers. In the morning, an author handler named Marge or Betty will pick you up in her late-model Toyota with used Starbucks grande cups and McGriddle wrappers littering the floor of the passenger seat. Marge will know all of the gossip on every author on tour over the last five to twenty years, and she can tell you who's nice, who sleeps with bookstore managers, who takes uppers before she does the local morning show, and what bestselling spiritual author let his ratty little dog poop in the back of her car and didn't even offer to clean it up.

Marge will have slung over her shoulder a giant tote bag, obtained free at a book fair, stuffed with whatever she's reading, a knitting project, bottles of water, a wrinkled, marked-up copy of your schedule, and, at the very bottom, a cereal bar or a bag of airline peanuts, which she will share with you if you've had a really long day and you haven't had a chance to stop for food or if you're not that author who let his dog poop in her car. She will drive you to a radio station to do a morning drive-time show, or a local TV station to do *Good Morning Little Rock!* or *Good Morning Tupelo!* or *Good Morning Wherever the Hell You Are!* and will sit patiently in the waiting room while you do your six minutes with a host who is graciously small-talking with you on the air, despite the fact that he probably doesn't know or care who you are or what your book is about. Then, Marge will drive you to your bookstore signing, where even if you're well known, you can expect to sit at a faux wood table, looking a lot like those survey people in the mall, hoping to God that at least ten people will show up so the bookstore manager won't believe your appearance and frankly, your existence, to be a complete inconvenience and utter waste of her time. Typically, you'll just be sitting around for two hours trying to catch any customer's eye as they enter the store so that you can psychically will them to your table. Mostly, though, you'll be giving them directions to the bathroom.

Whenever there are breaks in your day, you and Marge will hit the drive-thru for coffees or sandwiches, then drop in at bookstores en route to your next gig, where you'll introduce yourself to as many unfazed bookstore employees as possible and offer to sign any copies of your book they happen to have in stock. Which, if you're a first- or second-time author with a major publisher, will probably be one. After you sign the single, lonely copy, they'll rummage around the desk for one of those gold foil "signed by the author" stickers to slap on the front.

After your day is done, Marge will drop you off at the airport. You'll grab a quick slice at Sbarro before your nine P.M. flight, and you'll head (in coach) to your next glamorous destination.

I'm kicking off my tour this morning in Chicago. The logistics of touring are hard but the people I meet are great. I always dread being away from home for so long, but as soon as the plane takes off, I can feel myself getting excited, thinking about everyone I'm going to see. Touring is probably the hardest, most exhausting part of being an author (you miss your family, you're schlepping from one anonymous place to the next), but it can be the most exciting part as well. Whenever I get too tired or feel like I just want to go home, I suck it up, put on a smile, and carry on. Touring is when you get the chance to meet your readers—the people who thought enough of you to spend twenty dollars of their hard-earned cash on your book, and who are nice enough to tell you that your work means something to them personally. For me, that's enough to get me through the lonely hotel rooms and the six A.M. cab rides.

Risa, my author escort for Chicago, is waiting for me at baggage claim with a little cardboard sign that reads DARBY VAUGHN. She's short, not even five feet tall, with olive skin and curly black hair that just touches her shoulders. She is smiling, and she's got the most amazingly white teeth I've ever seen.

"Hiya!" she says as soon as she spots me.

I smile back and stick out my hand to shake hers. "Hi! I'm Darby. So nice to see you!" She looks at me inquisitively for a brief moment and says, "*Secrets to Make the Guys Go Gaga,* right? I was your schlepper four years ago."

"I thought so!" I say, glad to have a friendly face on my first stop. We hug briefly, chitchat about what we've been up to since the last time we met, and she offers to watch my carry-on bag while I drag my suitcase off the carousel.

"Big bag, eh? How many cities are you doing?"

"Eight, on this trip. I'm in New York for four nights after Chicago; I have two two-night stops, and the rest are one-nighters. No dry-cleaning."

She hands my carry-on back and I load it and my laptop on top of the rolling suitcase. I follow her toward the doors that lead to the parking deck.

"You've got a ten-fifteen call at *AM Chicago*, but the studio's only twenty minutes away. No problem at this time of day." She takes one look at my high heels, bare legs, and short-sleeved wrap dress and says, "You gotta jacket?"

I tell her I do, but it's at the bottom of my suitcase, so I'll just suck it up until we get to the studio.

We step outside, and I'm practically blown over by a freezing gust of wind.

I'm not sure why, but I always have a hard time comprehending that the weather in other places is different from where I live. I realize it's ridiculous, but I board a plane, arrive at a new city, and some part of me (usually the same part that decides what I'm going to wear on the plane) expects the weather to be the same as the place I just left. I watch the Weather Channel before I go anywhere, I see the little snowflake icons over my destination state, and yet when I see the palm trees swaying in my own backyard, it doesn't seem real. Which is unfortunate, since I live in Florida, where it is generally a balmy 85 degrees in November. Risa laughs as I jump at the chill, stomping my strappy Jimmy Choos to warm up my bare toes, and informs me that the high temperature is expected to be around 23 degrees today. I'm a dork.

We have five stops today, a local morning show, *AM Chicago*, a radio interview at noon, a couple of bookstore drop-ins in the late afternoon, and then I'll be teaching a Dreamgirl Academy dating class at the Chicago Learning Annex. Classes and book signings are the only thing that keeps me alive between stops, because that's when I get to talk with the women who read my books. They tell me what they liked or didn't like, ask me for advice, trust me with the heartbreaking stories that caused them to pick up the book in the first place, introduce me to their friends. It's like one big girls' night in.

The next day is more of the same, a quick gig on the *Mancow* morning show, which is one of my favorites, followed by a couple more bookstore drop-ins, a quick lunch with a reporter from the *Tribune*, then another signing at the Barnes & Noble on State Street.

At the end of my day, Risa drops me back at the airport and I'm back on the plane, winging my way to NYC. When I land at La Guardia, it's after midnight. If I make it to my hotel before one, I'll get five whole hours of sleep before my appearance on the *Today* show. I'm so excited I can hardly stand it.

Thankfully, there is a Lincoln Town Car waiting with my name on it, so at least I won't be hailing a taxi in the middle of the night.

As a fan of glamorous, romantic Technicolor movies from the sixties, I was practically drooling when I found out I'm staying at the Waldorf-Astoria. I've dreamed of this art deco landmark for years, and now (cue orchestra), I'm finally here. While the accommodations on my other tour stops have been decidedly bourgeois, I'm in for glam, glam, glam in the city. The car rolls to a stop and immediately the bellman whisks the door open, extending his hand to help me out of the car into a far more glamorous era. Hello, Cary Grant. I watch the bellman hike my bag out of the trunk, and we step up into the lobby, past the most mammoth flower arrangement I have ever seen. A piano tinkles away somewhere, and the stunningly ornate clock in the center of the lobby chimes two A.M.

When I finally get to my room, I do a quickie birdbath in the fancy marble bathroom sink, an attempt to try to scrape off some of the pancake makeup and airplane smell, and then climb into bed. No sooner does my head hit the pillow than the alarm goes off, with Sonny and Cher's rendition of "I Got You Babe" blaring on the clock radio. Really? Sonny and Cher? Holy *Groundhog*

Day. I sing along (off-key, I'll admit) and giggle to myself. "I got *you*, babe." Today is my day.

Fortified by four hours of sleep (plus an airplane nap and a car nap), I feel fabulous. Or, at least, functional. I look out my window at the city blinking to life below me. After a quick call to room service for a $65 plate of bacon and eggs and a Coke, I pop in to the shower.

My author escort, a fortyish Italian woman called Babs, meets me in the lobby at 6:45 and tells me the car and driver sent by the *Today* show is already waiting outside, and just a few minutes later we arrive at the studio at Rockefeller Center. I'm in awe, but Babs, who has been here a number of times with dozens of other authors, seems unfazed and escorts me through the entrance over to the guard desk. A twenty-something blonde production assistant carrying a clipboard appears to retrieve us, and whisks us through the hallways back to the green room. Which is, interestingly enough, not in the least bit green.

"Why is this called the green room?" I ask.

"Nobody knows," Babs replies with authority, "but you'll never find a *green* green room."

"Really?" I ask, thinking she might be pulling my leg.

She smiles and raises an eyebrow. "It's bad luck."

Lovely. Just then, another energetic production assistant appears. She introduces herself as Mackenzie, offers Babs and me coffee, and tells me she's here to escort me to the makeup room.

Thank God. After just four hours of sleep and not nearly enough caffeine I definitely need professional help.

I ask Babs to hold my suit jacket so it won't wrinkle while I'm in the makeup chair, and follow Mackenzie down the hall, flipping through my note cards and powering down my phone so it won't ring while I'm on the air.

We've all heard the old saying that a TV camera adds ten pounds, but no one tells you that it makes important parts of your face just blend into a puddle. Like your eyelashes. And your chin.

It usually takes a couple of really terrible appearances before you realize that the key to looking like a human being while appearing on television is to tart yourself up to look like a hooker. Page Six columnist Paula Froelich calls the look "TV tranny."

I think it might actually be some secret initiation process into the wild world of television. Like hazing. It's why amateurs look so bad and professionals look so good.

False eyelashes. Black eyeliner. Seven pounds of lip-gloss. I learned my most important lesson in TV makeup when I made an appearance on the same day as Rachel Weingarten, a celebrity makeup artist I met in a Philadelphia green room. She was promoting her new book, *Hello Gorgeous!,* and after informing me, in the nicest way possible, that I was about to appear on television with six chins, she did an emergency face fix five minutes before I was supposed to go on the air. Three minutes later, I had a visible smear of bronzer encircling my throat, rendering my double chin(s) invisible to all in TV land. In person, I looked like a recently strangled streetwalker with really expensive shoes.

"Trust me, darling," she said reassuringly, "you'll look fabulous." And I did.

Today's makeup artist is clearly on board with the whole hooker = normal plan, and I emerge from the makeup room freshly spackled and ready to be miked.

Mackenzie pops by to warn me I'm up in eight minutes, and I ask her if I have enough time to make a quick stop at the ladies' room. The green room sink is out of hand soap, so I make a dash to wash my hands at the makeup room sink next door. I'm about to meet Matt Lauer, so this is not exactly the time to skimp on the hand washing.

I turn the cold faucet a half turn to the left and am immediately blasted in the face by an out-of-control water sprayer. Water shoots all over the room, drenching me and most of the staff, before a quick-thinking guy armed with a hairdryer wrestles the errant hose back into the sink and shuts the thing off. The shampoo sink. The hair and makeup staff stand back with their mouths agape, trying hard not to laugh.

Just then, Mackenzie pokes her head into the room. "You're on in five." She does a double-take, then puts her hand up to her mouth. "Oh crap."

My pale pink T-shirt is sopping wet and now transparent. The eight coats of painstakingly applied mascara run in black rivers down my face, while a single false eyelash sits perched on my boob like a spider. My shoulder-length red hair, which I had spent half an hour meticulously straightening this morning, looks like it has been caught in a car wash.

Mackenzie snaps into action. "She's in the chairs with Matt in four minutes, folks."

Dryer-man, the saint who had mercifully turned the wretched sink off, comes to my rescue again, drying the front (and most of the back) of my hair, slicking it back into a chic knot, while both makeup artists go to work on cleaning up the damage done to my face.

Mackenzie stands in the doorway, eyes glued to her watch. "I need her on the set in two."

"Done," the makeup girls say simultaneously.

"What are we going to do about her clothes?" someone asks.

"There's no time to find her different wardrobe, I need her on the set now so she can get miked."

I then have an idea that seems simultaneously moronic and genius at the same time: "I've got a jacket," I say, "can I just wear my shirt backwards?"

"That works, if you can do it while you're walking. Otherwise, you gotta go on wet," says Mackenzie, and I follow her hurriedly to the set while slipping my arms out of my soggy shirt and twirling the shirt around sort of like that bra-removal trick we all learn in college. As I put on my jacket, the sound guy snakes the microphone wire underneath and clips it to my lapel about five seconds before we go on the air. I flop into the chair next to Matt Lauer just a breath before he begins to introduce me.

"With us on *Today*, we have bestselling author Darby Vaughn. She's got a new book out this month on how to snag the man of your dreams. The book is titled *The Dreamgirl Academy*. Welcome, Darby Vaughn."

"Thank you so much for having me on the show," I say enthusiastically.

"So, what made you decide to write another dating book?" asks Matt, with just the hint of a grin.

"Well," I say, easing into standard interview territory, "I've always been the one who gave dating advice to all of my friends, and now all of us are happily married." I laugh and smile. "I think it was a combination of two things: It's really fulfilling to me to help other women find relationships, and once we all got married, well, I really missed the girl talk."

Matt leans forward, his eyes fixing on mine in a sort of "brainlock" that all truly gifted interviewers share, the one that makes you forget you're on TV and feel as though you're just chatting with your friendly neighborhood mind reader. "You said you're *all* happily married?'" he asks.

"Yes," I respond, pausing, not quite sure if there's another question coming, or if he's wanting me to elaborate on marital happiness.

His eyes crinkle for a brief second, and then he asks, "What do you have to say about the article that appeared in this morning's *USA Today*?"

"Gee, Matt," I joke, hoping he'll give me a bit more to go on. It's always a bit of a challenge when interviewers bring up some obscure article or study without warning, expecting you to be able to comment on it intelligently without having read it. I give him a big smile and reply, "I have to say, I was so excited about appearing on the *Today* show this morning I didn't have a chance to read the paper."

"The article states that your husband, publicist Will Bradley, is filing for divorce and that he has reconciled with his ex-wife, Gigi Bissanti, former Miss Arkansas and star of the hit reality show *Castaway*. A representative for the couple confirms the report. Do you have a comment regarding your impending divorce?"

The room starts spinning and my stomach begins to lurch. I press my lips together as tightly as I can, the bile pushing its way through my body as I try to will it back into submission. Too late.

Panicked, I scramble to reach for the only thing I can see—a small basket of chrysanthemums on the coffee table in front of me—just a nanosecond before puking up my entire breakfast.

Live. On national television.

And then, everything goes black.

When I come to, I am lying on the floor wedged between the *Today* show couch and the *Today* show coffee table with an ice pack under my head. Mackenzie and several other staffers are huddled around me, and as I look around, trying to gain my bearings, I can see from a nearby monitor that Matt, Anne, and Al are out on Rockefeller Plaza talking about the weather. An intern is standing by with an unopened first-aid kit and a bottle of water.

Matt's question echoes in my brain, I feel the room go woozy again, and the last thing I hear before everything goes black is Babs's nasally voice asking, "Is she all done? 'Cause I gotta get her down to KROC for a nine-thirty."

The Dreamgirl Academy: It's Not Me, It's You

by Darby Vaughn

Dear Darby,
What's the best way to break up with my girlfriend? I don't want to hurt her, but I don't want to sit through a thirteen-hour "what went wrong" discussion either.
Looking for the Easy Way Out

Dear Easy,
Maybe you don't want to hurt someone you've been close to, or maybe you're dealing with a nut and you don't want to be the trigger for an economy-size bottle of Prozac and a six-week stint at the Bendy Willow Psychiatric Center. So what do you do when it's obvious you're just not meant to be together? The key is to have a plan, a good plan:

- **Don't drag it out.** The longer it takes, the worse it is for everybody.
- **Pick a good strategic breakup setting.** The best places are both public but fairly private (such as a park) with a convenient escape route.
- **Make your reasons relevant only to you, and stick with them.** Say, "This is not working for me." She can't argue about reasons that pertain only to you. If you say "we fight too much" or "you don't seem happy," she may offer to change, taking all the air out of your breakup and landing you right back in the relationship.
- **Time it perfectly.** If you're ending the relationship at a restaurant, do it only after the check has come and you've paid for dinner. (And by the way, if you're about to dump someone, you should DEFINITELY be buying dinner.) There's nothing more horrifying than being dumped and then having to sit around making small talk for another 20 minutes while you're waiting for the check to come. (As in, "Hey Lula, so what are you doing later tonight? Laundry?")
- **Never break up with someone within two weeks of a major holiday or her birthday.** There's no faster entry to the Jerk Hall of Fame than permanently destroying the holidays for your soon-to-be-ex. You don't want that what-goes-around-comes-around thing biting you in the ass when your turn as the dumpee rolls around.

Chapter 6

I'm startled out of my mental wooze with ice water splashed on my face. When I open my eyes, an even bigger crowd has gathered around me than before. I search the swarm for a familiar face and spot Mackenzie near my feet.

"Is it true?" I croak, meeting Mackenzie's eyes but barely able to form the words.

Mackenzie looks at me pitifully, the first human crack in her ultra-efficient persona. "I'm sorry," she says quietly. "You didn't know?"

I shake my head no, too stricken to speak more, as warm tears begin to pour out of me. I will them to stop, and steel myself not to lose it again in front of this crowd of strangers. Oh God, I feel my stomach churning again.

"Jesus," whispers a crew member setting up for a kitchen shot nearby. "How could her damned publicist not warn her when this story broke?"

"My husband is my publicist," I say quietly, and silence falls over the set.

I see Babs coming toward me, her short, stocky frame elbowing through the throng like a freight train with kind brown eyes.

She gives me a motherly smile as she helps me to my feet. "Well, girl, I think you just got spun."

Babs shepherds me through the crowd like a club bouncer, loaded down with her shoulder bag and the handbag I'd left in the green room, announcing, "She's fine folks, thank you all for your help."

Mackenzie follows us outside to the street. "Again, I'm so sorry. We thought you knew and since you were coming on the show anyway, you were trying to do a little PR spin. Matt, me, everybody . . . we all feel terrible that you found out this way. We never would have knowingly put you in a position like this."

I try to force myself to smile, even a small one, to let her know that I don't blame her for what's just happened, but my face is unable to do so on its own and my soul is too shattered to make it happen.

"Thank you," Babs pipes in, "she appreciates the thought." Our driver pulls up to the street in front of us, and Babs yanks open the door, throwing our things inside. "Hop in, sweetie," she directs me firmly.

I climb into the car. Babs follows me in and directs the driver to take us back to the Waldorf. On the way, I stare out the window, the gray buildings all blurring into each other. I'm trying to make sense of what I've just heard, but I can't.

Babs yanks my schedule out of her bag and dials my publisher on her cell phone.

Although Babs is sitting next to me, I'm so locked into my own brain that I can barely hear wisps of what she is saying: "Cancel the interview." "Family emergency."

The driver pulls up to the Waldorf-Astoria. Babs pays the fare and helps me out of the cab, and then takes me to my room. She draws all of the drapes closed and puts her arm around me kindly.

"Do you want me to stay," she asks gently, "or do you want to be alone?"

"Alone, please," I whisper hoarsely.

She takes the ice bucket and my room key off the marble-topped nightstand and heads down the hall to find the ice machine. She returns a few minutes later and places both on the desk.

Scribbling a number down on hotel stationery, she says, "Call me if you need me. Your publisher is canceling all of your interviews for the next three days; the only thing we can't get you out of is the Dreamgirl Academy class you're supposed to teach at the Learning Annex tomorrow. We've got a call in there, but you've got a hundred and eighty-six women who have signed up and paid to hear you speak, so we'll see what we can do."

I hear her call down to the concierge for a bottle of tequila and a copy of *USA Today* to be delivered to my room.

"I know it's only ten A.M.," she says gently, "but when the shock wears off you're going to need something to dull the pain."

"Thanks," I say, curling myself into a ball and pulling the covers up to my chin. The pristine white sheets are soothing, and I'm comforted by the fact that the Waldorf makes a bed the same way my grandmother did, with a warm blanket sandwiched in between two top sheets.

Road Signs to Splitsville: Six Signs You're About to Get Dumped

by Darby Vaughn

When you're together, his toes are pointing away from you. Our bodies line up when we're in love (heart to heart, face to face). When things start to go wrong, the feet are one of the first places you'll see it. He may be with you now, but if his feet are heading out the door, or worse, toward someone else, he may be looking to walk.

He's no longer interested in sex, or worse, he has a new bag of tricks and a shrink-wrapped trapeze. Barring medical problems, a dramatic change in sexual behavior (less sex, or different sex) usually means he's learning it somewhere else or getting it somewhere else.

When he hugs you, he gives you that little pat-pat-pat on the back. Patting you on the back is a signal he's uneasy, and the bigger the pat, the more discomfort he feels.

He starts picking fights about stupid stuff, like which way the toilet paper roll goes. We find reasons to argue when we want out. If you find yourself bickering over such pressing issues as why Hulk Hogan, not The Rock, should be crowned King of Wrestlemania, your partner is trying to make you look like the bad guy so he doesn't feel so bad when he leaves. "That's it!" he'll scream, after another paper-versus-plastic bout. "I can't take this anymore! I'm LEAVING!"

If he's looking left, something's not right. When someone looks up and to the left when they're speaking to you, it usually means they're lying. The look left is an indication we're using the "creative" side of our brains and a good indicator he's telling you a whopper.

Want to know when you're most likely to get the ax? Experts agree it's somewhere in the neighborhood of the first three to five months. So, stock up on tissues and chocolate if you find yourself heading down the wrong road.

Chapter 7

The phone is ringing. The room is dark, except for tiny seams of light where the curtains break away from the walls. I have no recollection of where I am, what time it is, or how long I've been curled up on this strange bed. And then, I start spiraling as snippets from the *Today* show flash into my mind like tragedy updates on CNN.

Damn it, I should have known this would happen.

It feels like I'm sitting in the middle of the interstate, my life strewn around me like shattered glass. I finally gain enough focus to pick up the phone but can't manage to get the word *hello* all the way out of my mouth. It sits stuck somewhere in the back of my throat.

Jules is on the other end of the line, "Darby darlin', can you hear me?"

A low, foreign sob escapes my body.

"I'm so sorry," she soothes, "so, so sorry. Honey, I did *not* see this coming."

"When did you hear?"

"The same time you did," she says gently, "right there on national television. Come home. You can stay with us until you figure things out."

"I can't," I bawl. "I can't leave, I have a class to teach. I can't leave New York until tomorrow night." I just want to crawl back under the covers and die right here.

After a second's pause, she says, "We'll get you home tomorrow night, then. There's a ten-forty flight. Can you make it to La Guardia by then?"

"I think so. The class should be finished by eight-thirty; I'm pretty sure I can get to the airport by nine-fifteen." The sobs crash through me in violent waves. "I don't know how I can possibly face a room full of women and tell them how to meet Mr. Right when I've just been humiliated on national TV. They'll think I'm a stupid, pathetic fraud. I can't face it."

"Then don't go," Jules says matter-of-factly. "Just cancel the class."

"I can't." My head is pounding away, and my face feels so stretched and swollen from trying to keep in the tears that it hurts.

We talk for a few more minutes, and the usually sweet-natured Jules tries to figure out if she knows anyone who can put a contract out on Will's head. After much deliberation, she concludes that the most evil person in her circle of acquaintances wouldn't be capable of much more than flattening his tires, although she's pretty positive she can get him shut out at the really good dry-cleaners.

A tiny laugh escapes, and then I'm wracked with sobs again.

"An honorable man wouldn't have hung you out to dry on national TV. It's just cruel. An honorable man wouldn't do it," she declares. "God doesn't like ugly."

Exhaling in frustration, she listens to me cry some more, tells me to hang in there, and offers one last piece of advice before we hang up: "Don't turn on the TV."

I set the phone down on its cradle and stare numbly into the dim room. I pull the covers up to my chin. The tears swell out of me, and for once, I just let them. I try to make sense of what has happened and can't. Not after the beach the other day. Not after the last four years. Not after spending my *entire life* working to ensure that this very thing wouldn't happen. I've been completely blindsided.

I pick up the phone to call Will. Every fiber of my body is howling that it's over, but three tiny cells in my brain are unconvinced; I want to hear it straight from his mouth. I dial his cell phone and it transfers directly to voicemail. Fucking jerk. He just orchestrated the most humiliating moment in the history of television, the least he can do is pick up. I leave a message for Will to call me, and try him at his office. Kendall picks up, but instead of answering "Will Bradley's office" she just says, "Hello?"

I debate whether to hang up.

"Kendall," I say, fighting for my words to win out over the mounting lump in my throat, "is Will in? It's Darby."

"Ohmygod," she exclaims, her voice graveled with pity. "Darby, I'm so sorry, I had no idea he was capable of something so horrible."

"Do you know for sure?" I ask, hopeful that this is some dreadful, cruel mistake and not the end of my life. "Is it really true?"

She sighs. "Have you read the article in *USA Today*?"

"Not yet."

"He called me at home right after the *Today* show and told me you'd need a list of publicists right away, and that he couldn't handle you as a client anymore. He was, I don't know, cryptic. He wouldn't say any more. The jerk actually hung up on me."

"What?" That fucking bastard. Did everybody in the universe know before me?

"The *Today* show, *USA Today,* E!, all on the same day?" She says angrily, "He has to have been planning this for weeks."

I feel my limbs go to jelly and the bile rise in my throat. "What happened on E!?"

"Gigi had a press conference today at nine-fifteen, just a few minutes before you passed out on *Today*," she continues. "They were together at the studio. Gigi had on full TV makeup and her hair was blown out. And Will was definitely wearing pancake and maybe eyeliner. I think he planned this. I think he planned the whole thing."

"What did he say?"

"Nothing," she says. "He just stood there like an idiot."

How could this happen?

"I tried to warn you," she says, "but your phone was turned off. I was leaving a voicemail for your author escort when Lauer introduced you." She takes a breath before continuing. "I'm so, so sorry, Darby."

The room starts swirling around me again and I grip the phone for dear life.

"I told him I quit," she says angrily. "I can't believe he could do this to you. By the way, I spoke with the travel agent. Will hasn't been making those trips to Atlanta."

"Where was he?" I ask, afraid to hear the answer.

"On six of the dates in question he was in LA. On the other missing dates he didn't go anywhere, at least not on a plane. I still haven't learned anything about the Ritz, but as soon as I do, I'll let you know."

"Thanks, I really appreciate all you've done."

"One more thing," she says, tentatively.

"Oh God," I can't take it, "there's more?"

"Just don't turn on the TV."

"Why?" I ask.

"Just don't." Kendall promises to call me later, once she's cleared her things out of Will's office.

I say good-bye, hang up the phone, and drag myself over to the table that holds the newspaper and a massive bottle of Jose Cuervo. I unscrew the cap, take a munificent swig out of the bottle, and sit down on the edge of the bed to read the paper. The story is placed on the third page of the Life section:

DATING BOOK AUTHOR'S MARRIAGE HAS UNHAPPY ENDING

It's a love triangle that sounds like a movie of the week: Divorce papers are being filed today by *Secrets to Make the Guys Go Gaga* author Darby Vaughn's husband, publicist Will Bradley. The reason given for the split is irreconcilable differences. They have been married for three years.

Bradley is reportedly reconciling with his former wife, Gigi Bissanti, the stunning star of last season's hit TV show *Castaway*. The pair have two children together from their marriage that ended in 2002.

Bissanti said in a telephone interview Thursday, "Will and I never stopped loving each other. We want to put our family back together."

Vaughn, who is currently on tour for her book, *The Dreamgirl Academy*, could not be reached for comment.

Thursday? She fucking knew on Thursday? I throw the paper across the room, and it hits the silk drapery and falls to the floor with an unimpressive thud, as the various sections float down to the carpet.

Shame wraps itself around me, and the sick chases my stomach around in a circle, as every feeling of unworthiness, disappointment, and humiliation I've ever known do a jamboree in my gut.

I take another swig of the Cuervo, then another, and another. It's the only thing I can think of that will give me a rest.

The Dreamgirl Academy: Penniless Playboy

by Darby Vaughn

Dear Darby,
I have been seeing a guy for about six months now. When we first met, he asked me to go to Miami with him for a modeling competition that he was in. Once we got to Miami, he said he didn't have any money, so I ended up paying for everything. He's really a nice guy, but lately there has been a lot of inconsistency in our relationship. Whenever we go out, I always have to pay because he says he doesn't have any money.

For the past month, he's been going out of town every single weekend and when he goes, for whatever reason, I don't hear from him. When I finally talk to him he tells me his cell phone wasn't working, or he left it home along with his pager. One weekend, I actually caught him coming out of his house with a girl. When he saw me pull up, he ran in the house and had his cousin tell me he wasn't in there. I really don't know what to do about him. I think he feels like he can do anything that he wants to me. It seems like I show all the feelings and he doesn't. How can I get him chasing after me?
Chasing Him

Dear Chasing,
Wow, this guy sure does do a lot of traveling for somebody who is always broke.

You'd better sit down for this one, because I'm going to give it to you straight up: Your guy is sleeping with other girls.

The reason he feels like he can do anything and it is okay is because you are allowing him to treat you that way by putting up with it. The reason you never hear from him when he's out of town is because he's with another girl. Really. Nobody's cell phone just goes dead on the weekends. You say that you are the one showing all the feelings, but that isn't really true, is it? He's showing you his feelings on a daily basis: He doesn't care about you and doesn't respect you.

You are a woman, not a doormat. Dump him; you deserve much, much better.
Kisses,
Darby

Chapter 8

The first thing I do when I wake up again is turn on the TV.

I look at the alarm clock, askew on the nightstand, and it's 6:04. I flip through the channels, past news and more news: NBC has me as the third story from the top; they're showing the clip of me projectile-vomiting on the *Today* show, and they finish up with the details of my humiliation and a quick piece of the clip from Gigi and my prick of a husband Will's press conference from hell, at which she declares their undying love. Kendall was right, Will is definitely wearing makeup, and the sight of Gigi with her perfectly blown-out beauty queen hair has me seething.

The anchorman perkily rattles on about the end of my life while a photo of me smiling and perched on top of a trash can hovers in the air over his left shoulder.

Stupid picture. Will talked me into it; he thought it would be a great publicity shot (something about representing women climbing out of the dumpster), available in a variety of hi-res formats for easy downloading by members of the media. Clearly he was right: As I flip through the channels, I see CBS, FOX, and E! are all using it.

I'm filled with something big and awful, anger maybe, viciously humbling, and trampling through me. I flip through the channels, soaking up every gruesome detail of this mess, my fucking life.

I am everywhere.

I've never been one to wallow, feel sorry for myself, give myself over to being overly emotional. Turning off the TV, I force myself to block the humiliating images and riptide of self-doubt from my consciousness.

Then, I do the same thing I've always done in a crisis. I form a plan.

If I could just talk to Will. I pick up my cell phone, check the screen with the faintest flicker of hope, and see the voicemail icon flashing in the corner. The ringer is still off from this morning. I have seventy-three messages, all from various media outlets, except two: one from my agent informing me I've been fired from my radio and TV shows; and a marginally sympathetic message from my publisher, informing me that my Dreamgirl Academy class for tomorrow night has been called off because of the media circus, and that my book tour has been canceled unless I want to share my *reaction* (read: cry on TV) to my very public humiliation on all the shows. No thank you, I didn't sign up for the Jerry Springer tour.

How did I go from being a media darling, with a pal at every show, to feeling like I'm surrounded by a bunch of rabid jackals?

Fuck. No message from Will.

I open up my laptop to see if maybe he's sent me an e-mail. Fifteen minutes later, my computer is still cranking, with 937 new e-mails and no signs of letting up.

Most of the messages are media requests for interviews, which I delete, but there are more a than a hundred reader e-mails forwarded from my website:

TO: fanmail@darbyvaughn.com
FROM: jelly432@goweb.com
SUBJECT: Best Wishes

Dear Darby,
I'm a big fan of your books and I always listen to your radio show. You've made such a difference to me—not just in my dates, in my life! I was so sorry to see what happened to you today. Remember, there are a lot of dreamgirls out here pulling for you!
Sincerely,
Jan Ellis
(Dreamgirl in Training)

I'm so touched that so many of my readers thought to reach out to me that I start to sob. I don't deserve them. Scrolling through a few dozen more heartening e-mails from wonderful fans, I'm lifted by their encouragement until I reach this one:

TO: fanmail@darbyvaughn.com
FROM: yerda5423@hotmail.com
SUBJECT: You

Darby,.
You're pathetic. How can you tell me what to do with my life when yours is such a mess? How dare you preach to all of us how to find a great guy when you can't even do it yourself? You make me sick. I think you got what you deserved.
Yolanda

Shame burns my face, and I bury my head in my hands. What if she's right? Should I really be telling anyone else how relationships are supposed to work?

I try Will's cell again, still no answer. I call back once again, just to hear his voice on the message. God, I miss him. I need to talk to him, hear this straight from him. He owes me that. My brain is whirling like a maypole with a thousand strings of logic on why this can't possibly be true. *Maybe Gigi cooked this whole thing up for publicity. Maybe Will can't tell the press it's not true because of the divorce court order. Maybe I'm being pranked on one of those stupid shows where all of your friends get together to torture you for ratings. Maybe he got abducted by a mob of angry divorcées and can't answer his phone.*

This can't be true, it just can't. Reality is gnawing away at me, but I won't let myself believe it until I hear it from Will. This can still be fixed, I just need to figure everything out.

After a dozen more tries on Will's cell phone throughout the night, I decide to go to the source. I'm getting desperate, and I know just how to find him.

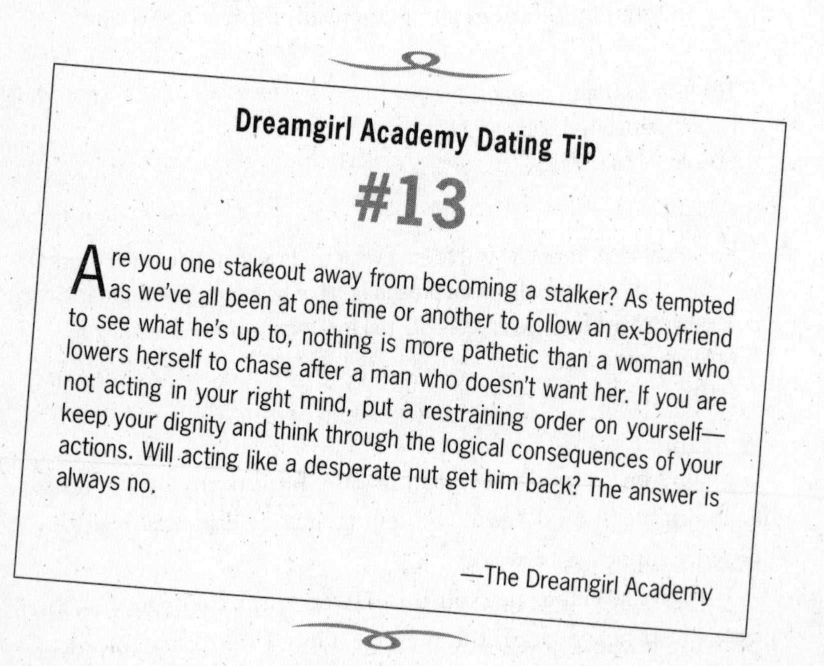

Dreamgirl Academy Dating Tip

#13

Are you one stakeout away from becoming a stalker? As tempted as we've all been at one time or another to follow an ex-boyfriend to see what he's up to, nothing is more pathetic than a woman who lowers herself to chase after a man who doesn't want her. If you are not acting in your right mind, put a restraining order on yourself—keep your dignity and think through the logical consequences of your actions. Will acting like a desperate nut get him back? The answer is always no.

—The Dreamgirl Academy

Chapter 9

I just barely make it to JFK in time to board the red-eye to Los Angeles. It's after eleven, and despite the fact that the sun has been down for a good five hours, I'm wearing the biggest pair of sunglasses I could find: My face is so bloated and red from the crying and the Cuervo, I look like I'm in dire need of a speedy intervention and a twelve-week stint at Betty Ford. I skulk onto the plane, hiding behind a *People* magazine, and take my seat, in coach.

Miraculously, the flight is nearly empty, and the attendants scurry about, preparing the plane for takeoff. I sneak a small bottle of Bailey's out of my purse, acquired at the last minute from the hotel mini-bar, and take a quick swig. Then I settle in to read my magazine, but have a hard time focusing on the latest antics of Tom Cruise. I must have drifted off because I'm startled awake as the plane jiggles down into a landing at LAX.

Renting a car at the airport, I pay an extra twenty bucks to get the GPS, and plot my way over to Gigi's to track down my husband. I'm certain that if I can just talk to Will, we can figure out this whole misunderstanding and make it go away.

I pull into Gigi's exclusive neighborhood at precisely 5:15 A.M. Slowing at the guard shack, I exhale in relief as the ruddy, overstuffed security officer takes one look at me and waves me through. Thank God for small favors. I'm not sure exactly how I would explain this situation. As I drive slowly down the street, scanning for her house number, I'm struck by how much Gigi's neighborhood looks like my own, except instead of being populated by plastic surgeons and politicians, these homes are inhabited by all manner of subfamous celebrities and Hollywood hangers-on—people not quite on the B-list but working their asses off to get there.

Tasteful, Mediterranean-style homes with red tile roofs, accessorized with the mandatory palm trees and bougainvillea. The street is dark, the pavement gleaming and devoid of dirt or leaves, as though it's just been wetted down by a film crew for a movie shoot, or as if I accidentally wandered into the back entrance at Disneyland.

The only discernible difference between her neighborhood and mine is that in addition to the manned gate at the entrance of Gigi's neighborhood, each and every mini mansion boasts a ten-foot decorative security fence of cast-iron bars around the property, every inch wired with closed-circuit security cameras. According to Gigi, many of these fabulous homes are rentals, occupied by the flavor-of-the-month ingénue, reality-TV star, or TLC supermodel/carpenter. People like Gigi herself. People who don't actually need double-security systems now, but who hope to have their very own stable of crazies and stalkers in the very near future, a sure sign they've made it to the big time.

I find Gigi's house and sit in my car for a minute, my heart thumping wildly. I'm here, but I haven't exactly figured out what to do. GET HUSBAND BACK is the extent of my master plan, and I'm unsure how to execute it. The sun is just starting to peek out, dragging streaks of pink sky with it. I check myself in the rearview mirror. *Oh God, not attractive.* I'm puffy and disheveled. I run a quick brush through my hair and pat on some lip gloss, not that it helps. My skin is parched, my lips are chapped and crusty, globs of gloss pool in the cracks. There are serious black rings under my eyes, but when I try to wipe them away, they won't budge. I'm not sure if this is relocated smudgeproof mascara or the last twenty-four hours. Easing out of my rental Buick and into the darkness, I walk quietly to Gigi's gate. I push the buzzer on the keypad, looking straight into the security camera, attempting to look like a normal visitor and not someone who drops in unannounced, from across the country, at five o'clock in the morning. Damn, I should have brought doughnuts. You can get in anywhere with a box of doughnuts.

After a few minutes, a woman's sleepy voice crackles over the intercom: "Hello? Who is it?"

"It's Darby Vaughn . . . Bradley," I add quickly. "Darby Vaughn Bradley. Will's wife. I need to speak with him right now, please."

"Um, jussa minute," the voice sputters back.

I stand there for five minutes that seem like sixty, peering into the camera with my face frozen in a smile. My TV face. If he's here, I don't want Will's first vision of me in four days to be puffy-faced *and* scowling.

"Darby, why are you here?" The surprise of hearing Will's voice slices through me.

"Will, why are *you* here?" I ask, my voice surprisingly shrill and dripping with panic. *Keep it together, keep it together, keep it together.* I take a deep breath through my nose and resolve myself into calmness.

"Darby, just go home. It's over between us."

"What? Why?" I am coming apart, sobs pressuring their way

out of every seam of my body. There is no answer from the other side of the speaker box.

"Will!" I call out to him; there is no answer.

"Will!" I scream into the box, hanging on to the keypad box for dear life as my perfect life spins away from me. Tears pour out of me, burning my face. "Please, please," I beg, "tell me what's wrong? We'll fix it! Please, please, come out here so we can talk." I can't stop crying, and I stare hopelessly into the camera, not even sure if Will is still on the other side.

"Just talk to me!" I shriek. "Damn it! Will, you fucking owe me that! Just tell me what is going on!" Suddenly, I'm blinded by lights in every direction, floodlights beam from the top of the fence, and I see that there are no fewer than three camera crews on the sidewalk ten feet away. Coming from the other side are a few photographers. I stop where I am, unable to speak or move. Then Will's unmistakable voice spills out onto the street.

"Go home, Darby. I can't be with you anymore."

What the hell? The camera guys rush me, and I scramble to the Buick and lock the doors as soon as I can pull myself inside. They are everywhere, banging fists on the windows and pointing their nasty cameras at me. One maniac jumps on the hood, and from every angle the bright beams of flashbulbs and night-lighting surge into the car. I lean on the horn to warn them I'm going to start moving—the last thing I want to do now is to run over the foot of some upstanding member of the paparazzi. What the hell! Where did they come from? There are no cars on Gigi's street. Did they sneak over the security wall like ants? Were they dropped from a helicopter under cover of darkness like gossip-gathering paratroopers? I drive slowly to the end of Gigi's street with an army of camera-wielding psychos following me.

Finally, I turn the corner onto the main road, and when I'm

certain I'm clear of stalkarazzi, I stomp on the gas and peel out of Gigi's neighborhood, almost clipping the gate at the guard shack. What the fuck is happening with my life? It's finally getting light outside, and the windows have begun to fog up—probably the combination of hysterics and high-speed chase. Reversing the directions on the GPS, I head back to the airport. I dump the car off at the airport drop-off, pull my hair up into a ponytail, and don the giant sunglasses again for a ride à la shuttle back to the Delta counter.

Changing clothes in the airport bathroom, I rummage through my bag for a hat of some kind. I add a pink baseball cap emblazoned with DREAMGIRL (ha!) to the ponytail/big glasses ensemble and change quickly into a pair of jeans, flip-flops, and a T-shirt.

Heading back to the counter, I try to buy myself a ride back to Florida, but the agent informs me that the eight A.M. flight is full, and she can't get me a flight out until two in the afternoon.

"Winter break," she explains. "You really should plan ahead if you're going to try to go to Florida in November."

Ah, now, why didn't I think of that?

There's only one seat on the afternoon flight. In first class. For $2,100.

"Thanks, I'll take it," I tell her, slapping my credit card onto the counter. I don't care, I just want out of here. I check my suitcase and head over to the coffee shop for something to eat. I feel sick to my stomach again, and can't decide whether food is a good plan or a bad one. Grabbing a bagel and a Coke from the display case, I take a seat in the corner.

In every airport in the country, the channel of choice is CNN. Except in LA, where E! substitutes for hard news. They even have the little news ticker at the bottom of the screen, just like the real news stations, so Californians can be updated immediately if Nicolas Cage signs on to play John F. Kennedy, or Pamela Anderson decides to change her nuptial status.

I bite into the bagel just as the video hits the screen: Me, of the bloated, tear-stained face, bawling and begging a security camera to take me back. The title below reads: BREAKING NEWS: ROMANCE EXPERT DARBY VAUGHN, OUTSIDE THE HOME OF GIGI BISSANTI. Then, a "news report" proclaiming Will and Gigi to be "resting comfortably after the incident." Oh, no. After a quick commercial break extolling the comparative virtues of shiny hair versus shiny, strong hair, E! is back with more news and another run of a slow-mo clip of me vomiting on the *Today* show. Boy, that thing just never gets old.

Stuffing another bite of the bagel into my mouth, I dump my tray in the nearest trash can and slink off to the ladies room. I'll be okay if I can just keep it together until I get home. I figure I'll barricade myself in the bathroom for the next five hours, if I have to. I wait patiently for an open stall in the back, drag my carry-on bag behind me, and cover every visible surface with seven or eight layers of toilet-seat covers. At first, I set myself up on the commode, but the automatic toilet keeps flushing and I have to jump up every time so I won't get splattered with toilet water. After a few rounds, I squat on the floor near the door, hovering in tissue paper. I pull my phone out of my bag to call my agent, Holland, and she picks up on the first ring.

"Where are you?" she asks. "*What* are you doing?"

"I'm hiding out in the bathroom at LAX," I sigh. "Have you seen E!?"

"No, just a minute," she says, and I hear clicking and the sound of channel changing. I can hear her breathing on the phone, and I assume her silence means she must be watching the latest development in my luge from dignity. "Jesus, Darby. Why in the world would you do this?"

"Well, I thought the whole I'm-leaving-you-we're-getting-a-divorce thing might be a mistake, and, truthfully, I wouldn't have acted like such a pathetic loser if I knew I was being filmed." I'm crying and, frankly, feeling pretty damned sorry for myself. This is so unfair. "Why do they keep torturing me? Why do they keep talking about this? They barely covered it for a day when that *Rules* girl got divorced, and when that *Get Perfect Love* author was on her seventh divorce nobody even cared. Why do they keep running this crap about me over and over on every channel?"

"Darby," Holland says incredulously, "are you kidding? This would be over for any other love guru in a day, but you keep giving them fantastic tape. You puke in Matt Lauer's chrysanthemums, you're begging a security camera to give you another chance. How could they *not* run it? It's a fucking train wreck, it's mesmerizing. Every time you're near a camera, you're a disaster."

Oh, God. I've become the O. J. of my generation.

The Dreamgirl Academy: And Baby Makes One

By Darby Vaughn

Dear Darby,
I met a man and he pursued me like crazy for five months. Every day, he called me from wherever he was in the world. He learned my sister is having a child and he assumed that I want a child with him. Because he already has two children, he said he can't give me what I want. But he already gives me everything I want.

I never told him that I want children! Last Sunday, he told me that he doesn't want a relationship with me. But he is the one who asked me to be his copilot! He is the one who repeatedly told me, "I have a dream in my life and you play an important role. I am rich because I have you in my life. You are the best woman I've met in my life. I can call you a PW: a perfect woman." I haven't heard from him, what should I do?
Baby Talk

Dear Baby Talk,
I'm sure it was better in person, but the whole "PW, be my copilot" thing sort of gave me a Scott-Peterson-strawberries-and-champagne-at-the-Holiday-Inn vibe. In other words, something just isn't right.

He's told you that he doesn't want a relationship with you. It doesn't matter if his reasons aren't valid to you, his reasons for not wanting a relationship are valid to him. And, in the game of love, it takes two to play.

I'm sure his feelings for you were genuine at the time, but for whatever reason, he doesn't see a future with you. Don't try to talk him back into the relationship—he doesn't want to be there. I sympathize with you, I really do. Everybody has been in this kind of relationship situation at least once—we feel if we could just explain our side a little better, or line up the proof like they do on CSI, the person dumping us would have an "Aha!" moment and come to his or her senses. All would be well and romantic bliss would be restored.

Unfortunately, the fact that we really want someone to love us doesn't make it happen. Move on with your life. Someday, you'll meet a man who wants the same things you do, who doesn't need to be reminded that he really does love you. He'll remember it every day on his own.
Darby

Chapter 10

I finally get back home, only to find that Will has pretty much cleared out our entire house. At first I think we've been robbed, but then I realize that the burglars have either very discriminating taste or a very specific list of pre- and post-wedding purchases.

All that's left are my clothes, a few pieces of furniture in the garage, and the photos on the walls. I'm basically leaving the marriage with exactly what I brought into it. It's eerie, as though the last four years never happened. The kids' rooms are barren, stripped of everything but the paint and the carpet, matted with impressions of where their furniture once sat. A lone, sparkly fairy hangs from Lilly's soft pink ceiling over where her bed used to be. I weep, remembering the day Lilly and I sat at our kitchen table littered with craft supplies, snuggling and laughing while we sprinkled glitter on Fairy Yolanda's vellum paper wings.

What crushes me is their absence, the unfamiliar quietness of the house, the overwhelming nothingness. I sit on the floor of Lilly's room, tracing with my finger the indent in the carpet of where our rocking chair sat, the story chair. How many times have we read *How Fletcher Was Hatched* or *The Kissing Hand* while snuggled up together in that chair, her silky head resting on my shoulder? An ache creeps its way inside of me, dragging with it a jagged awareness that I might never see Lilly and Aidan again.

I have to get out of here, I can't bear to stay in this house. Everywhere I look, I'm reminded of what's missing.

I force myself up off the floor and try to figure out what to do next.

This is Will's house; it was his before we met. And although I have tried to make it my home, looking around the rooms stripped of all evidence of our lives together, I feel more like an unwelcome visitor.

Divorce. My mind is reeling, sputtering with a montage of moments of our doomed relationship: The first time we met. The way he looked into my eyes with such profound emotion on the day we got married. The petty little arguments and life-flattening blowouts over credit card bills, political affiliations, and whether I should inform one of our well-liked neighbors that I suspected her husband was cheating on her. (There's some irony for you; I let Will talk me out of telling her.)

And the horrible, horrible end when my world as I knew it was suddenly over.

Part of me still thinks this will be just another argument. That the heat and anger will blow over and settle delicately into a truce. And once a few weeks have passed, all will be forgotten (or at least ignored) as the rhythm of PTA meetings, trips to the vet, and progressive dinners overtakes us once again, and we become too busy or too tired to fight another day.

I haven't talked to Will since the security-cam incident, and I'm not sure what I would say if I could. Plus, a part of me feels as though any phone conversation I would have with him would probably end up on *Howard Stern* by tomorrow. Do I really need that kind of exposure? I don't think so. My heart feels like it's been cut right out of my chest, but I've got to be pragmatic. I want answers from him: *Why did you do this to me? How could you leave me? Was our whole relationship a big fucking lie? What were we doing for the last four years? Did you ever love me? Are you even sorry for what you've done?*

Can you be an old maid at thirty-one? I feel so old, ugly, unlovable. Horribly, irrevocably damaged.

I am alone again. It is not an unfamiliar state of being. I felt this way after the last of my aunties was gone, at every Thanksgiving and Christmas in my twenties sitting at the dining table of some boyfriend or friend, watching someone else's dad cut the turkey and serving myself a scoop of cranberry sauce that looked and tasted all wrong. I felt this way when I had my first period, bought my first prom dress, learned my first book was being published, wishing I had my mother with me to share the news, and knowing that having family members who love you from heaven is not the same thing as having someone who loves you *here*. Someone who loves you profoundly, who'd wrap their arms around you and tell you how proud they are. I wish I knew my mother, and I wish my grandmother was still here with me. I pull the sacred bottle of Chanel No. 5 out of a small box and inhale deeply. It is the scent my grandma wore all my life, and the only thing that can bring her back to me. I need her, need someone, anyone, I belong to. It is almost gone, just a few droppersful of the precious liquid remain, and I use it sparingly at times like this: times when I am completely and utterly alone. Times when I really need my mother, my father, my grandmother, or my aunties, and all I have to love me is a thirty-year-old bottle of perfume.

What Is a Dreamgirl?

When we say Dreamgirls, we're not talking head-in-the-clouds, residing-in-Fantasyland kind of girls. We're talking knock-down, drag-out, fabulous, smart, funny, sexy, fearless, I've-got-it-all-together-and-I-know-what-to-do-with-it women.

We're talking kick-ass chicks here.

The reference to Dreamgirls is aspirational. If you can believe it, you can be it. It's the best version of ourselves, the one we aspire to be. You know, the one who has a fantastic job and the best girlfriends on the planet, who spends three days a week helping out at a soup kitchen or whose apartment looks like a magazine layout, or who always has the right shoes, no matter what the occasion. Your own version of a Dreamgirl is anything you want to be.

It's in you. And I just know you can pull it off.

—The Dreamgirl Academy

Chapter 11

My Dreamgirls have arrived. They pile out of Jules's giant SUV, laughing and toting luggage, empty boxes, and pastries, early Saturday morning. I know I'm saved.

I'm deeply thankful and humbled by their presence this morning, knowing just how impossible it is to drop everything at a moment's notice when you have a life, a family, a career, and fly across the country. Of course, they know I'd do the same for them.

Jules, Tia, Kimberly, and Sarah have been my best friends since college. And while they may not be my family of origin, there's no doubt in my heart that they are the closest thing to sisters I'll ever have. We've supported each other through everything: We helped Tia clear out her offices after her first company went bust, we camped out in the waiting room when Kimberly had her miscarriage, and later, her baby. We've laughed and cried together through bad boyfriends, bad jobs, and bad times. I know everything about them, every secret, every fear, every accomplishment. We are all women now, with lives, families, and responsibilities scattered all across the country. But even when we're eighty, sitting on Jules's front porch sipping mojitos and telling stories, we'll always be the girls. The Dreamgirls. The name was first bestowed on our little group by a hilarious gay hairstylist we shared and adored, then cemented by history, friends, and the men in our lives. I have included the Dreamgirl moniker in all of my books, and in my radio and TV shows—I always hoped that my readers would find support and love from a close group of girlfriends as wonderful as mine. And that together they could see themselves for the wonderful, amazing women they are.

All of us are married now, except Tia, who has always been far more interested in her career than men, and, well, me now. There was one wild summer three years back that all of us spent criss-crossing the country, doing bridesmaid duty for one another. Four of us got married that year. Kimberly and her husband almost missed my wedding because their flight back from their Jamaican honeymoon was canceled due to bad weather. Then, we were nearly bounced out of the church by a choir director in sensible shoes when the girls and I got a little too rowdy singing an impromptu version of "Chapel of Love" ten minutes before Will and I were set to take our vows.

They pull their things inside the door and take turns hugging me so tightly my arms begin to numb.

"Thank you for coming," I say.

"Of course we came," says Sarah. "What did you expect? We heard you needed a little Dreamgirl Disaster Relief. Have a doughnut, sweetie. Pastry makes everything better."

"How long can you stay?"

"We're all going back on Tuesday," Kimberly informs me. "My kids will have torn the house apart by then. Lord knows, my husband can't be trusted to watch his own children for any extended period of time. Tia's got some big presentation on Wednesday. We've got four long days to get you back on track. Easy as pie."

My friends tell me how sorry they are and that they know I will make it through this. I'm so glad they're here. I cry a little, and they cry with me, and then Tia, as always, breaks up the bawlfest.

"I've ordered some moving men, they'll be here at eleven," announces Tia, in that commanding voice that turns board members into groupies. The girls break into giggles immediately, and within seconds they're laughing so hard that tears are streaming down their faces.

"What's so funny?" I ask, quite obviously the only one not in on the joke.

"Tia hired some male models from Miami to move your boxes," says Jules, playfully chiding Tia with a little twinkle in her eye.

"The neighbors will be watching," says Tia with her most wicked grin, tucking her short, dark hair behind her ear. "If they're going to tell Will anything, let it be that the cover boys from Abercrombie and Fitch were loadin' up your truck."

"With their shirts off," adds Sarah deviously, patting her seven-months-pregnant belly.

I roll my eyes and laugh for the first time in two days.

"Are you sure you want to move out of the house?" asks Jules. "Will's already out, this is your home."

"It's not my home without the kids here," I say. "I can't stay here. Everywhere I look is another reminder that my family is gone. If I stay in this house, I'll go crazy. I've got to get out of here."

Jules nods. "Okay."

The girls and I get to packing my smaller, more personal items. At eleven on the dot, the doorbell rings. The hottie brigade has arrived.

The guys, gorgeous and shirtless as promised, start loading boxes in the truck. Will's Bose stereo is long gone, of course, so Tia spins the radio dial on the cheapie fuchsia boom box residing in my closet and cranks up the volume to give us a little moving music. As we pack the remaining contents of my bedroom, Tia plays pop star, using one of my three-pound weights as a microphone, and the rest of us join in to sing backup. We dance around, giggling and flinging my delicates into boxes, and belting out the words to Brad Paisley's song, "Celebrity":

I'll make the supermarket tabloids, they'll write some awful stuff.
But the more they run my name down, the more my price goes up.

When the song ends, I'm laughing and crying at the same time.

An hour later, my things are all packed and the moving models have nearly finished loading the truck. The girls and I stand outside on my front lawn half supervising, half ogling. The guys' perfect, twenty-something bodies glisten from hard work and humidity, and they occasionally break to make the crowd of housewives giddy with their wickedly spectacular smiles. As Tia predicted, a throng of my neighbors gathers on the sidewalk to chat and see the show. They wave, tentatively, and I feel a hot blush of shame and embarrassment creep its way up my neck. The girls huddle around me protectively, but one by one, my neighbors step into the circle to hug me, wish me well, and tell me how sorry they are. I'm braced for cattiness and judgment, but find kindness and support from them instead. Jeannie Gerbaud, the neighborhood gossip monger widely known as "the talk of the block," is the sole exception—she waves from her post across the street while diligently inspecting her flowerbeds but does not make her way over to speak to me.

I nudge Tia, nodding my head subtly in Jeannie's direction, and say, "Mission accomplished."

Jeannie can be counted on to disseminate a full, detailed report of the teen-dream movers to every single neighbor within a two-community radius by the time the street lights come on. Her greatest pride is being not only the first to know but the first to tell.

Tia grins at me, then heads toward the house. "Well, then, my work here is done."

Jeannie shades her eyes from the sun with her hand, and shouts to me from across the street. "So sorry you're leaving, Darby. I thought this might happen when I saw Will and Gigi cozied up together last month at the Un-Gala Gala. Those two always did have a spark. We've *all* been so worried about you . . ."

I can feel my face flush and tears begin to sting my eyes as I digest Jeannie's not-so-subtle way of letting me know I've been the neighborhood Starbucks topic of the week.

I glance around at my neighbors, and most of them look down to avoid meeting my eyes. The few who do make eye contact exude such pity that I'm compelled to look away.

How is it possible that everybody but me figured out what was going on? Am I blind? Stupid? Just when I think it is not possible to feel any more humiliation. I wonder for a second why no one told me, but I don't need to ask out loud. Nobody wants to be the bearer of that kind of news.

Sue, another of my neighbors, reaches out to touch my arm. "I'm so sorry, Darby. We didn't know if it was true or not. I thought maybe Jeannie was just being catty."

A few hours later I'm fully installed in Jules's guesthouse, which may be the only positive thing about my life falling apart. (Okay, male models, so that's two things.) Jules and her husband, Mark, both hail from wealthy old Florida families, and Mark's made a killing on his own in commercial real estate. Their main house sits on a bay-to-beach plot on Lido Key, lushly landscaped with hibiscus, bougainvillea, and a variety of exotic tropical plants and trees, not to mention a saltwater pool and tennis court (grass, of course). Nestled near the beach and to the left of the main house is the guesthouse, a four-room Key West–style cottage painted cheery yellow with white shutters. The cottage has a comfortable great room, a small tiled kitchen, and a roomy bedroom with spectacular views of the gulf. But my favorite room of all is the turret room—a tiny round room perched on top of the house with 360-degree views of the bay and the gulf. From the time Jules and Mark bought this house, I have always loved to climb the narrow winding stairs to the turret, open up all the windows and prop up the shutters, listen to the roar of the gulf and the murmur of the palms, inhale the sea salt, and let the bay breeze cool my skin. Jules does too. I know for certain that despite the fact that she has a six-thousand-square-foot home at her disposal less than a hundred yards away (including a closet bigger than my last apartment), the tiny room in the guesthouse is her favorite place. It's everyone's favorite place, actually. I have a million memories of Lilly, Aidan, and Jules's kids playing Rapunzel in the turret, the windows thrown open as they run giggling up and down the curved staircase, laughing until they're all rolling in the sand.

Most of my belongings are now stashed in a storage unit off I-75, but my clothes, toiletries, the quilt my grandmother made, and a few personal items are heaped in boxes in the center of the living room. Sarah and Kimberly methodically unpack my clothes while Tia fires up the blender for a batch of margaritas.

"Make mine a virgin!" shouts Sarah, raising one hand and resting the other on her burgeoning belly.

"Too late for that . . ." cracks Tia, handing her an alcohol-free concoction loaded with fruit skewers.

Mark makes a brief appearance from the main house to check in on us, give Jules a tender peck on the cheek, and bring a tray of warm rolls and pulled pork. You've got to love a man who can barbecue.

"Do you ladies need anything?"

Jules gives him a wink and shoos him off sweetly. "We've got it covered, darlin'."

She grabs my laptop case and motions for me to follow her upstairs. Wedged between two overstuffed love seats laden with striped pillows are two new additions: a small mahogany desk and an elegant padded chair with a pale blue, tufted silk pillow.

"I had Mark bring this up here earlier. I thought it would be the perfect place for you to write," Jules said proudly, placing my laptop gently on the desk. "We love you darlin', you're family to us. I know this is hard for you, but I want you to feel at home here. You can stay here as long as you like."

Tears well up in me and I let Jules hug me tightly as I wonder if I'll even *have* a career when all is said and done.

"Besides," she jokes, patting my back, "if you stay forever, Mark's mother can't."

I put my head against her petite shoulder and let the roar of the waves from the open windows drown out the sounds of my sobs.

NOTICE TO OUR READERS

Relationship Columnist Darby Vaughn is on personal leave. Her column, THE DREAMGIRL ACADEMY, will return in two weeks.

PETROVA'S PET-TACULAR PET TIPS will run in its absence.

Chapter 12

For the next two days I sleep and cry, with Jules and Tia bringing me their own brands of sustenance at regular intervals. Jules comes bearing comfort food—mashed potatoes and corn bread, apple crisp and pecan pie. Tia provides running commentary on the sorry state of the American male and endless pitchers of mojitos. I'm on day three of the ratty tank top and oversize blue pajama bottoms (Will's) that I wore to bed on the first night we arrived. The five of us sit huddled together on the couch with the heavy drapes closed, in extended slumber-party mode. Snack trays and empty glasses are littered around the room as we doze in and out of the requisite breakup film festival: *When Harry Met Sally*, *Sleepless in Seattle*, and *Bewitched*, a continuous loop of Nora and Delia Ephron's greatest.

I wake up on the third morning, splayed out on the guest couch with a hangover and a feeling of dread. Sarah and Kimberly are sharing the bedroom, Jules is back in the big house with Mark and their kids, and Tia is passed out a few feet away on the other sofa. As I lie on the couch in semidarkness, listening for the ocean, the last few days swirl around in my head. I miss my life. I miss my husband (or at least what I thought was my husband). I'm afraid everything I've worked so hard for—my book, my radio show, my whole career—is ruined, gone, because of stupid Will. How could this happen? To me? God, I really miss my kids. I'm staggered at how much it hurts, more than losing Will, even. More than anything. Without my family, my house, my career, without all the things I've dedicated my life to over the last several years, who the hell am I?

Sarah lets out a thunderous snore from the bedroom, puncturing my bubble of self-pity. I can't help but smile. Sarah believes wholeheartedly that her obscene snoring was brought on by her pregnancy, but the rest of us know from years of roommate roulette that Sarah has been rocking the walls since college. Her snore wakes Tia, who shakes her dark hair and stretches from her nest on the other couch.

"Up you go, babykins," she announces. "Your bellyaching days are officially over. Today is the day we get your life back on track." I groan and roll over, yanking the quilt over my shoulders and burying my head in the pillow.

"My whole world just fell apart, I only get three days to recover?"

Tia says matter-of-factly, "That's how it works, sweetie. Life goes on."

I know from experience that I could probably talk the rest of the girls into a twenty-four-hour misery extension, but once Tia's made up her mind, she'll just torture me until I comply.

"Job one is a shower," she says. "We have an appointment with your new attorney, Holt Gregory, at eleven. Will got a bit of a jump on you with that Nup Buster guy, but this Holt Gregory is three for three against ol' Sol in court over the last six months. According to Google, he's handled the divorces for a bunch of celebrity clients, but he never talks to the press about them; he's smart, he's cutting-edge when it comes to family law issues, and he has a reputation for being a lawyers' lawyer. So, unlike Will's attorney, Holt Gregory is not the type to air your dirty laundry on the courthouse steps and then suck up to the press just to further his own career. He has some dignity."

Now, normally I make my own decisions, but my brain is so deep-fried in despair that I feel completely incapable of picking out what kind of toast I want for breakfast, let alone hiring a divorce attorney. "Type-A Tia" is one of the smartest people I know, and I have no doubt she's whipped up complete dossiers on every suitable divorce lawyer within a 250-mile radius.

I close my eyes, hoping for just a few more minutes, but Tia pokes me in the ribs and says, "Get up."

Dragging myself to the bathroom, I turn on the shower. A heap of wet towels is piled on the floor, and I wander into the hallway to see if I can find a fresh one. As soon as I step through the doorway, I see Tia walking toward me carrying a giant basket loaded down with fresh towels and a smaller basket of muffins. Probably baked from scratch. A note is taped to the top of the handle on Jules's signature pale blue Crane notepaper.

"From Jules. The basket was out on the front porch," Tia says. Digging through the basket, she pinches off a piece of muffin and pops it into her mouth. "Clean towels, baked goods. What is this, fresh lavender?" She laughs. "Our girl puts Martha Stewart to shame," she says, handing me a clean bath towel.

Heading back into the bathroom, I drop my depression-wear into the hamper next to the door and step into the steamy shower. The water beats onto me and I allow myself one more good bawl as I lather myself with Jules's custom-blended coconut soap. Twenty minutes later I emerge, legs shaved, hair clean, and all cried out.

I dress and dry my hair in the bedroom as Tia, Kimberly, and

Sarah take turns in the shower, and finally, I feel a little better having pulled myself together.

Two hours later, Tia and I are sitting in the downtown office of one Holt Gregory, attorney at law. The receptionist is a plump elderly lady, and she occasionally peeks over the wall that separates her desk from the client waiting area. The lobby is comfortable and eclectic with casually elegant, café au lait–colored sofas, sea grass rugs over marble tile, and watercolor seascapes framed on the walls—a definite departure from the Old White Guys with Money design scheme generally favored in these parts. After a few minutes, the phone atop her desk buzzes, and she rises to escort us to a small conference room.

"May I offer you ladies some coffee or sweet tea?" she asks, standing in the doorway.

"Sweet tea, please," Tia and I request in unison. Tia shoots me a look, as if to say, *See, anyone with sweet tea on tap can't be all bad . . .*

The receptionist scurries off to fetch our drinks, and Mr. Gregory appears in the doorway within a minute. I'd guess he's in his mid-thirties. He is tall, extraordinarily tall, maybe six-foot-four, with broad shoulders and dark brown hair that looks like a losing battle between unruly and curly. He's mesmerizing, really, gorgeous but in an offbeat way I can't put my finger on—sort of the antithesis of my husband. Where Will is slick, his image polished to glossy perfection, even in a suit Holt Gregory looks like he might have just stepped off a Jet Ski.

I imagine Mr. Gregory can count on a slam-dunk verdict anytime he manages to swing a mostly female jury. His eyes are intensely green, the color of lake water, and he glances back and forth between Tia and me for a brief second, probably to ascertain which of us is the impending divorcée, and which is the supportive friend.

He thrusts his hand in my general direction, all business, and says, "I'm Holt Gregory, you must be Darby Vaughn," with the smoothest drawling bourbon baritone I've ever heard. The puffy eyes must have given me away.

"Yes, nice to meet you. This is my friend Tia."

"Ah yes," he says, with just a glimmer of something that looks like mischief, "we spoke on the phone. The interrogator, I presume."

Tia and I exchange glances, and she smiles at him, "Well, Mr. Gregory, you hold up well under questioning."

"Thanks." He pauses and shifts his gaze back to me. "Miss Vaughn—"

"Darby," I interject.

"Darby," he says, in such a way it almost sounds like *darlin'*. "Call me Holt. How long do you suspect your husband's been cheating on you?" Damn, he cuts right to the quick.

"Actually, I'm not sure. A while, I think." I tell him about the airline miles, the undercover dinners at the Ritz-Carlton, and any other bits of information I can think of.

"All right, then, what are your concerns?" He says "what" in a way that makes it seem like it has two syllables, wha-aat.

"What about the assets? You all have any kids?" he asks, as he scribbles furiously on a yellow pad.

"We have two kids. They're his, actually, from a former marriage. My biggest concern right now"—I take a deep breath and will myself not to cry—"is them, Lilly and Aidan. I want them to live with me. Will's gone back to his ex-wife Gigi and taken the kids to her home in California. I've been their primary caregiver, though. Not Gigi. Not Will. Do you think there will be a problem with custody? Do you think we can get them back?"

"Is he abusive? A gambler? A drinker?"

"No!" I say forcefully. "He's a wonderful father." Oh, what the hell do I know? Until last week, I was pretty sure he was a wonderful husband.

"Then yes, ma'am, I'd say you have a big problem with custody. Hell, I doubt you'd even get visitation. No judge is gonna just give 'em to you—they're not your kids."

My heart plummets toward my stomach. "But I'm the one who's with them all the time! Gigi is off in Hollywood being a ridiculous TV star and their father travels four days a week for work! I love them! I'm the only one who spends any time with them!"

"I understand. Sorry, that's the way it works," he says matter-of-factly. "I'll be happy to fight it out for you, but lemme tell you now, you don't have a snowball's chance. We have four or five possible options here, none of them particularly promising. We could try to establish you as a psychological parent, since you were the primary caregiver for the children, but the rights of stepparents is a relatively new area of legal development. Getting visitation is not a likely possibility, and gaining custody is practically unheard of. It's going to be a tough sell. We'd have to show that Will and Gigi were unfit, that they abandoned the children, or that the welfare of the kids depends on them being with you. I want to be honest with you: It's gonna cost you, and you probably won't win."

"That's not fair to me or the kids. I'm the one who takes care of them!"

"You're a public figure, you could be a pioneer with regard to stepparents's rights, shine some light on the issue," he suggests.

"I don't want to be a pioneer," I say. "I want to be a mother." I also want to cry, but I can't let myself lose it in front of this cold-hearted jerk. I take a deep breath as my gut begins to flip-flop. I concentrate ferociously on not getting sick right here in the conference room, as my entire body tenses and lurches. Damn it. Not again. *I've just got to get through this meeting.* I take a deep breath to calm myself, letting just a few tears leak out. Miraculously, my stomach stops turning somersaults. Thank you, Our Lady of Vomit.

"God have mercy on those of us on the right side of a lawsuit," Holt says, his expression completely unreadable. Then, our eyes meet across the table, and for a brief second, I glimpse a flash of something that looks almost like humanity in his intense green eyes.

"Let's talk about the other issues," interjects Tia. "He ended the marriage on national TV. Darby is a relationship expert and he effectively killed her career with one shot. She's already been fired from her radio and TV shows and her book tour was canceled. And since Will was Darby's publicist before the incident, he left her completely vulnerable in the media with no protection."

Holt nods and says, "That is an issue we can work with. Notifying Darby in such an opprobrious, intentionally damaging way on national television was malicious. Did you sign a contract designating Will as your publicist?"

"I did before we got married, and I know my publisher paid him to set up the media for my latest book launch."

"Did you ever hire another publicist during the time you were married to Will?"

"No, he acted as my publicist during the entire time we were married."

"Did you pay him for continuous service during that time?" Holt asks, jotting notes on his pad.

"No," I say, "but my publisher did."

"Good. I'll need an accounting of the marital assets. And Will's business assets."

"The house was his before we married. He owns a business, which he owned before we married. My book royalties and the income from my radio show are in my business account," I explain, miserably.

"Who is residing in the house now?"

"No one. Will took the kids and moved out while I was out of town last week. I moved out three days ago."

"I'd advise you to stay in the house," he says. "You have a legal right to be there, and it's far easier to claim the residence in the divorce if you live there."

"I can't go back there."

"That's a mistake. You need to reconsider. Did you ever sign anything releasing Will from service as your publicist?"

"No," I say.

"Well, after this, he's definitely fired," says Tia.

"I need to see your contract with him, but I think we're probably looking at breach of contract, which brings his business into play. You hired him, and he not only didn't fulfill his professional duties to you, he sabotaged you professionally." Holt asks me to produce bank statements and income information about Will's business, my income, and the rest of our assets. I do my best but tell him Will's home office was cleared out with the rest of the furniture before I made it home from California. God, I wish I'd paid more attention.

"Has your husband hired an attorney?" Holt asks.

"I'm not certain, but I know he's been meeting with Sol Weinstein for a few months." Holt raises his eyebrows when I say Sol's name.

"Will told me that Sol was a new client," I explain. "But he was billing Will, not the other way around."

He looks to be deep in thought as he scribbles down a few more notes on his pad.

"What do you know about Sol?" I ask.

"Sol is aggressive," Holt replies, carefully measuring his words. "He's not one who tends to settle cases, and Sol probably isn't going to mind too much if the press shows up at this hearing, but we can deal with that. We've got a strong case with the divorce, but with regard to the custody issue, the law is overwhelmingly in your husband's favor."

The words *no visitation* keep ringing in my ears over the next forty-five minutes, and my heart burns. I feel helpless, hopeless. What if the kids can't live with me? The idea of not even being able to see them, snuggle them, inhale the sweet scent of their freshly washed hair, kiss their soft little cheeks, or watch them as they lie sleeping, smiling in dreams. Never to hear them call me "Dar-mama" again. It's too much to bear. I sit fixated on the thought, barely hearing what is going on, while Tia and Holt cover the low points in my marriage.

Mr. Gregory's detached dissection of my marriage is strictly analytical, completely devoid of kindness, sympathy, or emotion. He efficiently rattles through the details of my life like he's picking specs on a new car.

It's almost two o'clock by the time we finally leave Mr. Gregory's office, and it feels like the longest day of my life.

"I like him," announces Tia, as we walk down Main Street and head for the car.

"I hate him," I say, sulking. "He doesn't care one bit about helping me get custody of Lilly and Aidan."

"Whoa," Tia says, calmly putting her hand on my shoulder.

"That is not what he said. He's being realistic with you, and he has a point. You may act like the mom and feel like the mom, but you're not the mom. Fair or not, you're the stepmom. And now you're the ex-stepmom. You've got to face facts here. He's giving you a realistic picture of what your odds are, which is a lot better than some lawyer who makes all kinds of big promises about full custody and drains your bank account when you don't have a shot in hell."

Her words cut through me. "You don't think I have a shot in hell?"

"No, I don't," she says kindly. "I love you, I know how much you're hurting, how much you love those kids, and I know it's not fair. I just think you'd be wise to listen to someone who gives you the facts. I'd rather see you go into this with your eyes open, as painful as that is. Mr. Gregory is not being cruel or insensitive. He's being straight with you. Wouldn't you rather have him tell you the truth? Now you know the facts, and you can deal with this. You can either try to make some arrangement with Will, take him to court and blow every dime you've got on a losing battle, or you can move on with your life and try to resuscitate your career, which is what I'd do, by the way. Your choice."

I feel beaten, and yet, I know she's right. It's easy to blame Holt Gregory, but the truth is, my predicament isn't his fault. He's just calling it the way he sees it. Plain and simple.

"Buck up, Miss Darby," Tia says as she squeezes my arm in the parking lot. "We're going to a party tonight."

"Party? Oh, no, I can't . . . I don't want to go anywhere," I say.

"It'll be fun," Tia says, ignoring me. "Do you remember Laura? She's hosting some little thing tonight. You must get back out in the world. No more moping around the house for you." I really want to just go home and climb into bed for another three days, but Tia and the girls have been so great this week, the least I can do is show them my appreciation and go along. I nod my head and Tia grins victoriously, as we head back to Jules's house.

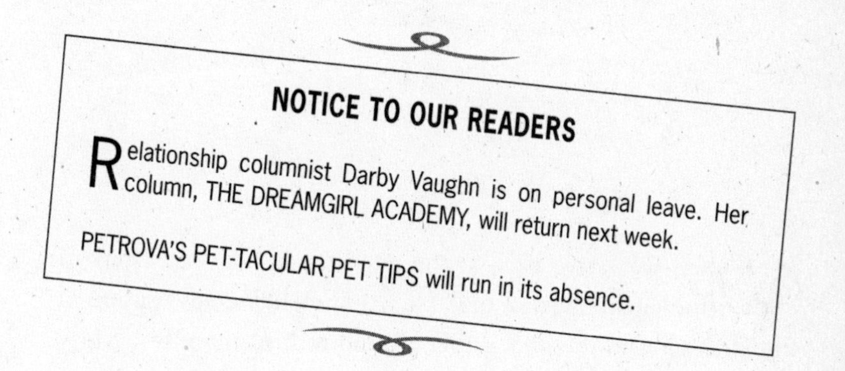
NOTICE TO OUR READERS

Relationship columnist Darby Vaughn is on personal leave. Her column, THE DREAMGIRL ACADEMY, will return next week.

PETROVA'S PET-TACULAR PET TIPS will run in its absence.

Chapter 13

When we arrive back at the guesthouse, Jules has a tray of homemade guacamole and warm tortilla chips waiting in the kitchen, and the girls gather around to hear the play-by-play on the meeting with Holt. Tia fills them in, including my pathetic odds of getting the kids back and high probability of a decent monetary settlement, given that Will not only cheated on me but attempted to maim my career in the process. Tia whips up a batch of margaritas and we volley between serious divorce talk and altogether fluffier topics.

"Have you seen Holt Gregory?" Tia asks Jules.

"No, we've never met," Jules says, "but I keep hearing his name come up at parties."

"He's gorgeous," Tia proclaims. "Green eyes to die for. Big, strong, tall, manly. Drool-worthy. I could *not* take my eyes off the man. Darby, didn't you think he was hot?" Tia wiggles her eyebrows devilishly, in a way that always makes me laugh. "Smart. Great hair—that sort of wavy, Patrick Dempsey look. The guy is total man candy. *Law* man candy."

"Tia!" chides Sarah, waggling a finger. "Darby has a lot more on her mind than whether or not her divorce lawyer is hot."

"Well," I say, a smile breaking for what feels like the first time all week, "he was reasonably attractive. But he seems really cold. That guy is all efficiency, no emotion. A law-bot."

"Which is exactly what you want in a divorce lawyer," interjects Tia, "Reasonably attractive? You've got to be kidding. I'd sure as hell rather be looking at Holt Gregory six hours a day in divorce court than some balding, chinless, middle-aged member of the tennis club."

She has a point.

Despite the fact that I moan and groan about not wanting to leave the house ever again, Tia insists that as this is our last night together before the Dreamgirls head back to their respective lives and homes, a girls' night out is mandatory.

The five of us get dressed to go out, our perfumes and wardrobes intermingling, taking turns in the small guest bathroom and lending each other earrings, lipstick, and stories, just as we did all through college and through most of our twenties. This togetherness is what I missed most in my married life, Dreamgirl soup, the fun and energy of five women staying together, laughing, dressing up, and hanging out.

An hour later we're seated on the deck at Marina Jack's, sipping cocktails while we watch the boats and nibble on fresh oysters and shrimp. After dinner, we head to a party hosted by one of Tia's former business acquaintances.

The gathering looks exactly like every other Sarasota cocktail party, except for the odd fact that there are no men in attendance. (Fine by me. I'd like to do without any more men for a while.) Our hostess, Laura, is a striking fifty-something woman, with elegant salt-and-pepper hair and the figure of Audrey Hepburn circa *Breakfast at Tiffany's*. She is exactly the type of woman you see smiling down, wearing a sun visor with a 9-iron thrown jauntily over her shoulder from all of those golf-course-community billboards scattered throughout the city. She ushers us into the living room, which is blandly elegant, with a feel that's more "model homey" than actually "homey."

The house has the look of being professionally done, in the eternally popular south Florida Naples-Tuscany look: shades of brown, tan, chocolate, and beige. Marble-tiled floors. Romanesque columns. Gilded frames. Travel volumes artfully stacked. A look, as Tia would say, that is "often imitated, always boring." A spry, smiling octogenarian and a group of women ranging in age from mid-twenties to mid-fifties cluster around the cocktail table, devouring the trays of hors d'oeuvres and knocking back cocktails like they've just been paroled. Our group joins the throng, with introductions all around and a few "hi, how are you's" to vaguely familiar acquaintances. In this city, like many others, the same forty-seven people make the rounds at all the parties. You're hard-pressed to go anywhere in town without running into someone you know. Usually, it's all the same people you know. As Jules's mother used to say, "a town full of social climbers and no ladder."

"I've never been to a party like this, have you?" asks a fidgety woman with a green cocktail in one hand and a skewer of coconut shrimp in the other.

"Well, it's interesting," I say, not sure what she means. Just as I'm about to ask Tia about it, the hostess appears in the doorway with a few stray guests, and rings a tiny silver bell to get our attention.

"Now, if you'll all take your seats, we'll get started!" says Laura enthusiastically.

Jules, Kimberly, and I shoot Tia a look. She stares straight ahead, unable to keep from giggling.

It is just like Tia to think it's completely hilarious to drag us all unknowingly to a coming-out party for middle-aged transvestites, or a fund-raiser to save a certain discontinued lipstick from extinction.

Moments later, drinks are refreshed (we've only been here ten minutes and I'm already on my second margarita) and catalogs are passed out. Ah, a home party. Jules and I exchange looks as I breathe a sigh of relief. No transvestites tonight, just some scented candles or kitchen accoutrements. Our hostess, Laura, hands me a catalog emblazoned with a Pure Romance logo. Hang on. That's not a spatula.

I'm more than a tiny bit surprised as I flip through the catalog. Inside are pages and pages overflowing with pink flower-shaped vibrators, creamsicle-flavored lubricants, and tummy-camouflaging lingerie.

I close the catalog, slightly embarrassed, and glance quickly around the room. I guess I'm expecting to see some shock or surprise on the faces of the other guests, but apparently Jules, Kimberly, Sarah, and I were the only ones in the dark about the evening's activity. Even the eighty-year-old woman on the sofa across from me flips through the catalog casually, like she's browsing for wool socks or book selections. Tia has apparently been waiting to see my reaction, and once she gets it she laughs and nods her head in Jules's and Sarah's direction. They are huddled together, apparently deeply engrossed in something offered on page three.

"Glory!" says the senior sex-toy shopper to no one in particular. "Does this stuff come in mango?"

Tia cracks up, as Laura emerges with an elegant silver platter (Tiffany, I'd venture) loaded down with bedroom toys and a taste-testing selection of flavored lubricants on mother-of-pearl caviar spoons.

The party gets downright rambunctious from there.

Toys are passed around, first-time, worst-time, and not-in-this-lifetime stories are told, and cocktails are consumed with increasing enthusiasm.

Soon the conversation turns to exes, and one churchlike partygoer waves something called a "magic bullet" in the air and proclaims, "Once Walter ran off with the elementary school librarian, this little sucker kept me sane . . ."

"I don't mean to speak out of turn, but you sure do look a lot like that gal who lost her cookies on TV," the elderly woman says to me.

"Yes. That was me," I say, singed by the realization that I'm going to be facing humiliation everywhere I go.

"You're a strong woman to live through that. Be proud of yourself," she says. And all of a sudden, I realize she's right. I have nothing to be ashamed of. My reaction, televised or not, was just . . . human.

Our hostess, pats me on the shoulder, handing me something that looks a little bit like a purple spider with a battery pack, and advises, "Take care of yourself, sweetie. That way, you won't be tempted to jump into a relationship that's wrong for you . . . just for"—she pauses—"comfort."

Everyone starts giggling, and I sit there, watching these women laughing and having so much fun together, and in that moment, surrounded by the gaggle of smut-buying ladies, I get my power back.

Buoyed by the support of my girlfriends, my new friends, and a few margaritas, I hash out a plan to take back my life. I will fix my broken career. I will join a gym. (Okay, I will actually go to the gym I already belong to.) I will donate more time and money to charity. I will get over Will. I will move on and someday, maybe in seven or eight years, I will meet someone who deserves me, who loves me, who will treat me the way I deserve to be treated. I will get my hair highlighted every six weeks, and not wait until

I have a root emergency. My thoughts begin to take on a Gloria Gaynor backbeat, as I vow to be a better, stronger Darby.

"I'm taking my life back," I say.

First, I decide that no matter what the risk, I'll do everything I can to get Aidan and Lilly back. Fucking Gigi. She's selfish! She abandoned her kids, she has a trashy career, and then she steals back the husband (my husband!) and the kids (my kids!) that she unceremoniously dumped, ruining four lives in the process because Her Highness decided she wanted him back. I'll be damned if she's going to set me up to do the same horrible thing to the kids that she did—she may think it's just fine to walk off and leave them, and then show up four years later like fucking mom of the year, but I don't. Lilly, Aidan, and I are family. Just because I didn't give birth to them doesn't mean they're not mine. And I'm theirs! I've lived without a family for too long to give that up. It's not fair. And Will! What kind of jerk just sits back and lets it all happen? What was all that "Good luck on the *Today* show, Darby" and "I'm really proud of you Darby" crap on the morning I left for my tour, when he knew full well I was heading into an ambush? What a shit.

I felt completely abandoned after my mother *died*, how crushed must Lilly and Aidan have felt when their mother just waltzed out for a low-budget TV contract?

I'm haunted by a memory of the time right after Will won custody of the kids from Gigi. She simply took off, disappeared into her career. She sent presents regularly and came back for visitation every few months, and Lilly and Aidan watched her religiously on television every Thursday night, blowing kisses to the TV and telling stories to her videotaped image as though she could hear them. But the calls came less and less frequently, she had to cancel visits a few times, and her bimonthly visitation was pitifully inadequate for two kids aching for their mother.

When Lilly was about three, she looked at me one night with tears glistening in her soulful little eyes and asked, "Why didn't mommy want us to live with her?" Will was gone that night, some work function, and I remember being terrified of saying the wrong thing, cursing Gigi in my head, holding Lilly's tiny body as she sobbed. I was helpless to make her hurt go away, and I was absolutely, tear-her-hair-out enraged with Gigi for putting her own children through so much sorrow.

It takes everything I have not to completely hate Gigi, and the only reason I don't let myself is that I know it would be bad for the kids. The only reason.

I can't bear the thought of Lilly or Aidan ever having a single doubt that I wanted them, that I loved them. I collect my thoughts and push my rage for Gigi back where it belongs. Even if I don't have a chance in the world of winning custody, at least they'll know I did everything possible to be with them. I am not going to be one more person to disappoint these kids.

On to disaster number two: My career is a mess. If I have any chance of saving my hard-earned reputation, I need to stage a very public comeback. Fast.

"I need a plan," I say to the group. Tia whips a pen out of her purse, ready to jot notes on a cocktail napkin spotted with little pink hearts.

The ladies brainstorm my options: I could change my appearance and continue writing under a false name (unlikely); I could quickly find a new, fabulous replacement husband (no thanks); I could convince my legions of marriage-minded fans that we don't really have any use for men (now *that's* a tough sell, and besides, even I don't really believe it); I could hide in an apartment in Duluth until it all blows over (this sounds like the best idea yet, but I know Tia will never let me); I could ignore the media and pretend everything is fine; or I could challenge Gigi and find a way to win Will back.

"You need to date a movie star. Or a sports star," Tia says matter-of-factly.

"I don't think I want to jump into another relationship."

"Who's talking about a relationship? I'm talking about 'spin dating'—dating for publicity. You need to be seen in public, happy and fabulous, with someone that the media perceives to be a better catch than Will."

"Which means," says Jules, "someone rich or famous. Preferably both."

Tia adds, "It's the only way to hang on to your credibility as a relationship expert. Onward and upward. You've worked too hard, and for too long, to let it all go without a fight. Once you've established to the public that you're not sitting around crying in your soup, Will and Gigi's reunion, and more important, your fifteen minutes of shame, will all be forgotten."

I ask, "Am I the only one who thinks it's bizarre that the only way to get my credibility back as a relationship expert is to pretend to date?"

"You'll just go on a few dates. You're not staging a wedding, or even a sleepover. We're not talking about reality here," says Tia, "we're talking about TV. Damn, Darby, kill me if my life ever gets so tragic I have to date a movie star."

And so it was decided. I would put "The Hollywood Plan" into action immediately.

Three hours later and several hundred dollars lighter, we emerge from the Pure Romance party gripping goodie bags brimming with samples and the promise of a future delivery wrapped in plain pink paper. Who needs a husband?

The Dreamgirl's Breakup Survival Guide

by Darby Vaughn

Maybe you knew it was coming. Maybe you didn't.

You've been dumped.

So, other than moping around in your pajamas or spending quality time with Ben & Jerry, what can you do?

The First 48 Hours

Give yourself at least one full weekend to cry your eyes out, eat junk food, and lie around on your couch in a brokenhearted coma watching sappy movies. Throw a few comedies into the mix; laughter is good for you.

Whatever you do, don't call your ex. Don't e-mail your ex. Don't see your ex. Screen your calls. Give yourself at least a month to build up your resistance.

The First Week

After your first 48 hours, get off the couch and take a shower. Not just for hygiene reasons (trust me, by this time you'll really need it), but because it's now time to start taking action. Take down all photos that include your ex, and put them in the garage. Have a ceremonial snapshot torching if you need to. Don't call your ex. If you feel yourself weakening, sit down and make a list of all the things about him that really annoyed you—the more humorous, the better.

- The way he gave the exact same 22-minute response to every single person who asked how his job was going for three solid years.
- The psycho-squirrel noises he made when he laughed.
- The cheap, ugly, green, plastic phone he gave you for Christmas.

Take an extra 20 minutes with your appearance this week. Sure, you may not feel like getting dressed at all, but if you look good, you'll feel even better. And nothing smooths the ragged edges of a recent breakup like a few well-timed compliments.

Make a detailed list of all your good qualities. Remember, you're a unique, wonderful person, and someone (probably several someones) will fall madly in love with you, and you with them. Treat yourself to a little something nice this week (massage!) and every week for the rest of the month.

The First Month

Make plans with friends for every Friday and Saturday night for the next month, and stick to them. Focus on taking care of yourself. Now is the time to make long-range plans: one for a vacation (even if it's three years away) and one for your life. You have a clean slate, so what do you want to do? Go back to school? Become a rock star? Learn how to make crawfish traps? No one is holding you back now. Write down your goals and the steps you'll need to take to reach them.

Holy moly! Before you know it, the entire month has gone by. You're through the worst of it now, and this breakup, which is so awful now, will just be one forgotten U-turn on your path to true love.

Chapter 14

The next morning, Tia, Kimberly, and Sarah pack up and head to the airport. They have careers, families, and lives to attend to, and their work here is done. They know—and more important, I know—I'm going to get through this just fine. We hug and get misty at the security gate, and we promise to get together soon, at the very least when Sarah has her baby. We tentatively plan for a girls-only trip to Mexico in the spring, to tide us over until our next visit. Jules and I walk silently back to the car after we drop them off, missing the others already.

After they're gone, Jules squeezes me at the front door of the guesthouse. "Call me if you need anything," she says.

I thank her and she heads back to the main house, back to her husband and her children. She is my closest friend, and in this moment, I have to try really hard not to envy her.

I drop my bag on the living room sofa and head up to the turret room.

First, I call Will's cell phone and leave a calculatingly sane message on his voicemail that I'd really like to speak to Lilly and Aidan. I miss them, and I'm sure they miss me. It seems unfair to the kids to cut off contact with me. I promise to be brief and positive, and then I say a prayer for a quick call back after I hang up.

A few hours later, my cell phone rings and it's Lilly, with her sweet little-girl voice, telling me what a wonderful time she and Aidan are having in California.

"Disneyland is just like Disney World, except smaller," Lilly says. "We rode on the Mad Tea Party, and I knew you'd be sad because you weren't there, since it's your favorite." I flash back to our last ride together, spinning around and around until we thought we might lose our cotton candy, our little family squashed together in a whirl of centrifugal force.

Aidan talks next and tells me how he and Will played soccer in the park.

"I accidentally got ketchup on my blue pants when we went to eat hamburgers," he confesses.

"That's all right," I say. "What happened?"

"I was trying to hide the ketchup from Lilly, and put all the ketchup packets in my pocket, and then I forgot about them when I sat down."

"That's okay," I say.

"And they squished."

We laugh together, and I'm surprised at how babyish and tiny their voices sound. I lap up their little words like I'm drinking from an eyedropper after being stranded in the desert for a week.

I hear my heart banging in my chest as I tell them both I love them and that I'll see them as soon as I can. I wonder what Gigi and Will have told them, and hope they understand that it is not my choice not to be with them. I am true to my word, however, keeping the tone light and cheerful, even though my heart is breaking in ways I never thought possible. I blow them kisses and tell them a dozen times how much I love them. Lilly gets on the phone one last time to say good-bye.

"I love you so much, Dar-mama," she says.

My voice shakes as I answer her in the way I always do. "Dar-mama loves you too, Lilly Bean."

Will gets on the phone as I'm about to hang up with Lilly.

"Darby?"

"Will?" My chest tightens. It is strange to hear his voice. It is familiar but changed, the same feeling you get when you go to your childhood home after becoming an adult. Everything seems smaller somehow; the same, but different.

"The kids were missing you. I'm glad you called," he says cautiously.

"I miss them," I say, leaving "and you" unsaid but floating around my brain. Fuck, how can I miss him after what he's done to me? *Focus, Darby. He humiliated you, wrecked your career, and stole your kids. Stay strong.*

"Will, it's not fair to just take the kids away from me. I love them, you know."

"I know," he says quietly. "I'm sorry, I just don't think it's a good idea for you to see them."

"*You* don't think it's a good idea . . ." I say, my anger rising. This from a man who thought humiliating his wife on national TV was a good idea. This from a man who thought yanking his kids away from their home, their friends, their school was a good idea . . .

"I just want to see the kids," I say with conviction. "Do they even know what is happening, or do they just think you're all on vacation?"

"They're fine," he mumbles.

"Well, I'm not fine. For all intents and purposes, I have been their mother for the last four years. You can't just take them away from me." I take a breath. "Please, I need to see them."

"Gigi will never allow it," he says. "Darby, you're not their mother."

"Really? You could have fooled me. Where was their mother, or for that matter, where were *you* two months ago when Aidan spiked a fever of a hundred and two, and I was up all night with him while he threw up every ten minutes? We didn't get to sleep until four in the morning and I passed out with vomit in my hair! Have you ever slept with vomit in your hair? Where were you that night? You said you were working, but were you actually working? Or were you and Gigi off screwing around while *I* took care of *your* kids? The kids I thought were *ours*. The kids I loved, and cared for, and hugged when they cried over her. There have been dozens of nights when one or both of the kids were sick, and I can't remember one night when you were there. Not one. And Gigi certainly wasn't there. Who made Lilly's ballet tutus? You? Gigi? No, it was *me*. Who spent weeks helping Aidan memorize his multiplication tables? Me! Who's been there for everything, every single thing, for the last four years? Not you. Not Gigi. Me. I love them; they're mine, too. I want to be with them." I'm so angry I barely recognize my own voice, and by the time I finish I'm out of breath.

"You think you're going to take them away from me?" Will yells back.

"No!" I say forcefully. "But I want to share custody."

"Darby, you're dreaming," he says. "No court is going to take them away from their mother and father. Drug addicts get to keep their own children, for fuck's sake! Lilly and Aidan have a mother and a father, and we're going to be remarried. Just leave it alone, Darby."

"How could you do this to me? I thought you loved me."

"This situation didn't happen the way you think, Darby," he says warily.

"It didn't happen the way I think?" I'm way beyond angry now. "Gee, Will, *I think* you let me find out on national television that you were dumping me for your ex-wife. Are you telling me it *didn't* happen that way?"

"I . . . I can't talk about this now," he mutters, and then he hangs up on me.

End of conversation.

I know for a fact that this is the act of a person who is trying to gain control when they feel they've lost it. And it just pisses me off.

I am bound and determined to be with Lilly and Aidan. Crap, I need to get my career back on track so I can afford to pay my new attorney and make this happen.

I place a call to Holt Gregory's office and let him know that I will be sending over a retainer later in the day, and that we are going to fight for my kids. That decision made, Holt offers some suggestions on strategy.

"I've been thinking about this a lot," he says. "We do have a number of different options, but I think our best route is to try to assert your rights as the psychological parent, to protect the best interests of the children. We'll try to prevent a permanent move to California, give you some say in how the kids are brought up, and try to gain custody, or at least, legally enforceable visits with them."

"Thank you," I tell him. "I trust your judgment." There's something about his confidence that makes me feel like maybe he's the one person who can guide me through this mess. By the time we hang up, I am feeling marginally hopeful.

Time to get to work. I sit at the small desk and pull my Rolodex out of a box. I know, I know, I'm a throwback. I just love the visual reminder of a big circular merry-go-round filled with names of friends and business associates. Will used to harangue me about putting all of my contacts into a BlackBerry, but I don't see the appeal. What if it dies? Or falls out of your bag at the airport in Toledo? Everyone you know just vanishes.

I twirl up the P's, and flip through the cards of every publicist I've met over the last three years. First things first, I need to find a new spin doctor. If I'm going to put the Hollywood Plan into action, I'll need someone who can make the appropriate introductions and wrangle the party invitations. Plus, with all the damage done to my reputation in the last few weeks, I'm going to need professional help if I have any hope of recovering. I call Holland, my agent, to tell her I'm alive and well, and ask her if she has any suggestions for my new publicist. She reels off a few names and tells me she's glad I'm back. I update her on what the attorney told me, ask her to fax Will's publicity contract to Mr. Gregory's office, and tell her I'm putting a plan into action to get my career back on track.

"That's my girl. It's about damned time," Holland says.

"What are you talking about? It's only been a couple of weeks."

"The longer you lie down, the harder it is to get up. Are you mad yet? Or are you still feeling sorry for yourself?"

"I'm over mad. I'm taking back my life." I say.

"Attagirl. You've finally worked through the five stages of grief: anger, denial, ice cream, chocolate, and acceptance. You'll be fine. On to damage control."

Next I call Kendall, Will's former assistant, to ask her to put together a list of Will's business assets. She's still reeling from his treachery and eager to help me. I think that in some ways, Kendall was hit as hard as I was by this whole situation. She worked for Will for nearly six years, and she considered him a friend. He pulled off this deception under her nose, too, and I'm guessing she feels almost as betrayed as I do.

"Obviously, I need to find a new publicist," I tell her. "Is there someone you'd recommend?"

Kendall pauses for a few seconds and says, "Me."

I'm surprised at first, but it makes sense. Kendall did most of the day-to-day dealings with the reporters and clients, while Will spent his time schmoozing bigger fish and, as we now know, porking his ex-wife at the Ritz-Carlton. Also, Kendall not only tried to warn me, but quit her job when she found out what Will did. Loyalty would certainly be at the top of my list of important skills for my *next* publicist.

"I know you have a lot of media contacts," I say.

"I have my own media database, but I have more day-to-day dealings with the reporters and producers than Will anyway. He hasn't pitched his own media in a couple years."

"What do you mean?" I ask.

"Most clients want to deal with Will directly, the big gun himself. If they think they're assigned to a more junior publicist, they won't pony up his three hundred bucks an hour. But if Will's *assistant* is making their calls and sending out their pitches, they feel like Will's doing the work. I'm just the elf that has been making it happen."

"Really?" What she's telling me makes sense. Will was always more of a face guy than a detail person. Could he have been any more full of crap? "How are you with writing press releases?"

"How did you like your last press kit?" she counters.

"It was great. You?"

"All me. Actually, your last media campaign was me, too."

"God, I remember telling Will what a great job he did boiling down the parts of my book that my female readers really related to." I thought maybe Will was the one guy who really "got" women. Clearly an error of epic proportions.

"The only media contacts Will deals with himself are the national shows. Which is why I didn't know about *Today* or E! until it happened," Kendall says regretfully.

"You're hired," I say. I like Kendall, I trust her, and, frankly, it doesn't surprise me at all that she's been doing the bulk of the work at Will's agency. "What was in it for you? Why did you settle for an assistant title when you were doing all the heavy lifting?"

"Three reasons. First, Will really does know his PR. He taught me everything, and his name opens a lot of doors. Second, he paid me really well—there's no way I would make that kind of money anywhere else as a junior publicist. And last, he promised to help me set up my own shop if I stayed with him for two more years."

I'm stung by her sacrifice. We're friends, but no one could have blamed her for keeping her job, especially when she was so close to seeing it all pay off.

"I appreciate what you've done for me."

"You're welcome, but I did it for me, too. This business is filled with snakes. I love PR, but I don't want to work for anybody like that. I need to be able to look at myself in the mirror."

"This is going to be a tough gig, Kendall. My reputation is toast."

"No kidding. Your 'Hurl Seen Round the World' has been the number-one clip on YouTube all week," she says.

"Ugh."

"Don't worry, I've already got some ideas. Everybody loves a comeback. Look at Hillary Clinton. People couldn't stand her until it all came out that ol' Bill was messing around. Now women actually admire her for staying strong through everything. Look at Jennifer Aniston. Look at J-Lo, for God's sake."

"I'm open to anything. I've been giving it some thought, and I think I'm ready to start getting out in public again."

"You're right. I think we start with red-carpet photo ops of you looking fantastic at events and parties; no interviews to start. I'd like to hook you up with a couple of TV boyfriends."

"Spin-dating, you mean."

"Exactly," she continues, "and I know just who to start with. Tony Kullen is launching a new line of basketball shoes next week in Miami, at Vix. I know his rep; I'll set it up."

"Perfect," I say, and he is. Tony Kullen is a professional basketball player, the gorgeous blond-haired, blue-eyed, six-foot-six, all-star center of the Miami Heat. He's a regular on ESPN, *Letterman*, and *TRL*, appears in commercials for everything from sneakers to Jell-O, and is notorious for dating the hottest models or starlets du jour.

He's also Will's favorite basketball player of all time.

Two hours later, Kendall calls to let me know I'm all set for my date with Tony Kullen next Saturday night at his launch party.

"Wear tall shoes," she advises. "I'll stop by later and we'll go over wardrobe selections." Well, this is a switch. As my publicist, Will's never made any contribution to my wardrobe, except on the rare occasions when he'd mutter, "*No*, that dress *does not* make your butt look big." Kendall tells me she'll arrange for a stylist to drop a few selections by, and asks whether I want to schedule my own hair and makeup people, or if I'd like her to do it.

"I usually do my own makeup. Do you really think I need someone for this?"

"I think after your last two appearances, we need every advantage we can get," she says gently. I agree, and she promises to make the arrangements for the glam squad to be at my hotel a few hours before the event. I wonder: Are we just delirious, or can this Hollywood Plan actually work?

The Dreamgirl Academy: Drive-By Dating

by Darby Vaughn

Dear Darby,
What do you do if your date doesn't pick you up at the door, and just calls from his cell to have you come out? Should you say something about it so he will (or won't) do it next time?
Ring or Ring the Doorbell?

Dear Ring,
It dismays me to hear that with all of the recent improvements in modern men (thank you, Queer Eye *guys) your Romeo is not schooled in dating etiquette. Is drive-by dating really acceptable? The answer, of course, is no. Your date should absolutely come to your door to pick you up. The last-second cell call to meet you on the street is the modern-day equivalent of honking the horn at the curb.*

(The exception, of course, is made for big-city dates on the rare occasions that one actually is picked up in a car—we all know parking and walking the eighty-seven blocks to pick up your date at her apartment would take several hours longer than the date itself. However, if we're talking public transportation, a cab, or a car service, the standard pick-her-up-at-the-door rule still applies. It is, after all, the gentlemanly thing to do.)

Fortunately, you have the power when it comes to deciding how you will allow yourself to be treated. Understandably you are not enthusiastic about being paged like a call girl at the convenience of your date. Try these trouble-free approaches:

If he calls and asks you to meet him on the street, either tell him 1) you prefer he picks you up at the door, or 2) be sneaky (if you must) and tell him you're not ready and ask him to come on in for a minute.

After two or three dates, he'll realize the "Come on down . . ." approach doesn't work with you and he'll soon be on his best behavior whenever he comes to pick you up.
Darby

Chapter 15

The road to Miami is paved with Lincoln Town Cars.

From Sarasota to Miami is usually a three-hour drive. Unless you plan to drive down during the high season, November through April, when Alligator Alley is paved three-across with retired ophthalmologists from Cincinnati driving luxury cars bearing curb-feelers, cruising at a sprightly 37 miles per hour. Then, it takes seven hours and sixteen minutes.

On the night of Tony Kullen's launch party (and my coming out), I'm stationed at the Shore Club, an über-trendy hotel on Miami Beach, where the rich and famous come to look bored. The lobby of the Shore Club is ultramodern, with sleek areas for conversation and billowing sheer white curtains hanging from the ceiling, creating random little pods of privacy throughout the lobby. The Shore Club is home to one of Miami Beach's hottest nightclubs, Sky Bar, full of cozy alcoves teeming with celebrities and heiresses.

My room is freezing cold, but has a great view of the beach. (Which, frankly, is pretty much all it takes to make me happy.) The floor is made out of some sort of treated cement, and every other surface is plastic, laminate, ceramic, or wood. I get the feeling that they could just turn on big sprinklers after every guest checks out, instead of bothering with housekeepers. It is sparse and modern, and it creates an echo every time I set down a bag, move a magazine, or take a step. The bathroom shower is sort of open-plan, which feels strange, and it looks a bit drafty—a nozzle pokes out of a wall in a room made entirely of Mexican sandstone, with a big drain on the floor. Welcome to modern luxury.

The only fabric in the room is on the bed, a pristine white duvet with pristine white sheets. Even the pillows are oddly firm, as though they, too, might be made of plastic. This place is a little too cool for me. Call me bourgeois, but I like a nice comfy couch, preferably one that isn't made of recycled pop cans or shredded tires.

My hair and makeup team arrive at six P.M. so they can have me coiffed and spackled for my big entrance with Tony at nine. The stylist has picked out a gorgeous long mermaid gown in red, a power color, to be sure, with elegant shirring at the bust, and fitted from the waist all the way down to my knees. So fitted, in fact, that she has to sew me into it to avoid any excess bulges or wrinkles showing up in the pictures. Jules insisted that I wear her favorite pair of shoes, silver python and rhinestone Beverly Feldman stilettos, indisputably the most fabulous shoes ever created. On the stylist's advice, I'm wearing not one but two pairs of Spanks, the tummy-squeezing undergarments sure to disguise any hint of my guacamole compulsion. My hair is up, with tendrils cascading around my face. The color of the dress plays nicely against my auburn hair. I feel beautiful. And compressed. Like my kidneys have been vacuum-packed. I was hoping to ditch the girdles in the ladies' room after Tony and I made our big entrance, but the stylist decides to stitch my dress to my Spanks, in order to keep the girdles from riding up or my dress from bunching. Damn, I'm going to be stuck in these things all night.

I try to call Lilly and Aidan before I go, and I end up leaving a message. Heading down to the lobby at precisely 8:45, I stand outside the hotel waiting for Tony's car. Or rather, Tony's car service. Which is late. A tiny spark of dread shivers through me, and I say a quick prayer that Mr. Basketball will not stand me up on my first non-Will date in four years. Outside the front entrance of the hotel are deep white sofas covered in some sort of weather-resistant fabric, and I'd like to sit down, but I'm afraid I might wrinkle. Or bust a seam. So I just stand around, attempting to look glamorous. My main goal for the evening is not to do anything to humiliate myself.

I'm nervous about tonight. Although I am (sort of) famous, I'm more of a faux celebrity. I'm on TV a lot, I'm quoted in magazines pretty often, but, generally speaking, my life hasn't been that glamorous. I've never actually attended a red-carpet event before. I'm far more likely to be curled up on the couch with the kids with a tub of microwave popcorn and a DVD on a Saturday night than attending some big celebrity party. Will has been to some, but that's mostly because he was working them. And once when he "had to" attend the Emmys with Gigi. Jerk.

After a few minutes, the limo pulls up. The hotel doormen jump to attention and scramble over to the car, looking somewhat disappointed to learn that it is going, not coming. The limo driver hops out, beats them to the door, and helps me into the car, despite the fact that I seem to be having quite a bit of difficulty bending at the waist. Damn. There is not one spare inch of room in this gown. Unladylike as it may be, I sort of stretch my legs out into the middle section of the car, until I'm practically reclining. At least I can breathe. Tony, seated way back in the rear of the car, is similarly situated, although not because his formal wear is too tight. He's just so tall. The man has the biggest feet I have ever seen. I have to angle myself sideways to avoid kicking him.

Tony leans forward, greeting me with a glass of champagne. I accept the bubbly and thank him for inviting me to attend the event with him. He is a gracious host, and neither of us mentions the fact that this is a red-carpet marriage.

I'm feeling a little jittery, so I suck down the champagne pretty quickly. Tony does not talk for most of the car ride over to the event, except for the rare and random comment.

"Nice shoes," he says.

"Thank you," I say. He is great-looking, but not nearly as handsome as he is on television. His blond hair is ruffled just so, in a way that makes him look carefree and adorable in pictures but probably took a professional stylist a couple of hours of strategic spiking to achieve. His teeth are whitened to a Chiclet sheen with a sort of bluish cast, the result of one too many hours (or weeks) spent under the Zoom light. And when he speaks, I notice that he has no discernible accent. Not Midwestern, not Southern, not Eastern . . . nothing—obviously the product of extensive speech training.

We arrive at the club thirty-five minutes later, and the chauffeur pops out of the car to open the door. Tony does a quick check of his hair in the mirror of a small compact emblazoned with his jersey number in red and black crystals, which reminds me a little of a gift-with-purchase I once got at the Estée Lauder counter at Macy's. He tosses it on the seat when he's finished checking himself out, completely blowing my manly man image of professional athletes in one fell swoop. He gets out of the car first, his long legs sort of unfolding out the door. He leans in and extends his hand to help me out of the car. Thank God. I'm so tightly encased in this dress, I don't think I could manage to free myself from the limo without assistance. After some stealth maneuvering by the driver and Tony, I'm finally upright on the red carpet. There is a small throng of photographers and cameramen, all the local news networks are represented, and, closer to the door, I see staffers from E!, *People*, *US Weekly*, *Entertainment Tonight*, *Access Hollywood*, and a bunch of others I don't recognize. There is also a shirtless guy wielding a microphone wrapped in the *Naked News* logo. I'm hoping we can get through the interview before he decides to remove his pants. I feel a tiny twinge of panic—the last time I saw so many photographers they were chasing me down Gigi's street in LA like I was an escaped felon.

"Smile and keep your head tilted toward me at all times, so we won't get nailed by the body language experts in the weeklies," Tony whispers to me as we head toward the entrance. I plaster on a smile, as he slips his hand around my waist and rests it in the small of my back. This is clearly a man who knows his way around a woman's body. It feels at once completely natural and oddly foreign. I realize in a fleeting moment that Tony is the first man other than Will to touch me in four years, and even though this "date" is strictly professional, I feel a weird little tingle shoot through my body. He leads me expertly through the crowd, with stops at each media outlet, pausing to hug me closer to him occasionally or whisper little jokes in my ear. I laugh appreciatively and try to project the feeling that I am having the time of my life, going to a fabulous party with a handsome and eligible bachelor.

"Darby, how are you holding up since your husband left you for Gigi Bissanti?" asks a local reporter wearing a smear of pink lipstick, her highlighted blonde hair pulled back into an aggressive French knot. I brace myself for humiliation but hope for the best. Tony steps in to answer the question for me, the plan as arranged by our two publicists.

"Darby's so gorgeous, every man in America is wishing he was me right now. She's the guest of honor at the hottest launch party of the year and she's got a closet full of the new Tony Kullen Flyers. Darby's on top of the world," Tony says enthusiastically. Nice work. It's a talented guy who can compliment a woman and sneak in a plug for basketball shoes at the same time. I wave and grin at the reporter as we move along to the next stop.

The reporters flip-flop between wanting to talk to me about my divorce (or, more accurately, my personal experience with projectile TV) and wanting to talk to Tony about the shoe launch. Each time a question is directed to me, Tony steps in to answer it, while I smile and gaze up at him adoringly, or stare off into the crowd, earnestly searching for an invisible friend and pretending not to have heard the question. It's just plain weird. Like I'm having some sort of out-of-body dating experience, floating above the crowd watching someone who looks like me snuggled under the arm of a famous basketball star, laughing and smiling for the cameras as though she doesn't have a care in the world.

This is not my beautiful date. This is not my beautiful life.

We stop for a few minutes in front of the shoe logo for pictures, and we stand first together, then separately while the photographers snap away. I have no idea what I'm doing, but I wing it, posing like I'm channeling Drew Barrymore.

Just as we are finishing up, Tony pulls me into his arms unexpectedly and plants a big kiss on top of my head (not a stretch, after all, as he's almost a full foot taller than I am, even in stilettos). I'm a bit stunned—this was not part of the game plan—but I continue smiling and try not to look surprised, as though my new fake-boyfriend Tony is simply prone to such outbursts of public affection.

"That's a money shot," he whispers in my ear, "and ten bucks says it's the cover of *People* next week." Something Sharon Stone once said pops into my head: *Women may fake orgasms, but men can fake entire relationships.* We wave to the reporters and the small crowd that has gathered outside, and finally, nearly forty minutes after our arrival, we head inside to the party.

I'm sort of expecting that now that the media show is over, Tony will ditch me, but he sticks by me, introducing me to the athletic-shoe reps and marketing people as though we really are a couple. I smile and chat easily with the clients, reps, and their spouses. I'm surprised at how rapidly Tony and I fall in step with each other. I did a million client dinners of this type with Will, and it feels a little like déjà vu with a replacement hubby.

Waiters clad in sequined tuxedos and basketball shoes bring round after round of champagne. After my third one, I decline, fearful that one more bubble would put the seams of my dress in jeopardy. Tony, however, keeps knocking them back, with a few Glenlivets thrown in for good measure. The liquor really does loosen his tongue, and a native Boston accent starts seeping out beneath the carefully crafted façade of speech coaching.

"You rawk and yaw husband's a maw-rawn," he slurs. I thank him for his kind words and steer him out to the terrace for some fresh air. I need a place to park him while I try to round up a waiter to bring him a plate of food. I prop him up against a mass of black and white throw pillows in one of the wicker and canvas cocoons that dot the terrace. The area is deserted, except for one giggly couple a few cocoons over who may or may not be having sex. I head back to the buffet table to load up a plate with some good old-fashioned, alcohol-absorbing carbs. Sadly, there's not a roll or piece of bread to be found anywhere (damned South Beach diet), so I settle for some sort of crab ravioli, and hope the pasta is enough to soak up some of the scotch. By the time I get back outside to the terrace, Tony has passed out, and he's lying down, flat on his back with his head resting against the back of the cocoon. Only his long legs are visible, stretching off the patio furniture, as though he's being eaten headfirst by a humongous wicker Venus flytrap.

I set the food down on a tiny table nearby and try to get Tony vertical, but he is big and heavy, and thanks to my ultraglamorous gown I'm barely able to bend at the waist. (I am useless! But I look fabulous!) I pull sideways at his arms, trying to maneuver him back into a semisitting position, using all of my weight and strength to get him upright. He shifts position and I lose my balance, falling headfirst into the cocoon. Tony does not move or wake up, and I wiggle around, facedown, trying to get myself out. I'm basically mummified in sequins, squirming to escape like a trout flopping around on a dock.

I manage to flip myself onto my side within a minute or so, but since I can't really bend, my feet don't reach the ground. They just sort of poke sideways out of the cocoon. I start inching toward freedom, perched on my elbow, and find myself temporarily blinded by a photographer's quick flash.

"Thank you," she says, as she scurries off toward the beach. Great. Nothing says photo op like a basketball player passed out in evening wear. The blinding bulb wakes Tony, and he groggily announces, "I'm starved." It dawns on me that heading outside, away from the protection of Tony's full team of publicists, was a mistake—the media are not allowed inside the party, but they are free to roam the property.

Tony sits upright, awkwardly helping to sort of push me out of the wicker prison, and grabs for the plate, scarfing down delicate raviolis like he hasn't seen food in a week. I'm starting to get hungry myself, but I'm afraid even a single shrimp would be glaringly obvious in this dress (and jeez, who can eat just one?). I'd probably just wind up looking lumpy, like a snake that's swallowed a fresh rat.

The rest of the party is uneventful. Tony switches to Perrier and sobers up pretty fast (oh, to have the metabolism of a professional athlete!), and we head out the back entrance, where his car and driver are waiting. Sitting in the limo on the ride back, I become acutely aware that I haven't used the restroom all night, and now my bladder feels like it might explode. We pull up to the Shore Club and I thank Tony for being such a great date, then rush inside, hoping I can make it to my room without creating a puddle in the lobby. I walk as fast as I can in four-inch heels, jam the card key into the door reader, open the door, and kick off my shoes as I run to the bathroom, yanking at my dress. It sticks, just below my hip, and I remember that the dress is stitched to my girdle. Holy bathroom emergency.

I grab the phone hanging over the toilet and punch in the number for housekeeping. It rings. And rings. And rings. Damn! I hang up and dial the front desk. No answer. I call room service. No answer. Crap! I call the front desk again; after fifteen or sixteen rings, a man with an unplaceable European accent answers. I tell him that I have an emergency in my room, and that I need a female desk clerk, concierge, or housekeeper to help me cut off my dress.

Without missing a beat, he says, "We have no female employees on the property at this time of night. Will a gay waiter from room service do?"

"Please! Tell him to hurry! And bring scissors!" I plead.

A few minutes later, there's a knock at my door. I fling it open and drag the twenty-something waiter into my room.

"Don't worry," he says with a strong Cuban accent, "I'm a professional." Flourishing a large pair of scissors, he assures me, "I had two and a half semesters at the Miami Institute of Fashion."

He uses one blade of the scissors as a seam ripper, creating an escape route and allowing me finally to unzip. I yell "thank you!" as I scramble into the bathroom just in the nick of time. Two minutes later and fully relieved, I unload my purse and give him a $137.48 tip, all the cash I have, and worth every penny.

I'm beginning to think the glamorous life may not be for me.

Dress disaster averted, I fall into bed, grinding my head into the extra-extra-firm pillow to find a comfort spot. I try to settle myself into sleep, but I can hear drunken voices laughing and shouting from the pool below. Tonight went well. It was weird, for certain, but at least I'm on track to put my life back together. I fall into a sweet sleep, savoring my first small victory in what feels like forever.

The phone is ringing.

I look over at the clock and it's 6:34 A.M. I've been asleep for only three hours. Crap. This can't be good. No one ever calls with good news at six-thirty in the morning.

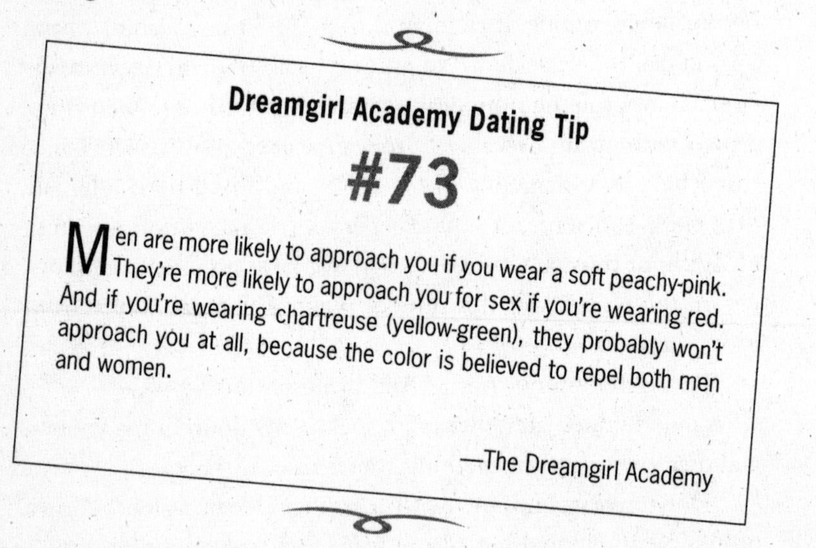

Dreamgirl Academy Dating Tip

#73

Men are more likely to approach you if you wear a soft peachy-pink. They're more likely to approach you for sex if you're wearing red. And if you're wearing chartreuse (yellow-green), they probably won't approach you at all, because the color is believed to repel both men and women.

—The Dreamgirl Academy

Chapter 16

"Darby, are you up?" It's Holland, my agent.

"I am now. What's going on?" I say, shaking my head to regain focus, and bracing myself.

"Sorry to call so early, I'm about to catch a plane and I didn't want to miss you. I have fantastic news. It's perfect timing, really. This could be exactly what we need to turn your career around."

"What's going on?" I ask. Now I'm up.

"I received a call from some development people at NBC about doing a new show with you." I can feel myself exhale, which is weird, since I didn't realize I was holding my breath.

"What's it called? What is it about? Tell me everything." A huge sense of relief floods over me, and I get the most wonderful inkling that things are going to work out just fine.

"The show is tentatively titled *Dating a Dreamgirl*. It's a reality show. Basically, the camera crew will follow you around while you go on a series of dates, following your own advice. The network is really on fire about the show, they think it could be huge."

"Wow" is all I can think of to say.

"We have a meeting set up in New York with a producer and

a few of the development folks next week. You *need* this one, Darby."

"They've seen what happened on *Today*? And they don't care?"

"That's what gave them the idea in the first place. But you've got to show them you're back on your feet, over Will, moving on with your life as a fun, fabulous, single girl. No more screwups."

"Well, I'll certainly do my best."

"See that you do," she says, her tone softening. "How are you holding up?"

"I'm moving on. I'm still hurt over what happened. Mostly, though, I miss Lilly and Aidan. I just hope I'll be able to at least win custody of the kids."

"Custody? What are you talking about?" she asks. She seems surprised. Or maybe irritated.

"I'm going to court for partial custody of the kids. Just because my marriage is over doesn't mean those kids aren't still my family." Why does this seem obvious to only me?

"Darby, I think it's a big mistake. Do you even have a chance of winning?"

"Not much," I admit.

"Why put yourself through a big, nasty court case when you have no chance of getting custody? Not to mention, being a single mom is not exactly the publicity move you make to enhance your reputation as a dating expert. You could blow your chances to get this show," Holland says sternly.

"I'm not doing it to enhance my reputation, I'm doing it because I love them."

"Rethink it, Darby, that's all I ask. A nasty custody battle could be the final nail in the coffin for your career."

When we say good-bye, my hand is tingling from gripping

the phone so hard. In the four years I've known her, she's never been wrong.

Dating Tips for Single Moms

by Darby Vaughn

I was flipping through the channels the other day and I got sucked into one of those sappy (yet popular!) Lifetime movies in which an attractive woman finds herself the single mother of two adorable small children after her husband has died tragically or run off with the town tramp. The first thing I wondered was how a single mom managed the upkeep on her Heather Locklear-esque blonde highlights. I also noticed that she had no problem meeting interested men in chance encounters at funerals, the gas station, or her sister's place of business. And last, the children (who were the center of Mom's universe) conveniently vaporized after sunset, so as not to spoil her big (but unplanned, because that would be too trampy) night of romance.

As a tear-jerking diversion from reality and a plausible excuse to eat frozen cookie dough right out of the tube, such movies are top-notch. But, as any single parent will tell you, the reality of dating is quite a bit different: Single moms often feel like dowdy, second-class daters just because they have children—believing they can't compete for the really great men. Single moms rarely have the time or money to blow on the elaborate beauty routines of their childless counterparts. And the date-scheduling challenge of custody arrangements (every other weekend and alternate Tuesdays), having to cancel at the last minute because a babysitter doesn't show, and being physically and emotionally spent (and possibly covered in Cheerios) before your date has even begun can make you wonder why you even try.

Parent-Friendly Dating Options

After drive-thru and DVD players in the car, the greatest boon to busy single parents is online dating. Why? You can search out Mr. or Ms. Fabulous at two A.M., weed out anybody who's not kid-friendly, and flirt like mad while your offspring are tucked safely in their beds. Plus, thanks to your fabulous date-ready photo, no one ever needs to know that you're flirting away in a ketchup-stained shirt and bunny slippers.

Fish-in-the-barrel approaches like Pre-dating, Speed Dating, and Lock and Key parties offer a quick way to meet lots of potential dates in one swift evening.

Once you make a date, don't spend the entire night talking about your kids, or what a pain it was to get out of the house. For a first date, names and ages only. After that you can add five minutes of kid talk during each date. And don't make the mistake of introducing your kids to your date too soon: A parade of disappearing uncles is simply too traumatic.

Finally, if your date can't roll with last-minute schedule changes, covert sleepovers that rival CIA missions, and more than a few rounds at Chuck E. Cheese, he's not the guy for you. Remember, it's your experience with your kids that has made you into the person you are today: Someone who is capable of great love. Someone who knows the meaning of responsibility. Someone who is making a contribution to the world. In other words, a great catch.

Chapter 17

Three days later, Holland and I are in New York City, bumping along in the back of a Town Car that is in desperate need of shock absorbers and a brake job. The interior, of course, is immaculate.

I've flown in this morning because we are meeting the *Dating a Dreamgirl* producers at a little Italian restaurant within spitting distance of Rockefeller Center. Holland has chosen the restaurant, I presume; she knows the location, menu, chef, and operating hours of every great Italian joint in the city. Possibly in New Jersey as well.

I'm ready for this meeting. I have worked out every day. (Okay, it's only been three days, but I feel more toned already!) I'm wearing a fabulous new outfit and fabulous new Christian Louboutin shoes. I should probably be conserving my money about now, in case the TV gig doesn't work out and my career continues in its free fall, but I really needed a little pick-me-up.

The restaurant is dim and narrow, with espresso-colored wood tables, a brick floor, and textured burgundy wallpaper: a linguini bunker in the heart of the city. It may be bright and sunny just a step outside at midday, but inside, it's always nine-thirty P.M. The producers have already arrived, and they're waiting for us at a large round table near the back of the restaurant. They stand in unison to greet us, introduce themselves, and then, as if on cue, return to their seats. There are two men, one woman. The men are interchangeable, named Steve and Mike, or maybe Mike and Steve, dressed in black suits, blue ties, their black hair slicked back. The woman sits between them, wearing a plum-colored jacket on top of a bright white blouse, with low-slung jeans and a wickedly cool studded belt. She is Olive, the would-be producer of the *Dating the Dreamgirl* reality show.

Olive's light brown hair is worn up in a spectacularly messy-yet-pulled-together 'do that women's magazines frequently tout as a "two-minute style you can achieve with a pencil"—a look I cannot pull off because it always makes me look like a demented receptionist with a writing utensil protruding from my head, Steve Martin–style.

We all chat about the weather, menus are passed out, and wine is ordered. The starters arrive and Holland reins us all in to get down to business.

"Darby," says Olive, "we think you're wonderful, a star, and we're so, so sorry about what happened."

"Thank you," I say, meeting her eyes directly, as I smile with my head held high. She gazes back at me from behind minuscule black rectangular glasses, searching for a crack in the armor. I'm ready for this line of questions and comments. I know that the network needs to see that I can hold up under scrutiny, and I'm up to the task.

"We think America would like to see what a relationship expert does *after* a very public breakup," Olive says.

"She gets on with her life," interjects Holland.

"Exactly," agrees Olive. "This show would follow Darby as she goes back into the dating world—we see her dates, we capture the 'doorstep moments,' we talk to Darby and her gentlemen for a post-date recap. We see the good, the bad, and the weird."

After our telephone conversation the other day, I'd told Holland that I would give the custody/career-in-the-toilet issue some thought. Out of respect. Even though every cell in my body was screaming "KIDS! KIDS! KIDS!" After thirty minutes and an extraordinarily detailed pros and cons list, I made my decision: I'm fighting for custody of Lilly and Aidan. (Okay, I'd already made that decision, sure, but my new pros and cons list was a valiant effort at reconsideration, right?)

Yes, I want the show, but I need my family.

Holland informed me I was making a huge mistake, and she advised me not to mention anything about the custody battle to the producers unless they asked me, point blank.

"Don't lie," she'd instructed, "but don't tell unless they hold a gun to your head."

Within the confines of the guesthouse, my decision to keep the kids seemed perfectly rational and doable; but here at the table with the network bigwigs, a little fear starts to creep in. What if I'm blowing my big chance?

OH. MY. GAWD. I just had an epiphany! *This is the EXACT same decision that Gigi made when she picked that stupid reality show over her own kids! This is the Gods of Parenting testing my resolve! Ha! Unlike Evil Gigi, I will make the right decision. I will fight for my kids. And if this TV show doesn't want me because I have kids, well, it's their loss.*

My brain rejoins the meeting, which is already in progress.

"We're concerned about the tone of the show," says Holland, ever the agent. "Until the untimely end of her marriage, Darby has always had a clean reputation, and despite this recent little bump in the road, we intend to operate in the manner in which she always has—Darby doesn't do sleazy."

"We couldn't agree more," says Olive. "*Dating the Dreamgirl* won't have that sticky 'reality show' feel to it. We'll have great production value, a real edginess, and an eye to romance. We're on Darby's side here. We want to make her America's sweetheart. This show, on a major network, in a prime-time slot, can put Darby back on top again. Like a real-life version of *Sex and the City*."

"We want full approval on the dates, location, and wardrobe."

"I'm not sure we can agree to that. We'll have to talk to some people at the network." says Olive.

I'm really intrigued by the idea of doing this show, but I'm also extremely apprehensive about signing on for anything that could potentially take me away from the kids. I run through a dozen scenarios in my head on how I could make this work with Lilly and Aidan, punctuated with little voices of reality screeching, *If you don't make some fast cash to pay that lawyer, you'll never have a chance at getting them back.* I feel a little tug of guilt as the career side and the mommy side of my brain battle it out. There are lots of working moms who are there for their kids. I'd never do what Gigi did. If I do this show, I can make this work with the kids. I *will* make this work. I'll do whatever it takes. And if I had to choose between living with Lilly and Aidan and getting this show, I'd walk away from the show in a heartbeat.

"Sounds good," I say. I'm trying to look nonchalant, but a little excitement starts to bubble up. Man, if this works out, it could really be amazing for my career. My mind starts popping with Hollywood fantasies: Me on the red carpet, arm-in-arm with

Chapter 18

Forty-five minutes later I'm at La Guardia to catch a flight back to Florida. I stop off in the airport gift shop to pick up presents for Lilly and Aidan, just like I always do when I'm coming home after a trip, and it hits me: They're not at home. God, I miss them so much. After selecting a tiny pink ballerina doll for Lilly and a book on magic for Aidan, I head over to the magazine rack for some light reading material for the flight home. On the wall are dozens of selections of my favorite brain candy, *US Weekly*, *People*, *Hello!*, *Star*, *In Touch Weekly*. How to choose? How to choose? And then I notice. I'M ON THE COVER OF *PEOPLE* MAGAZINE! Holy crap. The cover. It's the photo of me and Mr. Basketball himself, Tony Kullen, where he's kissing the top of my head. The headline screams DARBY REBOUNDS.

I pull a half-dozen copies of *People* down from the rack, as I scan the other magazines. Tony and I are on the cover (lower right-hand side, but still, on the front) of *US Weekly*. *Star* magazine has me and Tony on the cover with a screen shot of me on the *Today* show in a little bubble near the bottom. (Nice. Just in case I thought I might get off easy.) Basketball humor abounds; the headlines all offer some gem like DARBY NO LONGER ON THE BENCH! and DARBY'S FAST BREAK. All together, I've made the cover or the "party pages" of eleven magazines. The picture that was taken outside when Tony was passed out is published in one of the sleazier magazines, but I'm relieved that it's not as bad as it could have been. You can't really tell that we were lying down (or more accurately, that he was passed out and I was imprisoned in formal wear). We just look very, very relaxed. It's weird to see myself in all of these magazines. I'm so engrossed flipping through them all that I almost miss my flight. Holy smokes, Kendall's publicity plan really worked.

I run down the Jetway, yanking my phone out of my bag to call Kendall to give her the good news. My phone is turned off, and by the time the stupid thing powers back on the flight attendants are closing the doors on the plane. My phone chimes—I've got three new messages and not enough time to call Kendall. Damn, I'll call her when I land. Instead, I opt to check my voicemail: One, Kendall screaming with excitement about the covers. Okay, good, she knows. Two, Holt telling me we've got a court date set for February. A huge relief, this feels like progress. And three, Tia calling to congratulate me on sticking it to Will, Mr. Publicity himself, straight from the cover of *People* magazine. I power down my phone and relax in my seat. I've got a Hudson News bag crammed with $73 worth of magazines, and it's going to be a lovely flight.

By the time I land, I've got four more messages, including one from Will (ha!) and one from Holland, who had just spotted the *People* magazine cover at her office newsstand.

"Perfect timing, Darby. This should definitely help to swing the producers our way."

I call Kendall from the car to congratulate her on my fake-date coverage.

"Kendall, it's Darby, great work!"

"Thanks! I'm so glad you called," Kendall says breathlessly. "Can you get to Miami by ten tonight?"

"It's almost five-thirty, and it's a three-hour drive. I could make it by about nine-thirty if I swing by home to pick up my toothbrush and a change of clothes. Why?" I ask.

"I've got another high-profile date for you tonight. At a club opening. Have you ever heard of Kyle?"

"Kyle who?" I ask.

"Just Kyle, one name," she says laughing. "Like Madonna. Or Fabio. He's a model."

"That's funny. I don't know if I'd go with the 'one name' thing if I had the most common name on the planet for male models." I laugh and add, "I've never heard of him. Of course, that doesn't mean anything. Should I have?" I've just gorged my brain with a three-hour gossip magazine binge, but I can't remember seeing anything about him before.

"You'd know him if you saw him. He's being photographed a lot right now; he's very hot. Right on the edge of breaking out in a big way. I want you to go with him to the opening of a new club. The club belongs to a couple of A-list movie stars, so the celebrities, paparazzi, and groupies will be out in force tonight. It would be a good follow-up for you after the Tony Kullen thing."

"Kendall, at this point, I'll do anything you tell me to. What time will Kyle-the-one-named-model be picking me up?"

"Perfect! You're staying at the Shore Club again. Wear big glasses when you go in; there's some event there tonight and I don't want one of those photographers catching you before the glam squad arrives. We'll use the same stylist and makeup artist as last time. You looked freaking fantastic, so we want to stick with what works. They'll check in for you and head up to your room to set up—we don't want to lose any time. They'll get you all dolled up, and I'll have the car pick you up at eleven."

"Wow, that's late," I say. Four years on the minivan track and I'll never catch up to cool again.

"Late is when it all happens. I'll fax your itinerary and all the contact names to your hotel. The name of the club is F."

"F? Like the letter F?" I ask.

"Yeah, that's it," Kendall says. "Have fun!"

"One more thing," I say, "about the stylist . . ."

"Uh-oh. What happened?"

"It's nothing, really. Would you just tell her I'll need a dress I can pee in?"

"Picky, picky, Miss Thang," Kendall says, laughing, "I'll see what we can do."

I tell her that Will left me a message on my cell while I was on the plane.

"I'll bet he saw the *People* cover!" she snickers. "He's probably jealous! Are you going to call him back?"

"I have to. What if something has happened with the kids?"

I call Will next, and his voicemail picks up. I'm kind of relieved not to talk to him. Will and his little orbit of trouble is the last thing I want to deal with right now. I hope everything is okay with Lilly and Aidan. I really miss them. I leave a message for Will and tell Lilly and Aidan that I love them.

Four hours later, I'm back at the Shore Club for round two in a life that's way cooler than mine. I stop at the front desk to find out my room number and head up in the elevator. The second I open the door to my room, they pounce: The glamour girls have taken over. There are makeup and hair products spread all over the table by the window, a giant rack crammed with various outfits, a huge fabric steamer pumping away in the corner, and groupings of shoes and accessories blanketing every other surface.

The glam team gets to work, slathering my hair with product and blowing it out with big round brushes. Somewhere in the middle of the hairdo process, the stylist yanks open a big suitcase filled with fake hair in several lengths and every possible color. (I see something my grandmother would have called a "fall.") She holds two hairpieces up to my head, decides which one is the best match, and carefully returns the other one to its case.

She pulls a FedEx envelope out of the front pocket of the case and tosses it onto the nightstand by the bed. "Just put the hair in the prepaid envelope when you get back, and drop it at the front desk on your way out."

She works the fake hair into mine, which feels incredibly obvious for the first few minutes, and then miraculously nonexistent. The makeup artist goes to work next, which I find completely relaxing, like a delicate facial massage. Until the part where she sets my lips on fire.

"Ahh!" I say, clenching my teeth in pain, but trying not to move my face and disturb her work. "Could I have some water, please? I think I'm allergic to whatever you just put on my mouth—my lips are burning!"

"The burning sensation should go away in a minute or two," she assures me. "It will be worth the pain, believe me; the stuff I just put on you is a treatment that plumps up your lips, to give you that supersexy pout."

The stylist has selected a fabulously chic black dress with a high waist, deep V-neck, and billowing, three-quarter-length sleeves. I definitely won't have to worry about going to the bathroom in this dress—the thing is so short it barely covers my ass.

"Um, do we have anything longer?" I ask. "One tiny breeze in this frock and I'll be flashing all of Miami."

"This is perfect, it's the one for tonight," says the stylist firmly. "There will be lots of celebrities and models on the carpet tonight. If you want to end up in any pictures, you need a dress that will get you talked about. This dress is amazing, from Ule, a very hot designer. I could put this dress on a rack by itself and send it down the walk and it would get press."

"Uh, okay," I say, "I trust your judgment." Actually, what I mean is, I will *try* to trust her judgment. This is, after all, the woman who sent me to a cocktail party in a dress with no escape route.

"You'll have press on both sides of the carpet and an awning overhead," she assures me. "Unless there's a hurricane, you'll be protected from a breeze. When you stop for pictures, put your hands at your sides," she advises. "Also, you'll wear these," she says, handing me a pair of black boy-short panties. "If you do get caught in the wind, at least you'll have pretty lingerie."

Great.

She pairs the dress with some supertall black Jimmy Choos, and then puts accessories on and takes them off me, like I'm a Christmas tree. Finally, she settles on some big silver hoop earrings and a long Chanel chain. The three of them pronounce me ready to go, and I check myself out in the mirror: I must admit, the whole effect is pretty stunning. My legs look a mile long in this dress. My hair is big, glamazon big, expertly tousled and sexier than I could have ever pulled off on my own. And what the makeup artist has accomplished is nothing short of spectacular: My skin looks moonlit, it is so luminescent. My eyes are smoky and rimmed with a dramatic gray shadow that makes me look like a vixen, or at the very least, a really naughty Victoria's Secret model. And a cinnamon lipstick makes my teeth look whiter than

I have ever seen them. And even though they still sting a bit, my lips do look fantastic. Overall, it is a far vampier look than I could ever see for myself, but I like it for tonight. It's amazing what a team of trained professionals can pull off: I almost look like a movie star. Will would have loved it. For a second I wish that someone who cared about me could see me looking this way.

I add a little of my favorite perfume, a cinnamon-vanilla combo called Dreamgirl that was created especially for me after my first book became a bestseller. I dab it on my throat, my décolleté, and behind my knees, and I feel warm, sexy, and fun almost immediately.

I thank the miracle team and head down to the lobby with five minutes to spare. Even though I'm early, the car is waiting. Two of the valets stop in their tracks to give me a once-over, and I feel an odd mix of flattery and feigned glamour as I hop into the car with my name on a card in the window.

Inside is a young man who can only be described as beautiful. He is twenty-three, maybe twenty-four (please, not twenty-two), with blond, surfer-boy hair, bronzed skin, and brown eyes, deep as chocolate. Unlike Tony Kullen, who seems calculatingly casual, this guy looks like he just rolls out of bed every morning looking gorgeous. I don't see any obvious product in his hair. He's wearing some very cool jeans and a fitted shirt that shows off his perfect chest, perfect abs, perfect arms. I blink for a second, taking it all in, and hit the mental reset button to stop myself from staring at him like he's a spectacularly exotic animal. Or a hunk of meat.

To his left is a young woman, probably thirty. She's wearing black, with her warm brown hair in a sleek ponytail that highlights her ebony skin. A BlackBerry and a clipboard rest on her lap. Either Kyle has brought his own date, or he's brought his own publicist.

"Hi!" she says perkily, in a sweet English accent. "I'm Tanya, from QRPR, and I'll be escorting you tonight." She smiles at me perfunctorily, and then gazes at Kyle moonily.

"Hey, Darby, right?" he says casually, sticking his hand out to shake mine. "I'm Kyle. Nice to meet ya."

"Hi, Kyle, nice to meet you, too," I say, shaking his hand, unable to take my eyes off his face. How is it possible for any real human being to be this great-looking? I had never heard of Kyle before this afternoon, but I've definitely seen him before. This afternoon, in fact. Kyle, in his underwear, chiseled abs and all, gracing a giant billboard in Times Square.

"Dude, we're ready to hit it," he says to the driver, thumping the Plexiglas partition lightly with his fist.

The driver takes off, and we make our way down Collins Avenue an inch at a time. F is just a few blocks away, but the traffic is so horrific it takes us twenty minutes to get there. It certainly would have been more practical to walk, but I'm guessing that "hoofing it" is probably not the best way to make a red-carpet entrance.

Tanya chattily issues instructions as we ride. She'll get out first and let us know when the time is right for us to exit for optimum photographer attention. Then Kyle will exit the car and help me out. Jeez. Who knew this was all such a big production, just to get out of the car?

"Pull your dress down as far as it will go toward your knees before Kyle opens the door. Face forward in the car, keep your knees together at all times, right foot out first, then left foot, *knees together*. When your feet are out, swivel your body toward the door, *knees together*," she instructs. "Kyle will help you up to your feet. Kyle, take Darby's left hand, and *gently* help her out of the car." Kyle has a look on his face like he might be computing the molecular formula of Spam, and then the spark of understanding suddenly flashes in his eyes.

She adds sternly, "Darby, under *no* circumstances do you face the direction of the car door without your knees pasted together. We can't have you pulling a Britney." Ah, good advice. Tanya looks me directly in the eye, "You *are* wearing knickers, aren't you?" Kyle perks up with interest as I answer, a mischevious little smile on his face.

"Yes. Thanks for asking," I say, smoothing down my dress.

We pull up to the club, and Tanya hops out. A minute later, she pounds the top of the car, and Kyle and I make our big exit. I instantly feel like I've stepped into a 3-D IMAX version of the Academy Awards. There are dozens of celebrities, I mean big-time, A-list celebrities, milling around, and probably at least triple the number of photographers, reporters, and cameramen as there were at the Tony Kullen event. A massive line of people snakes all the way down the block. The front-of-the-line folks are pleading to gain entrance while three giant bouncers keep them at bay. There's a huge crowd of screaming fans on both sides of the carpet, and a line of police officers on either side keeping them off the rug. I'm rapidly overwhelmed by the sight of it all. This is *way, way, way* out of my league.

"And we're walking . . ." whispers Tanya, eyes fixed on her clipboard. Kyle and I start to move forward on the carpet, his arm casually draped around me. He's a complete ham, totally relaxed, mugging for the cameras, waving at fans and photographers like he does this every night. He probably does, now that I think about it. He seems completely at home in this crowd, angling me this way and that for photo after photo, zigzagging us back and forth across the carpet so we hit the photographers on both sides. I'm smiling so hard my face hurts, trying to keep my shoulders back and my head up, lining up to point my toe and my shoulder to the lens each time to make myself look leaner. There are no interviews this time; Tanya and the rest of the publicists shepherd us all forward toward the entrance of the club, as though they're herding a collection of sequin-and-stiletto-wearing cattle.

Inside, F looks like a million other nightclubs. Black suede banquettes, pounding music, flashing lights, and some sort of gold-specked Formica that is remarkably similar to something my grandmother had in her kitchen, installed circa 1943. The floor is stamped concrete embedded with white fiber-optic lights that flash in different patterns under our feet, and the whole club has a weird smell, like cloves. It's kind of hard to imagine what all the fuss is about. I'll bet the people who will be waiting outside in line all night would be pissed if they knew they were giving up their Saturday night to stand in the humidity in hopes of gaining entrance to a place that looks like about thirty other places right down the street. Tanya ditches us inside the door as soon as she spots a group of her PR buddies, so Kyle and I head to our table alone. I find myself acutely aware of an overpowering scent of lemon.

"Do you smell that?" I ask Kyle, shouting to be heard above the music.

"Lemon?" he yells back.

"I think so," I shout. "It's so strange, when we first walked in, I thought it smelled like cloves."

"What?" he asks.

"Cloves!" I yell.

"Thanks!" he yells back, smiling and bobbing his head to the music. I have no idea what he thinks I just said, but he looks enthusiastic about it, whatever it was. A few minutes later, I distinctly smell something that reminds me of meat loaf. It occurs to me that the club has created some sort of a "scent bar." It's an interesting idea, actually. Our sense of smell is second only to sight when it comes to evoking incredibly strong memories and emotions. The Dreamgirl perfume I'm wearing tonight is a perfect example—men are attracted to cinnamon and vanilla. I just slap on a little cinnamon mojo, and voilà! Catnip for men.

A waitress appears and takes our order: a beer for Kyle and the house punch for me. She's back in a blink with our drinks. The music is so loud it's almost impossible to carry on a conversation. Instead, Kyle and I hang out at the table together, smiling occasionally, listening to the music, but mostly sucking down our drinks, which are replenished with remarkable speed. A-plus for service, I must say. (Although I suppose no one could hear me.) I'm attempting to stare at Kyle discreetly (he's so pretty, I can't help myself, but at least I'm trying to be inconspicuous about it). Every time I look at him, he catches me and grins.

After drink number four, Kyle gets up and motions for me to come dance with him. He grabs my hand and leads me out onto the dance floor, which is completely packed. He dances in a way that is fluid, sensual: none of those herky-jerky, Elvis-hipped moves. I'm not surprised, really. I remember reading that good-looking men are better dancers because their bodies are more symmetrical. True or not, it certainly seems to be working for Kyle. After three or four songs, one of the pop stars in attendance takes the stage and starts belting out his latest ballad. Kyle pulls me close, and we dance to the slow song, his hips pressing against mine, his arms firmly around my waist. Suddenly the smell of orange blossoms is in the air, Kyle leans in, and I know he's going to kiss me. I'm holding my breath in anticipation, acutely aware of the code-red tingles shooting through my body. His full, perfect lips brush gently over mine, and something vaguely familiar stirs in me—the first-kiss swoon. God, the absolute bliss of kissing someone new for the first time. And damn, it's been so long since I had a first kiss. His mouth is so soft, so warm, so intoxicatingly fantastic that it muffles every rational thought my mind can toss out: *He's too young. I'm not ready. I just met him. I've had too much to drink. I'm going through a divorce . . .*

God, this guy can kiss. I'm completely sucked into the moment (literally) and then the pop star's ballad ends and the music stops. Kyle and I stop kissing and open our eyes at the same time, our mouths still centimeters away from each other's. Waitresses flood the floor bearing champagne flutes, which they quickly dispatch to the crowd. I take a small step back; Kyle accepts two glasses of champagne from the tray and hands one to me.

Three hours later, I can't remember the last time I had this much fun. The crowd has gone completely nuts. The movie stars have started to thin out a bit, now that the swag room, once laden with goodie bags and freebies for the celebs in attendance, has been pillaged. The crowd on the dance floor has become a bit more interesting. Kyle and I have been dancing to song after song after song, and I'm floating so high on champagne and lust I can't feel my feet.

"Should I take you home now?" he asks me, smiling sweetly. I'm just lost in those gorgeous brown eyes. My vision is blurry and my entire body is jumping with possibilities. Has a more loaded question ever been asked?

Okay, this is completely wrong, right? I don't know this guy, and he's so adorable, and I just want to kiss him again. I generally do not go home with guys I don't know. What kind of dating expert hooks up with a guy on the first date? I haven't kissed a complete stranger since college. (Okay, fine, one New Year's Eve when I was twenty-six, but that's it.) I may be drunk. Tipsy. Drunk. On a scale of one to ten, how pathetic/terrible/slutty would I be if I kissed this gorgeous guy for an hour? Just one hour. I will not sleep with him. I definitely will not sleep with him.

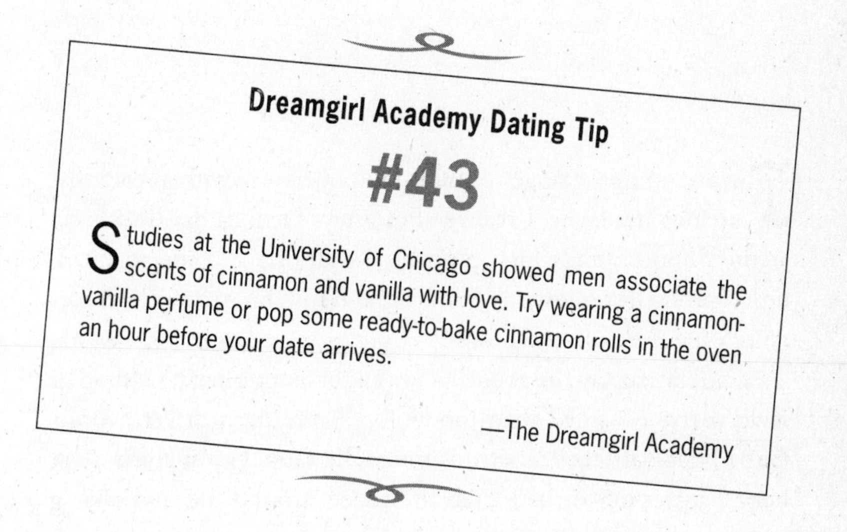

Dreamgirl Academy Dating Tip

#43

Studies at the University of Chicago showed men associate the scents of cinnamon and vanilla with love. Try wearing a cinnamon-vanilla perfume or pop some ready-to-bake cinnamon rolls in the oven an hour before your date arrives.

—The Dreamgirl Academy

Chapter 19

I wake up in a strange room in my underwear with a seriously vicious headache. I realize after a few seconds that I'm back at the Shore Club, which probably should have come to me a little quicker. My dress, my handbag, and my shoes litter the floor. And someone is in my shower.

I quickly replay the events of last night and realize it's either 1) Kyle the one-named-man-model, or 2) the limo driver, whose name I cannot recollect at this time. Oh, God. Last night is a bit hazy. I jump out of bed, grab the sheets around me, and take a quick peek in the mirror. I look like death's mistress. My fabulous smoky eye makeup, which made me look so mysterious and sexy last night, has migrated all over my face—like I just lost a sixteen-round bout for the welterweight championship of the world. One earring is missing. And the fake hairpiece, critical for last evening's glamour girl look, hangs limply from the left side of my head like a misplaced tail. Bad news. I hear the shower turn off. Oh crap.

I lose the lone earring, yank the fake hair off and toss it under the bed, and search around the room frantically for something I can use to clean my face. There is nothing but a half-empty can of Sprite, left by one of the glam squad yesterday. I quickly pour the Sprite over the bottom corner of the bedsheet and use the wetted sheet to frantically scrub away as much of the makeup as I can. Less than a minute later, my face looks better, but it feels infinitely more disgusting.

Breath.

My morning-after champagne breath is at toxic levels. I swish a little of the Sprite around in my mouth to get the woolly-socks-on-my-teeth out. Ugh, disgusting! There's nothing quite as gross as gargling with somebody else's old, used, flat soft drink. Except, maybe, using it to wash your face. A quick peek in the mirror reveals a vast improvement—my face is pink from the scrubbing, but at least the giant streaks of black eye makeup are gone. My hair actually looks good in that sexy, bed-head kind of way, especially now that my glamour girl toupee is hiding under the bed. I toss the can back onto the table, hide the soaked and disgusting sheet corner under the duvet, and rummage around in my suitcase for a robe. Too late.

Poster Boy steps out of the bathroom with a towel wrapped around his waist. Bare chest is a miracle of nature: smooth, tanned, with a perfect six-pack. He takes one look at me wrapped in a sheet, and a smile lights across his face. It's so unfair, he really does roll out of bed looking gorgeous.

"Hey Darby-girl," says Kyle, "how'd you sleep?"

Two thoughts cross my mind simultaneously. First, I *hope* that I did not sleep with this man that I have not even known for twenty-four hours. And second, if I did, I hope I wasn't too drunk to not remember every single minute of it.

"Great, thanks . . . and you?" I say, pulling the sheet a little tighter around me.

"Great," he says.

"Um. Did we, uh . . ." I stammer. Oh, the humiliation.

"Huh? Oh, no," he says, laughing, "you were a little out of it. Your publicist told my publicist to make sure I was nice to you. So, this is me being nice to you."

I sigh with relief. "Thank you, I really appreciate it."

"We did kiss a lot," he says. "Is that okay?" He looks a little bashful, which surprises me. I feel myself blushing. It's all coming back to me now. Kissing in the limo. Kissing in the elevator. Kissing on the balcony. I'm a little fuzzy on the part where I thought it was a good idea to sleep in my underwear with a complete stranger, but at least the rest of the night isn't a total blur.

"Um, yeah, that's okay," I say, smiling. "Good. It's good." I grab a change of clothes and a toothbrush out of my suitcase. "I'm going to go take a shower now."

"Cool. I'm going to order room service. Do you want anything?"

Okay, apparently Poster Boy is staying for breakfast.

"Um, scrambled eggs and bacon, some fruit, and a Coke," I say. I realize I'm starving, and that the last time I ate was lunch with the producers yesterday. No wonder I got so loopy. The closest thing to dinner I ate was the collection of pineapple chunks and maraschino cherries that came skewered in my drinks.

I head into the shower and try to remember every detail of the kissing part. There's a gorgeous guy in my hotel room, ordering me breakfast. The least I can do is have the good sense to enjoy it.

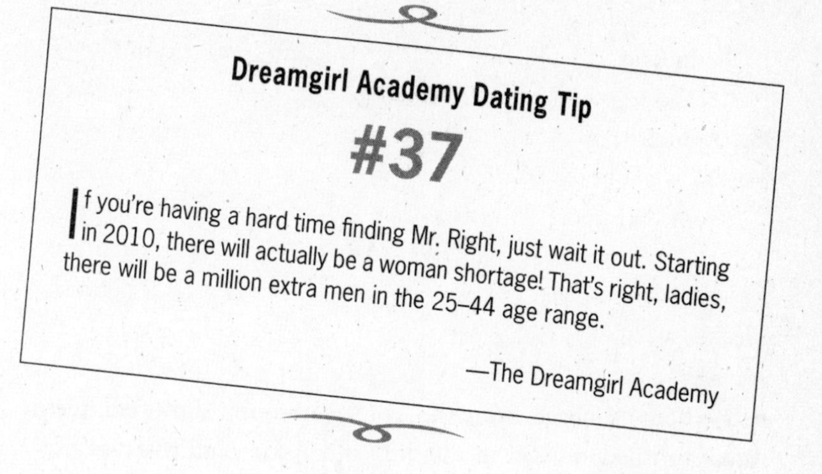

Dreamgirl Academy Dating Tip

#37

If you're having a hard time finding Mr. Right, just wait it out. Starting in 2010, there will actually be a woman shortage! That's right, ladies, there will be a million extra men in the 25–44 age range.

—The Dreamgirl Academy

Chapter 20

When I emerge from the hotel bathroom, showered, teeth brushed, dressed in a T-shirt and a skirt, and party-grime-free, I feel a thousand times better. Kyle and the room service waiter are out on the balcony, where the waiter has set up our breakfast on the table. As the waiter turns to leave, our eyes meet just as he turns toward me. Recognition is both instant and mutual: The waiter smiles and strides quickly toward the door, giving a little nod in Kyle's direction.

"I see you didn't need any assistance with your dress last night," he says, raising his eyebrows. He is the very same scissor-wielding savior who cut me out of my gown a week ago.

"No, thanks, I managed."

He winks and disappears through the door.

Kyle has ordered a little of everything on the menu—eggs, potatoes, pancakes, and fruit—and he chows down as only a twenty-ish male can. I dig in to my eggs and take a solid swig of the Coke. Breakfast has never tasted so good.

Twenty-five minutes later we have exhausted Kyle's entire conversational repertoire—parties, clubs in Miami, New York, and Los Angeles, other models (turns out that a few of his pals recently did a stint as moving men for a dating expert turned dumpee), celebrities, surfing, and gaming. I'm depressingly reminded of something Tia always says: "Smart people talk about concepts, average people talk about events, and stupid people talk about each other."

Although we spent most of the night together, we haven't really had a conversation until now—it was too loud to talk in the club last night, and after we left, well, we just didn't do much talking. I'm disappointed but not surprised; while Kyle is physically perfect, he is, well, not very bright. If intelligence were looks, he'd be a five-foot man with bad skin, a potbelly, and a comb-over. Damn, was it completely wrong of me to secretly hope that there would be a literature-reading brain surgeon lurking behind those soulful eyes and perfect pecs?

He leans over the breakfast table to kiss me, as I do a lightning-fast pros-and-cons list in my head:

PROS: He's fun to look at. He's a good kisser. He's really, really charming.

CONS: I will tear my hair out if I have to spend another ten minutes talking to him.

PROS: Maybe we could go to a retreat somewhere where you're not allowed to speak for seven days?

PROS: Maybe we could drive separately?

CONS: Damn. I can't do it. I just am not shallow enough to date someone only because he's hot. Incredibly, unbelievably hot. I need conversation! I need a point of view! I need a basic awareness of things that aren't covered in *People* magazine! Damn! How do men do it?

Our lips meet (bliss!) and I realize I need to figure out a way to get out of this. (In just one more minute. Okay, in two more minutes.) I can't keep him. So it's not really right to keep kissing him. Right?

Unless I tell him! I'll just tell him I think he's sweet and gorgeous and that I don't really see this going anywhere. *Except straight to the bedroom. Darby Vaughn, welcome to Trampsville.*

Blessedly, my cell phone rings. I break the kiss and scramble to answer it.

"Sorry," I say to Kyle breathlessly, as I snap the phone open. "Hello?"

"Darby? It's Holt Gregory. There's been a development in your case."

"Oh, hi, Holt," I say, feeling somewhat embarrassed. "What's up?"

"I just received a counterclaim from Gigi's attorney alleging you are responsible for 'alienation of affections.'"

"What does that mean?" I ask, confused. And wait, why is Gigi making claims in my divorce from Will?

"It means that Gigi is claiming that you interfered in her marriage to Will. That you broke up her marriage."

"I broke up *her* marriage?" I'm incredulous. "Is she kidding? She broke up my marriage! I didn't even meet Will until after their divorce was final! I think all those wrinkle shots have finally begun to seep into her brain!" I stare out at the balcony, dumbfounded and pissed.

"Darby, I need to know all the facts, even if they're not pretty. This is an extremely challenging case as it is . . ."

"Mr. Gregory, let me make it *extremely* clear that I *have* never and *will* never mess around with a married man. Will's divorce was final for *a year* before we ever *met*," I hiss into the phone, twisting my body away from the balcony so Kyle doesn't hear any more than he already has.

"Did you see the divorce papers?" he asks.

"No, Will told me on our second date. I remember because he said that we had met exactly one year after his divorce was final, and he thought it was some sort of sign. It was a date. A romantic date. I didn't exactly think to say, 'Hey, Will, thanks for the linguini. Say, before we order dessert could I take a peek at those divorce papers?' "

"Let's just hope he was telling the truth," Holt says.

"Mr. Gregory, do you ask to see divorce papers on the second date?"

"I don't date," he replies brusquely. "Anyway, it should be easy enough to verify."

"I don't appreciate that you don't seem to believe me."

"Most clients are their own worst enemy, Ms. Vaughn. What they don't realize is that the truth almost always comes out in the end."

"I'm telling the truth." I'm hurt and angry. Gigi lies and I'm the bad guy.

"For the record," Holt says quietly, in his most soothing Southern lilt, "I believe you."

"Thanks, I apologize. I didn't mean to snap at you." I feel genuinely sorry and strangely relieved.

"Don't you worry about it. I imagine you're starting to feel like the last sheep in a pack of wolves," he says kindly. "There's something pretty cockeyed about this deal anyway."

"What do you mean?" I ask.

"Well, Florida doesn't recognize alienation-of-affection laws, and not that it matters, but neither does California. Forty-three states, in fact, don't recognize such laws. Gigi has no standing to pursue an alienation-of-affections claim. The date of their divorce is a matter of public record, and it should be pretty easy to prove that you and Will met when you say you did. The claim doesn't apply here. They can't win on this; it will probably piss off the judge. It doesn't make any sense at all for them to file it." He pauses. "I don't know, maybe they're just trying to run up your legal fees, hoping they'll either scare you off, or you'll run out of cash before we get to court . . ."

"It could be, I guess," I say, disheartened. It's probably a good strategy. If I don't pick up this new TV show, I'm in big trouble. My books stopped selling after the *Today* incident, and the photos of Tony Kullen and me have only been on the newsstand for a day, not long enough to have any real effect on my book sales. If I don't turn my career around quickly, I'll burn through everything I've saved over the last few years. Damn it, I've got to get myself back on track. Then, another horrible motive springs into my consciousness:

"Holt, are these alienation-of-affection papers public record?"

"Yes, why?"

Oh, fuck. "They're doing this to kill me in the media. Rule number one in my first book is that a woman should never *ever* date a married man. Even though it's a lie, the media will have a field day with this. And by the time the truth comes out, my reputation, my career will be over." Crap. I'm going to lose everything I have, and no judge in his right mind is going to give a couple of kids to a publicly declared home-wrecking slut. I'm so screwed.

That bitch.

Dreamgirl Academy Dating Tip

#73

Should you put a hex on his ex?

Troublesome ex-girlfriends can put a damper on your new relationship: Maybe she just can't deal with the fact that it's over. Maybe she's really angry. Maybe she's plotting to steal him back.

Whatever the case, the smartest strategy is to steer clear of her drama. Like tantrum-throwing toddlers, most nasty exes are just looking for a reaction from him or from you. The fastest way to diffuse the situation is to refuse to play along.

And finally, if your guy labels all of his ex-girlfriends as psychotic, evil stalkers, take a step back and remember: The common denominator among all these whacked-out women is him.

—The Dreamgirl Academy

Chapter 21

An hour later I'm in my car on the interstate, speeding back toward Sarasota. I cannot believe this is happening to me. What is going on? Every time I think I see a light at the end of the tunnel, a rabid bat swoops down and bites me on the ass.

As soon as I hung up with Holt, I told Kyle I had to head out of Miami right away. He'd said, "let's hang out sometime" and kissed me one last time before I packed him up and sent him out the door. Then I threw all my stuff back into my overnight bag, dropped the fake hair in the FedEx envelope at the concierge desk, and got myself the hell out of South Beach as fast as I could.

Just as I'm barreling across the exit for Alligator Alley, my agent calls.

"Good news!" she says. "We've got the offer from the network. They want you to star in *Dating the Dreamgirl*. Congratulations!"

"Oh, thank God!" I say, vastly relieved. This feels like the one thing that could actually turn things around and get everything in my life back on track. Getting Lilly and Aidan back is my first priority, and this job will certainly pay a lot of legal expenses.

"The offer is too low," says Holland, "so we'll have to reject it until they come up with more money."

"We can't," I tell her. "We need to make the deal as quickly as possible, before the supermarket tabloids proclaim me as an evil husband-stealer." I fill her in on my conversation with Holt, Gigi's antics, and what I fear is going to happen. "Let's just lock down the deal now, and take what they're offering."

"Not a chance," says Holland. "First, none of this husband-stealing business is true. Second, if you jump at the first offer, they'll wonder what's wrong with you. We'll reject this deal, give them a twenty-four-hour timeline to respond, and have the whole thing wrapped up by Monday. If it comes up, we'll be straight with them: The allegations are false, and you can prove it, blah, blah, blah."

My stomach flips at the thought of losing the deal, but I trust Holland to know what she's doing.

"Okay," I say, "it's your call." I'm completely terrified that the media will be brutal and the network will bail out on me.

"Talk to your new publicist and see what she can do to minimize the press on this, or at least get your side of the story out first," Holland instructs.

"She's my next call." We trade good-byes and hang up, and I hit speed dial for Kendall. No answer. As I'm leaving her a message to call me back, my call-waiting beeps in. I click over to pick up the call and I'm surprised to find Will on the other line.

"Darby, we need to talk."

No crap. "What the hell, Will?" I say, pissed. "You know damned well that you and Gigi were divorced for a year when we met."

"What are you talking about?" he says.

"Don't be a jerk, Will. What are you trying to do?"

"I just wanted to tell you that Aidan made the baseball team out here. He was really excited about it and he wanted to talk to you. What's your problem?"

My problem? Just as I'm about to launch into a tirade about how he and Gigi are going to rot in hell for lying, for screwing me over, and, well, for just plain old evilness, Will interrupts and says, "Uh, I've gotta go. We'll call you later." And then he hangs up on me.

What? I dial his cell phone back and it rolls into voicemail on the first ring. Fucking jerk. What is wrong with him? God, they're both brain-damaged. My call waiting beeps in again, I leave a message for Will to call me back *immediately* so I can talk to Aidan, then click over to the other line. It's Kendall. I have no idea what publicity magic she has up her sleeve, and I can't even imagine how she'll spin me out of this one—I just hope she can. I start telling Kendall the details of the latest round of hell and find I'm so pissed at Will and Gigi that I need to pull over to calm down. I swing into a rest stop and concentrate on taking deep breaths.

"Gigi did *what*?" Kendall says. I repeat what Holt told me, and I can hear Kendall pacing on the other end of the line.

"That bitch!" she says. "Okay, okay, let's not panic." Even though she sort of sounds like she is. Panicking.

"What do we do?" I ask. "I just got the offer for the network show and I don't want to blow it. Plus, we've got such great momentum going with the Tony Kullen photos."

"How'd it go last night? Did you get any action?"

"What do you mean?" I ask, flustered. Who ratted me out? Kyle's publicist?

"Pictures? Did you guys get a lot of action from the photographers?"

"Oh, yeah, yeah," I say, relieved. "We were photographed quite a bit."

"I'll bet. Was he a good kisser?"

"Oh God, how did you know?"

"Hell-*o*, you locked lips with the hottest guy on the East Coast in the middle of a crowd of publicists and reporters. I've had thirty calls on it already. We're all jealous."

"Yes," I say. "Good kisser. Moving on, please . . ."

"Nice job. We're far more likely to get the photos picked up since it was a real hookup."

"Great . . ." I say sarcastically.

"Did you sleep with him?" Kendall gushes. "I have to know! Was he amazing? Or completely pathetic in that way that gorgeous guys are sometimes—you know, so handsome they never develop any, um, skills."

"Didn't sleep with him. I did pass out with him in my room, however. And I apparently kissed him a lot. He was a gentleman. He took a shower and stayed for breakfast. I would like to say for the record that if his kissing ability is any indication of his other 'skills' he doesn't have anything to worry about. Happy?"

"Envious." She sighs. "Is he great?"

"He's a sweetheart. Not much of a conversationalist, though."

"Yeah," she says, "those male models are like Irish setters. Stunning, but with the smarts of a sand gnat."

Kendall feels certain we can get a jump on Gigi's husband-stealing story because the court papers were just filed yesterday, a Friday, at the close of business. We'll probably have until Monday to preempt the story.

"We have three options," she says. "First, we can wait and see if this story gets picked up at all, hope it doesn't, and respond to it if it does. Understand, of course, that if they report that Gigi says you stole her husband, and you come out saying you didn't, most people are going to think you probably did."

"Okay, what's option two?" I ask.

"Second, we can leak the story ourselves with all the details of when you met, and state that Gigi and Will are using false information to try to make you look bad in the custody battle. But a number of people will likely still believe that you probably did it."

"Is there an option available where I don't look like a pathological home-wrecker?"

"I can call every reporter I know, explain the situation, and ask them to kill the story if they were planning on running it."

"Would that actually work?"

"It depends on how newsworthy they think it is. If the reporter is sympathetic and sees this for what it is, Gigi lying to harm your chances in the divorce case or the custody battle, they won't run it. But, if they think it's a big story, or if they think it's true, then the fact that we tried to get it killed will only make us look worse," she says.

"Again, making me look guilty," I say, feeling defeated.

"Yes," she says dejectedly, and then, thinking out loud, continues. "Maybe I could prepare a fact sheet, a basic timeline detailing the dates of Will's divorce from Gigi, when your book was published, when you and Will met, et cetera, and provide it *without* a statement to the media."

"Or, we could just do nothing," I say, with an epiphany sparking over my head.

"Oh, Darby," says Kendall, giving me a verbal pat on the back for this ridiculous notion. "I don't want you to lose hope. We'll figure something out. We have to fight this."

"I'm not losing hope. This just feels sleazy, so I'm opting out.

It seems like fighting this will only make it worse." It suddenly hits me that there's something much bigger at stake than whether or not I get labeled as a hypocritical, marriage-crashing slut.

"Well . . ." She falls silent.

"Kendall, have you ever heard the expression, 'What you think of me is none of my business'? I can't change what people will think about me when this comes out. Some people will believe it, and some won't, but gossip feeds on details. Whatever people think, I know what really happened. I just won't go on television and say that Lilly and Aidan's parents are liars, even though it's true. If the kids saw it, it would break their hearts, and I can't be a part of that. Gigi's claim is easy enough to check out—I don't think responsible journalists will report this story without confirming basic facts, and for those who only want a nasty scoop, well, they'll have more than enough to go on. We'll do nothing. If reporters call for comment, we'll give them dates and the means for fact-checking, but I won't comment. I won't make this any worse than it already is. We'll keep moving forward."

Kendall is quiet for a moment as she contemplates my decision. Then softly, she says, "You're much stronger than people think, Darby. I'm proud of you."

As I drive home I can't help but wonder why Gigi would tell an outright lie. In a legal document. She knows as well as I do that Will and I met long after their divorce. Could Will have lied to me about the divorce? Oh, God. He certainly wouldn't be the first married man to lie. I saw the divorce papers when Will and I applied for our marriage license, didn't I? I can't remember now. Holt's question rattles around in my head, and I make a mental note to ask him to pull Will's divorce records so we can double-check them. This can't be right.

It occurs to me that for Gigi, the queen of all drama queens, everything is all about her. How it affects her. How it makes her feel. How it inconveniences her. She is so self-absorbed that she probably doesn't even realize she's lying. She's just rewritten history in her own brain, and in the Gigi version of reality, *she* is the wronged wife and *I* am the other woman. The fact that she left him, or that Will and I were married, is irrelevant. Will always belonged to her. And when she decided she wanted him back, well, I was just in the way—the one thing standing between her and her husband.

How to Survive a Public Breakup with Grace

by Darby Vaughn

From Christie Brinkley to Jennifer Aniston to Heather Locklear to your favorite dating expert, getting dumped is a miserable experience—whether it's on the cover of *People,* live on national television, or facing all the other moms at Chuck E. Cheese after your husband is caught fooling around with the school librarian.

Public celebrity breakups are mirroring what's happening to women all over the country: It's the most embarrassing situation of your life. And everybody knows about it.

Surviving a public breakup can feel like you're treading water in a fishbowl. So how do you hold your head up high and have the guts to go out in public again knowing that the whole world is watching and every person there you is talking about you?

Don't carry shame that doesn't belong to you: Hold your head up high. Don't let yourself wallow in the crowd's pity. Bask in the support of your friends instead.

Retreat to a safe place where you can catch your breath: Go back to your childhood home, camp out in a pal's living room, or take a trip to someplace where no one has ever heard of you until you're ready to face the world again.

Get a breakup buddy for the first few weeks or as long as you need one: Whenever you have to make a public appearance, bring along a sympathetic friend until you're strong enough to stand on your own.

Pamper your body and feed your soul: Dress to the nines every day. If you look better, you'll feel better.

Chapter 22

On Monday morning I flip back and forth between the news channels, the entertainment channels, and the national morning shows, waiting for the crap to hit the fan. So far, so good. I did catch a clip of me and Kyle together on the red carpet on E! (damn, he's great-looking!), but I almost didn't recognize myself thanks to the makeover wonder team. I recognized the dress first, actually. (The glam squad was right; it did get attention all by itself.)

So far, there's been no mention of Gigi's court documents, a huge relief. I realize that this is probably only a short stay of execution, but I'm thankful nonetheless. I make myself a boring breakfast of scrambled eggs and dry whole-wheat toast (all the cocktails and breakup bingeing has made my favorite pair of jeans a little snug) and head upstairs to my office. Finally, I settle in at my computer and check my e-mails. In my inbox is a message from a reporter at the *Gwinnett Daily Post* that strikes fear in my gut. I say a quick prayer for mercy and hold my breath as I click it open.

TO: DARBY VAUGHN
FROM: JENNIFER DOUGAN / GWINNETT DAILY POST
SUBJECT: GIGI BISSANTI COURT DOCUMENTS

Hi Darby,
First, let me say how sorry I am about your impending divorce. I'm not sure if you remember me. I interviewed you about four years ago in Atlanta about your book, *Secrets to Make the Guys Go Gaga*. I had just gone through an awful breakup and you listened to me cry for two hours at Fat Matt's Barbeque Shack. Do you remember? I felt like such an unprofessional jerk for bawling my eyes out in the middle of the interview, but you were so nice. You gave me some great advice on how to get over the breakup and move on, and how I deserved someone who would really love me and treat me with respect. You really made a big impression—I felt hopeful again.

Anyway, I just received a press release this morning about Gigi Bissanti's claim that you broke up her marriage, and I recalled something from our interview: When we met, you said you were single, not dating anybody, and I remember reading in your newsletter a few months later that you'd met someone, and then later that you'd gotten engaged. I knew Will (sort of) because he's the one who set up our interview, and I specifically remember he said that he was pretty sure you'd be a good interview because although he hadn't met you in person yet, you were really great on the phone.

When I read the press release I was surprised. Messing around with a married man doesn't seem like your style (Chapter 12!). I did a little checking—your book came out in May 2003. Gigi Bissanti and Will Bradley's divorce was finalized on May 23, 2002. Am I missing something here?
Jennifer

TO: JENNIFER DOUGAN / GWINNETT DAILY POST
FROM: DARBY VAUGHN
SUBJECT: RE: GIGI BISSANTI COURT DOCUMENTS

Hi Jennifer,
Of course I remember you! How are you doing?

No, you're not missing anything. Gigi and Will had been divorced about a year before I met Will.
Best wishes,
Darby

TO: DARBY VAUGHN
FROM: JENNIFER DOUGAN / GWINNETT DAILY POST
SUBJECT: RE: RE: GIGI BISSANTI COURT DOCUMENTS

Darby,
I'm well, thanks for asking. Any idea why Gigi would file these papers?
Jennifer

TO: JENNIFER DOUGAN / GWINNETT DAILY POST
FROM: DARBY VAUGHN
SUBJECT: RE: RE: RE: GIGI BISSANTI COURT DOCUMENTS

Jennifer,
Yes, but I can't say.
Darby

TO: DARBY VAUGHN
FROM: JENNIFER DOUGAN / GWINNETT DAILY POST
SUBJECT: RE: RE: RE: RE: GIGI BISSANTI COURT DOCUMENTS

Darby,
That's all I need to know. Just one more thing, I thought you'd like to know I'm in love with a fantastic guy (another reporter actually) and we're getting married this summer. My life changed so much after I met you and read your book—I just wanted to say thank you.
Jennifer

TO: JENNIFER DOUGAN / GWINNETT DAILY POST
FROM: DARBY VAUGHN
SUBJECT: RE: RE: RE: RE: RE:

Jennifer,
Congratulations!
I'm so happy for you. You deserve good things.
Best,
Darby

TO: DARBY VAUGHN
FROM: JENNIFER DOUGAN / GWINNETT DAILY POST
SUBJECT: RE: RE: RE: RE: RE: RE:

Darby,
So do you.
Jennifer

Wow, that's nice. I always love a good, happy ending. (I guess that's why I was drawn to the "happy ending" business, huh?) My heart twinges a bit for the loss of my own happily ever after, but I'm glad for her, I really am. And knowing that I've helped someone makes me feel like what I've done with my life has some meaning, that I've made a difference to someone. It's been a while since I've felt like that.

Deleting the parts about Jennifer's personal life, I forward the rest of the e-mail exchange to Kendall so she can keep an eye out for the article. It seems as though at least one reporter will get this story right.

After leaving a quick "I love you, I miss you" message for Lilly and Aidan, I answer more e-mail, spend some time working on my column, and page through a bunch of photos that Kendall sent of Kyle and me at the club opening. I head back downstairs to the TV to see whether Gigi's court documents have hit the news yet. Nothing so far. If a tiny suburban paper like the *Gwinnett Daily Post* has already received them, then it's only a matter of time before the story hits the television. And the newspapers. And the Internet.

Holland calls me around four to tell me we have a deal with the network. We'll begin taping *Dating the Dreamgirl* in two weeks.

"Why so quickly?" I ask.

"They want to fast-track it for the summer season, which means we've got to get into production right away. As far as I'm concerned, the faster the better," Holland explains.

"Where are we shooting?"

"Miami. Lots of clubs, lots of celebrities this time of year. It will be perfect," she assures me. "This is just what we need to get your career back on track."

The timing is great. We'll probably be wrapped up with filming before my custody case ever gets to court.

She asks about the news coverage on the court documents and is relieved to hear that it's been quiet so far. She instructs me to sign the agreement the minute it comes in and fax it right back to her.

"Let's get this deal locked down as soon as possible," she says.

An hour later she faxes the papers, and I sign them and send them back. I'm hugely relieved, because getting this show means that I can afford to fight for Lilly and Aidan for as long as it takes. It also means that I may have a chance to resuscitate my career. It's only six by the time I finish signing and faxing the documents to Holland, but I'm completely worn out from waiting for the other shoe to drop. I call Lilly and Aidan again, and leave another message telling them I miss them. Then I decide to take a long bath and go to bed early.

I am wide awake at four A.M. This is, I suppose, what happens when you go to bed around seven. No wonder old people are always up at the crack of dawn. As I sit in the darkness, listening to the waves crashing outside, the covers pulled around me, I try to make sense of the jumble of events from the last few days. I pull a book from the nightstand and flip through the pages, but I can't concentrate. I slip on a bathrobe and head into the living room to turn on the television. I just can't get used to the quiet. Even when Lilly and Aidan were sleeping, I could always feel them in the house. There is an ever-present energy around children, crackling and buzzing, dipping to a breathy hum as they slumber. Now, it's just quiet. All the time, quiet.

I plop myself onto the couch with the book and an afghan my grandmother made, and keep one eye on the TV, watching for any mention of Gigi's court documents. I'm surprised, and hugely relieved, that there is still no coverage. Maybe, just maybe, I could be lucky enough for this to go away quietly?

Around seven-thirty I head into the shower. I've got a meeting with Holt at nine to discuss the custody hearing set for next month. I'll be so glad when all of this is finally resolved.

An hour or so later, I am standing in the reception area of Holt's downtown office. No one else is waiting, so I guess I'm the first client of the day. His receptionist leads me down the hallway, where a pitcher of orange juice and a tray of pastries is spread out on the conference table. Yum. I've vowed to eat less junk food, but there's a fat blueberry muffin that's calling my name, and I forgot to eat breakfast this morning. Just as I'm starting to unwrap the monster muffin, Holt bursts into the room with a look of pure irritation on his face.

"What the hell were you thinking?" he demands.

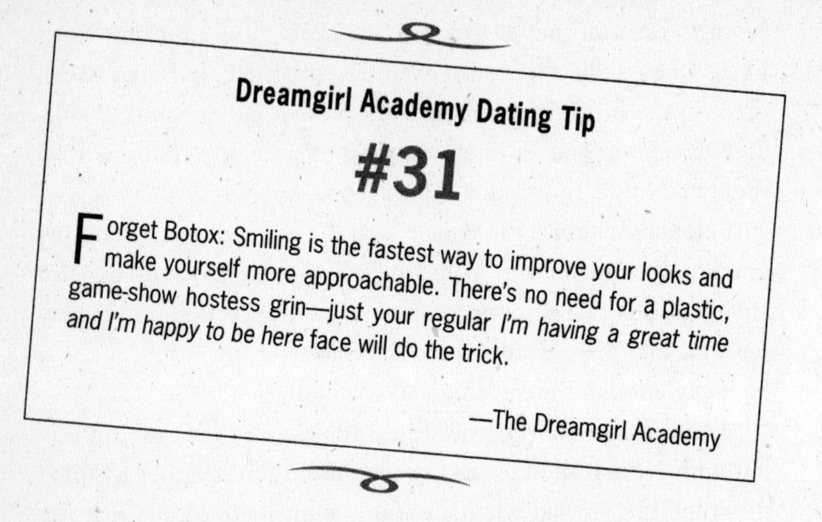

Dreamgirl Academy Dating Tip

#31

Forget Botox: Smiling is the fastest way to improve your looks and make yourself more approachable. There's no need for a plastic, game-show hostess grin—just your regular *I'm having a great time and I'm happy to be here* face will do the trick.

—The Dreamgirl Academy

Chapter 23

"Good morning to you, too," I say.

"What the hell is this?" Holt asks, his green eyes flashing as he tosses a stack of magazines onto the conference table. The pile makes a big thud when it lands and a few of the magazines skitter across the table to the other side. I recognize the photos of my date with Tony.

"Well," I say, completely smart-assed, "it looks like you've got *People*, *US Weekly*, *In Style*, and a few others. All the classics."

"Why are you *in* them, Miss Vaughn?" he asks, making every syllable count. God, that Southern accent: How can he sound so charming and polite, even when he's pissed?

"I'm trying to get my career back on track," I say defensively. "It's for publicity, to show book buyers that I've moved on, that I'm not the hopeless loser they saw on TV."

"You're not a hopeless loser," he says, his richly melodic voice softening slightly, "but you are making it incredibly difficult for me to convince a judge that your life and your livelihood have been irrevocably ruined, that all you care about is taking care of your children, when you and America's favorite basketball player are cuddled up on the pages of every magazine."

Fear shoots through me.

"Are there more pictures?" he asks.

"Yes, there was an event the other night, a club opening, lots of photographers. I attended with a model named Kyle."

"Great," he says sarcastically. "Anything else I should know about?"

A dreadful feeling hits me in my stomach. "Yes," I say, "there's one more thing."

"What is it?" Holt asks.

"I'm doing a show, a new show called *Dating the Dreamgirl.* It's sort of a reality dating show. The whole idea of the show is for the camera to follow me around on various dates."

He looks pensive for a moment, and he rakes his fingers through his hair, deep in thought. I'm mesmerized for a second and catch myself wondering if his curls are as soft as they look. A single dark lock catches around his finger, and he absentmindedly brushes it from his ear. *Focus, Darby.*

"Can you keep it from airing?" he asks.

"We haven't even started shooting yet, but I don't think I can get out of it. I've signed a contract."

"This is not good, Darby, not good at all."

"What are you saying?" I ask, fearful of the answer.

"This does not bode well for your custody battle. You've got to stop dating, especially in public, until the hearing is over." *Oh no, what have I done?* "You barely stand a chance of getting the kids back as it is," he states firmly. "You have to make a choice, Darby. If you continue to do this, I can't help you. If you don't stop right now, you'll destroy what little hope you have left of ever seeing Lilly and Aidan again."

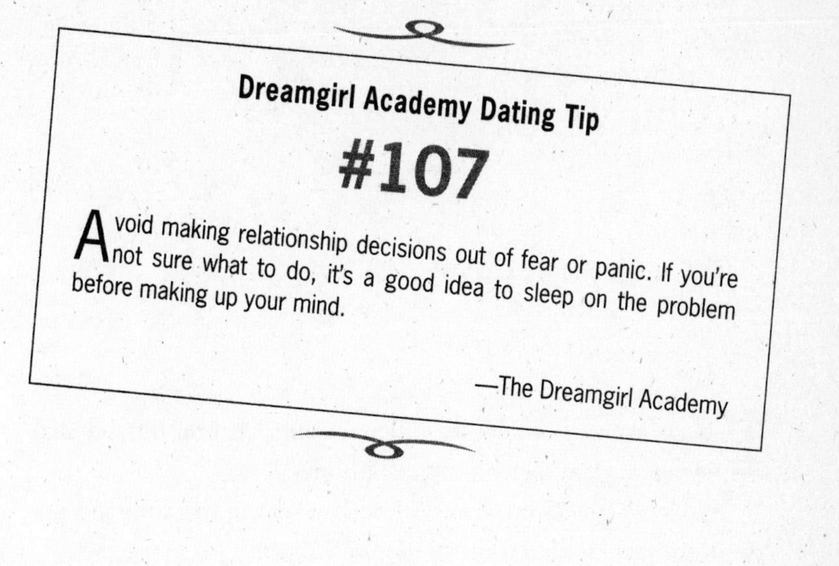

Dreamgirl Academy Dating Tip

#107

Avoid making relationship decisions out of fear or panic. If you're not sure what to do, it's a good idea to sleep on the problem before making up your mind.

—The Dreamgirl Academy

Chapter 24

I speed home from Holt's office, crying hysterically as I dial my agent's number on my cell phone.

"Holland, it's Darby," I say. "Have you sent in the contracts for the show yet?" I ask. *Please say no, please say no.*

"Yesterday. Why, is there a problem?"

"You've got to get me out of it," I plead. "I can't do it. I need you to get me released from the contract."

"Calm down," instructs Holland. "What exactly are you saying?"

I launch into an explanation of my meeting with Holt and tell her that if I do the show, I'll effectively be killing any chance of getting custody of the kids.

"Darby," says Holland firmly, "I think it's time for you to let this custody thing go. The kids aren't yours. I know you love them, but I hate to see you throw away your whole career over something you can't win. You need to be smarter about this. You need to think about the big picture here."

"I can't let them go," I sob, "I love them."

"Darby, are they worth everything you've worked for?" Holland demands. Her trademark cool demeanor is tinged with exasperation. "Are you willing to give up your entire career for these kids? If you sacrifice this show, it will all be over. I don't see how you can come back, otherwise. This is your last shot," she says angrily. "What happens when you lose the kids, too? You'll have nothing. Can you live with that? Is this really worth it?"

"Yes."

"What in the world are you thinking? How are you even going to support those kids? How are you planning to feed them and yourself, pay for your house? I think you'd be making a huge mistake, Darby."

I cry all the way home. It's strange . . . in the past this is just the kind of situation that would have made me sick to my stomach. I never used to cry, even when I was alone, and now it seems like I'm crying all the time. At least I'm not throwing up. Thank goodness for small favors.

I'm so confused. I'm terrified of screwing everything up, and for once in my life I have no idea what to do. If I give up the show, I probably won't have enough money to fight for custody. And if I take the show, I'm probably throwing away the only chance I might have to get my kids back. Why does this have to be so impossible? Digging through the glove compartment, I rummage around for something to blow my nose on, finding only a leftover drive-thru napkin. Wiping my face with the napkin, I stare at myself in the rearview mirror, all puffy eyes and blotchy skin.

I can't stop crying. What the hell am I going to do?

I head to Jules's house right away, and we spend the rest of the afternoon on her porch commiserating and drinking iced tea. She watches her children play, and I mourn mine. By the time I head back to the guesthouse it's after five in the afternoon, and I have eleven messages on my voicemail.

The first message is from Lilly, and her tiny, sweet voice catches me in my throat as she chatters on about the goat she petted at the zoo. Aidan's message is next, and I try to picture him talking on the phone, the phone squeezed between his ear and his shoulder, pacing the kitchen as he always does. I miss the tiny details of them: long eyelashes, round cheeks, Lilly's giggles, Aidan's impossible cowlick. In an instant, I find myself in tears again.

The phone rings while I'm listening to messages, and I can see from caller ID that it's Kendall.

"Darby, have you seen the paper yet?" Kendall asks breathlessly. Well, here we go.

Wiping my tears, I ask, "No, where? What does it say?" My heart races. Damn it, damn it, damn it.

"There's an article written by that reporter from the *Gwinnett Daily Post*, which is a little tiny paper in the Atlanta suburbs. It was picked up by one of the wire services, so the story is running in hundreds of papers all over the country—413, so far, according to the media monitoring service."

"Right, the one from yesterday. What does it say?" Jennifer was quite nice, but I know she has a job to do and I respect that. She's a good person. Take a deep breath. Whatever she's written can't be worse than what I've already been through.

"Long story short, the article claims that Gigi may be trying to use the divorce case to manipulate the media to jump-start her own floundering reality-TV career, and how she's filed court documents that are obviously, provably false."

"Holy crap," I say.

"There's more," Kendall says. "It says how well you have held up under the pressure of Gigi's smear campaign, and how you have shown, quote, 'class and dignity' by refusing to comment on the matter."

"Wow," I say, and then I start to tear up again. Through all of this, I've been a running late-night gag, a topic of water-cooler gossip; and my career, a landfill of humiliation—a giant receptacle for the world's pity and mockery. Now, to have someone who barely knows me defend my honor, stand up for me, to see the situation for what it is. I am so thankful, I feel so much relief, that someone else in the world sees the unfairness in all of this. It makes me feel like a person again, and not just the punchline of a cruel joke.

Kendall and I talk for a bit longer, and I pull myself together. She's pretty certain that the rest of the media coverage will go this way as well, especially since it's been reported in such a large number of newspapers that Gigi's allegations are false.

"I wonder how much of a backlash this will cause for Gigi," speculates Kendall. "The media does not like to be lied to."

"I wonder, too," I say. A tiny (okay, medium) part of me hopes she'll get what she deserves, but mostly I'm just glad to be out of the fire for a while. I hang up with Kendall and check the rest of my messages. There are two from Kyle and four from Holt. I skip the rest of the messages and call his office. Voicemail informs me that his office is closed, so I leave a message with my home number. I'll deal with the rest of my messages later.

Pouring myself a glass of sweet tea, I head out to the back deck to read a book and watch the gulf. I'm just settling in on the lounge chair when I spot my attorney jogging down the beach directly in front of me.

"Holt!" I yell toward the sand. He spins around, obviously surprised to see me, and sprints up to the guesthouse.

"You live out here?" he pants, out of breath from his run.

"For now," I say. "It belongs to a girlfriend. The guesthouse." Holt mops his brow with the front of his white T-shirt, giving me a quick glimpse of spectacular abs beneath, then wipes his hands on his pale gray shorts. I am not ogling my divorce attorney. Even though he has nice legs.

"What are you doing out here?" I ask.

"I run this beach every day. Six miles, rain or shine. I usually try to get my run in before I go to work, but I had an early meeting today. Nice place," he says, looking around. "I can see why you don't want to leave." He looks out across the gulf. "Great view," he adds.

I get a little tingle in my knees. God, what is it about that Southern accent? The sun from the window reflects just above his eyebrow, sending a little shimmer through his eyes.

"I was just calling you back," I say.

His breathing comes slower, as he steps toward me. "Right. I wanted to apologize, I think I was a little hard on you today."

"It's okay." I immediately feel bad for being so irritated with him earlier. "I'd rather know the truth."

"Well, you'll always get the truth from me. Still, I know I can be a bit harsh sometimes." His voice softens. "I really didn't mean to upset you."

I offer him some sweet tea, which he accepts, and we take our drinks over to the porch swing.

"I'm okay," I say. "Frankly, I appreciate your directness." And I do. I don't think I've ever known a man who was so brutally honest. And although it's taken a little getting used to, I'm starting to appreciate how straightforward he is. "I'm really more angry with myself than anything else. The last thing I want to do is jeopardize my chances of getting Lilly and Aidan—it never occurred to me that going out with Tony Kullen might affect the case. I couldn't bear it if I screwed this up . . ." I feel tears welling up, and I try to brush them away quickly with the palm of my hand before he can see them.

"Don't be so hard on yourself, Darby," he says, looking at me intently with those placid green eyes. "You didn't know." He pauses and the deck is quiet; neither of us speaks.

"Darby, are you crying?" he asks, moving forward and putting his hand to my face. His fingers are soft as he tenderly touches the skin on my cheek and our eyes meet. We stare at each other for a few seconds. Suddenly, he looks down at his hand like it's a foreign object touching my cheek and pulls back, as though he's been burned.

"It's fine," I say, suppressing my sniffles, and dabbing my eyes quickly with my shirtsleeve. "I'm fine. Thank you."

He pats me awkwardly on the shoulder and excuses himself, saying he's got to finish his run. As he stands up, he thanks me for the tea, then sprints down the steps to the beach. After he's gone, I sit on the swing for a good hour wondering what the hell just happened, and why I'm sort of hoping he'll come back.

Flirting 101—Five Tips to Make 'Em Drool

by Darby Vaughn

You don't have to look like Drew Barrymore to make the guys go gaga. All you need is your fabulous smile and a few surefire flirting tips like the ones you'll find below. The key is to look approachable enough for men to feel comfortable in taking a risk.

1) Lock Eyes Lock eyes with the guy you're flirting with for a full five to six seconds, then smile and drop your gaze. Don't stare a hole through his forehead, just give him a smoldering come-hither glance and look away. Do this at least three times in a ten- to fifteen-minute period. Why? Your target needs to know it's him you're flirting with, and eye contact is a universal signal.

2) Be a Vampire's Best Friend One of the most winning flirting techniques a woman can use is the exposure of her neck. This can be done with a head tilt to one side, the classic hair flip, or my personal favorite, the over-the-shoulder glance.

3) Lip Service Both men and women are subconsciously attracted to red, moist lips because they signal youth, sex, and fertility. To make the most of it, try wearing a red lipstick (red has been shown to increase a man's heart rate), which not only gives your lips that youthful color but also makes your smile more visible and your teeth whiter.

4) Let Your Feet Do the Talking To make yourself approachable, stand with your feet no more than six or seven inches apart, pointing your toes slightly inward. *Slightly* inward.

5) Hottie See, Hottie Do People mirror each other's body language when they are attracted. Try subtly mimicking your flirting target's behavior. If he leans forward, you lean forward. When you mirror someone's behavior, he'll begin to feel a connection to you.

Once he starts talking to you, use these tips to cement the attraction: Smile and maintain eye contact as he speaks, and focus your attention on what he's saying. Nodding and tilting your head signal that you're listening. Smiling and laughing are crucial—it's the quickest, easiest way to put him at ease and make a connection. Finally, seal the deal with some low-level touching, such as brushing the shoulder or elbow.

Chapter 25

Two days later I meet Olive and a crowd of assistants and crew from *Dating the Dreamgirl* for a preproduction meeting in Sarasota, at the guesthouse. After some back and forth with the network, Holland let me know that they'd promised to keep the sets closed, so no "date" photos from the show would end up in the press. They also pushed back the date of *Dating the Dreamgirl*'s premiere until the fall season, so that it would not affect my custody hearing.

Holt wasn't thrilled that the show was still going forward, but he was at least satisfied with the compromises.

With any luck, the media won't catch wind of *Dreamgirl* until after the issue of custody is settled. It's the best we can hope for.

Apparently there were a number of executives at the network who were not enthusiastic about the custody problems and wanted to find another dating expert. Holland has spent the last forty-eight hours working every contact she has at the network trying to keep this deal on the table. In the end, it was Olive, the producer and a single mother of two, who really pushed for me. Eventually the network agreed, on the stipulation that we keep this all as quiet and dignified as possible. And while I'm hugely relieved that the show is going forward, I'm still not quite sure that I've made the right decision.

The *Dreamgirl* crew measures me for wardrobe and quizzes extensively about the type of men I like to date. Hello? I haven't dated for four years! (Well, except for the two fake dates, but that doesn't really count, now, does it?) What the hell do I know about whom I'd like to date? I've been so focused on what getting this show could do for my career that I sort of pushed the fact that I'd have to go on dates to the back of my mind.

Two weeks later I'm back in Miami, installed on the ninth floor at the Tides in the Goldeneye suite, which I love because it has a private terrace and a fabulous marble bathtub in the sunroom overlooking the beach. We're shooting fifteen or sixteen hours a day, which works itself out to about three dates every single day. I had forgotten how exhausting it is to date, and it's even more exhausting to do it on TV.

Most of the men are nice, no one really spectacular, which is fine by me. I wonder where the producers find some of these guys: I'd like to think there's some complicated, exhaustive interview process, but for all I know they could be combing the bus stations. Anyway, my contract states that I can't date anyone outside the show, and if I do happen to hit it off with one of my "show dates" (a phrase that reminds me of "show dogs," and believe me, some of them are), we can't be seen in public until after our episode airs. It all feels a little James Bondish to me, but whatever.

After my conversation with Holt, I'd told Kendall that we were going to have to put the Hollywood Plan on hold until the show was over. Only Kyle-the-one-named-model is not on board with the new "no dates" policy. He's been calling three or four times a week since we met. And the more I tell him I'm not available to date, the more he persists. Isn't that the way it always goes?

He's sent flowers, champagne (a nice bottle of Cristal, actually), and even an aromatherapy kit. (I think that had something to do with the fact that we met in a scent bar; otherwise, it's just strange.) He's a nice guy, but even if I weren't under a dating moratorium, I'd have to say no. Otherwise, I might keep saying yes. He's just way too young and clueless for me.

The press coverage of Gigi's fake court documents has been brutal on her end, and barely a blip on mine. The media has apparently had enough of Gigi, and most of the stories of late have portrayed her as a publicity-seeking witch. They've become bored with her twice-a-week press conferences to announce her newest court filing or to rant about me, and since I'm not adding any more fuel to the fire, the press has moved on to more interesting news.

Winter is the height of the Miami Beach social season, yet I find myself alone in my room a lot. I just don't feel much like going out. After a fifteen-hour dating triple-header every single day, I simply want to be alone. I miss my kids, I'm not too crazy about living in a hotel room (even one as nice as this), and by the time we finish shooting each day, I'm so exhausted I just want to pass out in that spectacular marble bathtub.

I try to call Lilly and Aidan every night when I get back to the hotel, around eleven-thirty my time, which makes it almost bedtime in California. It breaks my heart on the days shooting runs late: If we're not done by midnight, it's too late to talk. I sneak in a few calls to the kids while we're filming during the day, but it's not enough. I miss their faces. I miss their hugs. I miss *them* so much.

I'm on the set at every morning at eight. We have a quick production meeting, and then I'm off to Hair and Makeup until eleven. We're taping three dates a day, all lunch or dinner dates, so I spend most of my time seated behind a plate of some sort of Italian food at a quaint table for two at one of Miami's many local hot spots. Then, my "dates" and I go skimboarding at the beach, or get our fortunes read, or practice our nail-gunning technique at a Habitat for Humanity house. At the end of the day's taping, I have three "doorstep" moments (one right after another, tell me *that's* not weird), which are supposed to be the end of each date. On a normal date, of course, the doorstep is where you have your first kiss (or the ever-popular awkward handshake) and make plans to see each other again. Or not. Since I'm staying at a hotel, the "doorstep" is actually a set. That's right, from eight to eleven every night, three strange guys try to put the moves on me in front of a cardboard door. As if.

Today's dates are Liam, a minor royal (he's something like seventh in line for the throne of a tiny European country I'd never heard of before today); Jess, a bra designer (seriously!); and Chadd, a semifamous music promoter.

My date with Liam is excruciatingly dull, as his main (and only) interest is himself and his royalness. Once I got past the initial three seconds of *Oh my god!!! If we fell madly in love and got married, I could be a princess!!!* my little castle fantasy deflated immediately when he managed a little half-lipped smile and generously told me that I could refer to him as "Prince Liam" for the duration of the date, rather than "Your Royal Highness." In the course of the longest forty-five-minute date on record, I realized that Liam—sorry, *Prince Liam*—was not only the dullest man I've ever encountered but also, quite possibly, gay. Why in the world he would want to date on TV is beyond me, but hey, it's his call. Whatever.

When we're finished with His Royal Highness, date number two arrives.

"Hi, I'm Jess," he says, sticking his hand out in my direction. I take a sip of my fake wine (can't use the real stuff, or I'd be napping under the table by the middle of the day) and shake his hand as he joins me.

"Hi, Jess, I'm Darby," I say. "Great to meet you."

We chat about Miami, about Jess's dog Marley, and a little bit about what I like best about being an author. A fake waiter stops by to refill our fake wine, as we smile back and forth over our penne with lobster.

"What size bra do you wear? You're about a 34B?" Jess asks nonchalantly.

"Um, yes, well, that's sort of a personal question, isn't it?" I choke out, unable to finish swallowing the sip of fake wine now bubbling in my throat. Great, I've just confirmed my bra size on national television.

"Hey, don't sweat it," he says. "I design 'em, so I can pretty much figure it out right away. You're wearing the right size bra, I can tell. A lot of women don't."

"Um, well, yes, it's hard to find a good bra . . . size," I say, trying to figure out how to steer the conversation anywhere but where it is.

"Hey, I'll be happy to send you a box of our newest models. You like the padded ones?"

"Thanks," I say. "I'm covered." Pardon the pun. "So, how did you get started in the bra business?" I ask. Anything to get the conversation off me. Please.

Jess explains that his grandmother opened the business nearly sixty years ago; his mother had worked there all her life, and he had practically grown up in the factory.

"I knew all the designers, all the sewing staff, the people who ran the packaging and the shipping department," he says proudly.

"Truth be told, I couldn't imagine doing anything else. I always knew I was going to be a bra man." I try my best to keep a straight face as he discusses various fastening methods and covers the high and low points of the great underwire debate. At the end of our date, I know more about bras than any person should. The active part of our date will be parasailing, which I'm infinitely thankful for. At least I won't have to spend any more time talking with him, although I'm certain he'll have some thoughts on the harness materials.

My last date, with Chadd, goes by quickly, mostly because he's such a charming, outgoing, fast-talking guy. He seems to know everyone in Miami, and he's the ultimate "hook-up" king: From discounts on jewelry to the best places to get fresh-caught seafood to entrance into some of South Beach's most exclusive nightclubs, Chadd's got friends everywhere. He's funny, interesting, knows a little bit about everything. He also has the shortest attention span I've ever encountered outside of a preschool. Every time he asks me a question, I'm two seconds into the answer when he goes off on some other topic. Our date activity is supposed to be salsa dancing lessons, but we haven't even finished the main course (this is pasta-rama number three for me) before he's throwing out all types of alternative activities.

"Have you ever been skydiving?" Chadd asks. "That would be really cool. I've got a friend who's a pilot and he could totally set it up for us today, or ooh!—you know what else would be totally smokin'?" he asks, not pausing for an answer. "Cigar rolling! I know this guy, he's like an authentic Cuban cigar roller. He's got this unbelievable story about Castro. You know, in Cuba, cigar rollers are, like, royalty or something. Like the ballet dancers in Russia."

By the time we move to the activity part of our date the crew is referring to him as "Chadd, with an A.D.D." During our salsa lessons, he's all over the place—talking music with the DJ, showing off his own moves to the instructor, chatting up the camera crew. By the time we get to the "doorstep" portion of our date, Chadd is so antsy he looks like he has to pee.

Jill, the makeup artist, touches up my face, and, out of the corner of my eye, I spot Holt standing near one of the production assistants. Jeez, he's early. He attended some legal conference in Miami today and asked if we could meet tonight to go over some paperwork for the case. I'm exhausted, but he's only in Miami for one night and he said it was important.

Against the backdrop of camera guys and crew members wearing ratty T-shirts and torn jeans, Holt is a picture of casual elegance: dark suit, crisp blue shirt, natty tie. Three or four of the female production assistants are buzzing around him, and he smiles graciously at one of the staffers, who has brought him a bottle of water.

One of the girls, Brooke, subtly points in Holt's direction and mouths to me, *Ohmygod! Cute!* I see Holt scanning the room, and when he spots me, he grins.

Wow. Great teeth.

I glance at my watch and see we're running about ten minutes behind schedule. I give him a quick wave and a smile as Jill finishes touching up my eyebrows and lipstick. Heading back to the doorstep set with Chadd, I flag down one of the set runners and ask him to apologize to Holt and tell him that we'll probably be about fifteen more minutes. A little shot of pride sneaks through me. For some reason, I'm glad Holt will have the chance to see me when I'm not crying my eyes out or acting like a pathetic loser. The studio lights dim as we get ready to shoot the doorstep scene, and another of the production assistants raises her eyebrow at Holt, giving me a discreet thumbs-up.

What is it with these girls? You'd think they'd never seen a man before. They certainly didn't get this excited about Liam, Prince of Dullness.

Back at the cardboard door, it quickly becomes apparent that Chadd has the mistaken impression that we've made a love connection.

Chadd rushes in for a good-night kiss, throwing me off balance, and I tumble into the plastic bushes. So much for not acting like a loser in front of my attorney. Brushing myself off, I notice that Holt has begun pacing behind the camera guy with an irritated look on his face. He's probably ticked off that we're running late.

We reset for another take, and this time, Chadd moves in carefully and deliberately. He may be a fast talker, but he's a slow learner.

"Chadd, thank you for a wonderful evening," I say, sticking my hand out.

He tries to maneuver my handshake into some awkward hand-holding gesture, but I remain firm. Undaunted, he uses his other hand to pull me into a hug. I pat him on the back, hoping he'll release me, and make a serious effort not to grimace while he has me locked in his embrace—every facial expression is being captured on tape.

"Don't tell me you don't feel it, Darby," he whines.

"Chadd," I say, "I don't feel it."

I thank him again and excuse myself through the cardboard door. Olive is on the other side of the door set, and she smirks in Chadd's direction.

"That Chadd is a piece of work." She laughs. "At least it makes for good TV. Who's the hot guy hanging out by camera two?"

"My attorney," I say. "Holt Gregory."

"No dating," she reminds me.

"Don't worry. After this job, the *last* thing I want to do is date," I say, rolling my eyes. "I may never date again."

She snorts a giggle, and we walk back into the studio together.

"Darby, you're done for tonight," she says, giving me a little wave. "People!" she yells. "That's a wrap!"

I make my way over to where Holt is standing, and he looks significantly more relaxed than he did five minutes ago. It's late, and he's probably just as tired as I am. I say good-bye to a few crew members as they pack up to leave.

"Where did you want to go to talk?" I ask.

"Are you hungry? There's a Cuban place just a few blocks from here," he answers. "I'm not sure how late they're open." I check my watch, it's 11:10.

"That sounds good. I'm starving." Holt calls the restaurant to find out how late they serve food, while I make a quick call to Lilly and Aidan. No answer on their end. I leave a message for the kids and tell them I love them.

We walk out of the studio into the warm night. The humidity is not overbearing, so we decide to walk the three blocks to the restaurant, which is open until midnight. A mingling of deliciously fragrant spices and traditional Cuban music spills out into the street and floats up the block.

Holt gently places his hand on the small of my back to lead me inside, and he requests a booth from the hostess. Most of the tables are occupied, but thankfully there's no wait. I'm famished.

A short, stocky waitress leads us to our table, slaps down a couple of menus, and reels off the specials. Holt asks what I'd like, and then orders us a couple of beers and some tamales to start. We both settle on the house special for dinner: *arroz con pollo borracho*, a traditional Cuban chicken and rice dish.

The beers come quickly, and Holt opens his briefcase while we wait for the appetizer to arrive.

"First," he says, "I did a check, and Will's divorce from Gigi was final when you met. Gigi's ridiculous claim that you interfered in her marriage goes away."

"Good," I say, taking a sip of my beer.

"Also, I'm adding Gigi as a party defendant to the divorce case on the theory that she has conspired to interfere with your career."

"I didn't know we could do that."

"Well," he says, "it's a progressive concept, but I think we can make a strong argument to include her."

"What about that whole alienation-of-affection thing that Gigi was claiming? Can we claim that? I didn't interfere in her marriage, but she definitely interfered in mine."

"No. Florida doesn't even have alienation-of-affection laws on the books. Those laws are a throwback to when women were still considered the property of their husbands. The laws are outdated, ridiculous; most states don't even have them."

I watch Holt as he thumbs through some papers, and in the warm light of the restaurant I can see why all the women on set were so gaga over him. There's something really intriguing about him. He's a good-looking guy, for certain, and he has that effortless charm that so many Southern men wear with ease. But there's something else . . . something, I don't know, a kind of a charisma, some sort of molten sensuality bubbling just beneath the surface. I can't quite figure it out.

"What's the situation with the Sarasota residence?" he asks. "Did you move back in?"

"As far as I know, it's empty. Will is still living with Gigi in California, and I'm planning on staying at Jules's guesthouse. At least for the time being."

"I'd like you to give some more thought to moving back into the house. It could help our position."

"I know. I'm sorry, but I can't be there without the kids," I say. "I just can't."

"Okay. I understand," he says kindly.

The waitress is back with the tamales, ice water, and another round of beers, and she tells us our dinner will be out in a moment. Holt pushes some documents across the table for me to sign and gives me an overview of what will happen during the next few weeks. I scrawl my name on the bottom of each one before sliding them back to him. Our fingers brush as I push the last of the papers back, and his index finger lingers on mine for just a heartbeat. He glances up at me and smiles as the waitress reappears with our dinner. He quickly files the papers back in his briefcase and she places the steaming plates in front of us.

"Perfect timing," he says.

"This looks amazing," I say, as we dig into the food. The chicken is delicious, searing hot and a little spicy.

"So, the show tonight," he asks, "is it always like that? Some guy making a move on you every single night?"

"No, usually there are three guys making a move on me every single night. You just missed the first two."

"Are you kidding?"

"Nope."

"How do you feel about that?"

"I hate that part. I'm ready for this show to end, but I really need the job. I've got a custody battle to pay for. So much for the glamorous life of a dating expert." He smiles again, and I notice he has a tiny dimple on his left cheek.

"How does one become a dating expert, anyway?" he asks, laughing. "I don't remember seeing that table at career day."

"I've always been good at seeing patterns in someone's relationship history. I can usually figure out the glitch in about two minutes. Most women make the same four or five mistakes over and over: They chase after some guy who doesn't care about them. They stay with someone who cheats, or hits them, and hope the guy will change. They give up their lives, their friends, their needs just to be with a man. They pick partners based on chemistry with no regard to the kind of person they are. Or the worst, they stay with anybody who will have them just because they're afraid to be alone."

He watches me as I speak, his green eyes sparking with interest. "What else?" he asks.

"I like helping people," I say. "I like solving their problems. I like showing people how small changes in their behavior can make a huge difference in their lives. I had a friend who dated one horrible guy after another. It never occurred to her that there was another option. I sat her down one night and said, 'Why are you putting up with this? You're a wonderful person, where did you get the idea you have to settle for these jerks?' That conversation changed her perspective and, eventually, her relationships. A lot of women have lived their whole lives without someone telling them they're special, or that they deserve to be happy. I like being the one to tell them that. It just turns a light on, you know?" I take a drink from my water glass and adjust the napkin on my lap. "What about you, why did you become an attorney?"

"When I was eight, my best friend's parents went through a horrible divorce. His father abandoned the family, and his mom had no way to support them. She put so much faith in her lawyer; he was supposed to sweep in and save the day. In the end, it didn't quite work out the way we'd all hoped: They didn't get enough support from his dad to be able to stay in their house. They had to move away to Michigan to live with my friend's grandparents, and his mom had to get a couple of jobs to support them. He was my best friend, and I never saw him again after the trial. The day before he moved away, we talked all night. We were certain, in our eight-year-old minds, that if the lawyer had done a better job, he could have saved the day, and my friend wouldn't have had to move away. I decided right then that I was going to be a lawyer when I grew up. And that under my watch, no kid would ever have to move away from his best friend."

"It must have been hard, feeling so powerless," I say.

"Well, the reality of being an attorney is not exactly what I envisioned when I was eight. But basically my reasons are the same as yours. I like to help people. I see folks at the worst times in their lives . . . when they're most vulnerable . . . when they really need someone to guide them. It's an honor, a good feeling to be that person."

"I know what you mean," I reply. This is the very thing I love about being a dating expert: helping people navigate through the rocky spots in their personal lives, steering them to better times. "What else?"

He smiles. "I've always loved the puzzle of law: how the same facts in the same case, under the same laws, can go one way or another based on the skill of the attorney, the mood of a jury or judge. I got into this to make a difference for families, but it gets complicated. Sometimes the law doesn't protect the people it should." He takes a sip of his beer and smiles. "Maybe I should have been a dating expert instead. I can always tell who's going to get a divorce."

"How can you tell?"

"The pre-nup. Anyone who suggests a pre-nup has a little seed in their mind somewhere that the relationship might not work out. They protect themselves. And then, when things start to get rocky, they know they're covered, and they feel they can walk away. I think that if you're protecting yourself, holding something back, it means your heart isn't committed all the way."

"Interesting," I say.

"With love you've got to be all in . . . or you're not really in it at all," he says, his eyes thoughtful. "You've got to say, 'Do what you will with my heart, darlin', it's all yours.' "

"Of course, if you're wrong, they get all your stuff. Right?" I laugh.

"Ah, but if you're *right* . . ." he drawls.

"Oh, this is hilarious," I tease, "somebody alert the bar association! Holt Gregory, killer divorce attorney, is a . . . a . . . *romantic*?"

"Keep it to yourself. That's privileged information." He grins and takes another bite of his dinner.

Now I'm intrigued. "Do you know anyone like that?" I ask.

"My parents," he says. "They've been married more than forty years. Sure, they've had their ups and downs, but they eat breakfast together every day. They hold hands at the movies. Dad still calls Mom his bride."

"So do you advise your clients not to sign a pre-nup?"

"Heck, no." He laughs. "If they want a pre-nup, they've already got that seed of doubt planted. Besides, it's my job to protect their assets. I always try to do a little damage control on their hearts while I'm at it, but, really, if something has to give, it's that. Most people, when their hearts are in jeopardy, start worrying about their stuff. I dunno, maybe it feels safer to fight over dinner plates than admitting that someone has shredded your life."

"Well, I don't care if Will keeps the assets or not. I just want my heart back."

"I know, Darby," Holt drawls softly. "That certainly makes you something different."

The waitress arrives with our check. "Can I get anything else for you?" she asks, glancing at her watch.

"Dessert, Darby?"

"No, thanks," I say, looking at my own watch. Midnight already! I can't believe we've been talking for almost an hour. Holt slides a few twenties into the little leatherette folder and hands it back to the waitress.

"Do you need change?" she asks.

"No, you keep it." He smiles. "Thank you very much, ma'am. The food was delicious." The waitress smiles at him dreamily, like a fifty-five-year-old schoolgirl.

"Thank you," she croaks. She fidgets into a move that sort of resembles a curtsy, then turns and scurries toward the back of the restaurant. Holt is unfazed. Do women always get so doe-eyed and goofy around him? Probably.

I thank Holt for dinner, and we stand to leave. He grabs his briefcase and leads me toward the door.

"Where are you staying?" he asks. "Can I drop you at your hotel?"

"The Tides," I say, "and that would be great. Usually the car service takes me back to the hotel, but I don't think they run after midnight. I can take a cab if it's too far out of your way."

"Well, that depends on your room number," he says with a laugh.

"What?"

"It's not too far out of my way," he says. "We're staying at the same hotel."

"Really? You're at the Tides?"

"Every time I'm in Miami."

We quickly walk the few blocks back to the studio parking lot, and Holt opens the passenger's side door of his car for me. It's not exactly the usual Sarasota lawyers' ride. While most of his contemporaries prefer the flashier Lexus and Hummer models, Holt Gregory drives a Toyota Prius, a hybrid vehicle. I glance around the car quickly as he walks to the driver's side. The car is orderly, and basically empty except for an overnight bag and a bright yellow skimboard resting in the backseat.

We drive back to the hotel, laughing and talking, and a thirty-minute ride feels like five. When we arrive at the Tides, he pulls in to the valet stop and hands the valet a few bills. Grabbing his overnight bag from the backseat, he swings it over his shoulder and the two of us walk through the door of the lobby to the elevators.

"Which floor?" he asks.

"Ninth," I say. "And you?"

"I'm on seven," he says, pressing number nine.

"Thank you for dinner," I say, fiddling with the contents of my purse.

"My pleasure," he answers, checking his watch. "Wow, it's almost one in the morning." When we arrive at the ninth floor, Holt walks out of the elevator and asks, "Which way?" I point to the left, and we walk together silently toward my room.

I have to be back on set in seven hours, but I don't feel sleepy at all. I've missed being with friends these last few weeks, and I had such a great time hanging out with Holt tonight, there's a part of me that wants to ask him in to continue the conversation. Maybe for a drink? I fumble with the plastic key card, then slide it into the lock. The door clicks and I push it open.

"Good night, it was fun." He leans in to peck me on the cheek, but pulls back quickly, and stiffly sticks out his hand to shake mine. "Uh, well, I'll contact you next week about those depositions," he says awkwardly. "Have a good evening, Darby." I take the step inside my room, turning to face him. He lingers uncomfortably for a second on the other side of the threshold. Then, turning quickly, he waves and takes a few steps down the hallway, back to the elevators.

"Thanks for walking me back to my room," I say, realizing I've just had a doorstep moment far more interesting than the ones I have on the set each day.

With my divorce attorney. *Good Gawd.*

He stops and turns back to me, slicking a dark curl back behind his ear. "It's late. I wanted to make certain you got back to your room safely," he says quietly. "What time do you do your show tomorrow?"

"I have call at eight o'clock," I say. "It's a tough gig, but somebody's got to show the women of America how to tell the nice guys from the bad boys."

Holt grins. "Which type do you peg me for?"

I give him my best smile as I raise a single eyebrow. "You, I'm still figuring out."

First Date Killers

by Darby Vaughn

Boy meets girl. You flirt. You make a date.

You eat, you drink, you connect. You have the time of your life. And then, you never hear from him again.

What makes a date go from a romantic possibility to "never again"? Chances are, it's one of these eight dating disasters:

1) You mistook your date for your therapist. If you need therapy, get therapy. Don't expect your date to listen to your problems.

2) You slept together on the first date. No judgment here, but the odds aren't with you for a long-term relationship if you get naked on date number one.

3) You tried to determine whether he was marriage material. No guy likes to feel like he's being interviewed for the position of groom-to-be.

4) You're holding him and the entire male sex responsible for the ghosts of boyfriends past. Do you have trust issues? Paranoia? Check them at the door.

5) You were jealous. One date does not a relationship make. Don't give him a hard time for flirting with the waitress: He's not yours.

6) You were trying to create a relationship out of a date. Wait and see where things go naturally, don't try to lock him into a commitment for the next month.

7) You made it clear he wasn't going to get sex, and he was only in it for sex. Don't stress about this one—he wasn't going to call you back for the second date anyway!

8) You just didn't click. You're a great girl. He's a great guy. But the vibe is more friendly than fiery. Don't take it personally.

Chapter 26

After three weeks and forty-five dates, I know for certain I could die happy if I never went on another blind date again. This whole endeavor feels pitiful and empty, and I'd quit in a minute if I didn't need this job. Something about triple-header dating in a fishbowl just sucks all the fun out of it. All my dates saw me get dumped on TV, every guy knows my story. My usual dating M.O., what used to be natural and even mysterious, now seems completely contrived, "by the book" (which, of course, makes sense, since I *wrote* the book). I know the producers were hoping I'd hit it off with someone (or a couple of someones), but, frankly, my heart (and oftentimes my brain) just isn't in it. I'm just so tired. I'll be glad to have the next month off. The custody hearing is only a few weeks away, and I'll be so relieved when all of this is finally over.

On my second day back in Sarasota, Jules finds me on the beach in front of the guesthouse. I'm so exhausted from the long hours taping the show that I just want to crash on a beach chair with some industrial-strength sunblock and a tote bag full of chick lit. Jules, ever the Southern belle, totters down to the beach wearing movie star glasses and a gigantic straw sunhat, a towel and a picnic basket slung over her arm. Oh good, snacks! She plops herself down in the chair next to me, pours a couple of glasses of lemonade from a jug in the basket, and hands one to me.

"Darby, darlin', we've got to talk," Jules says.

"What's up?" I ask. Shoot, I hope her mother-in-law isn't coming for a visit.

"It's Holt Gregory," she says quietly. "I'm not sure what's happened, but we heard from a number of people at the Oaks last night that he's closing his practice."

"What?" I ask, starting to panic. "Our custody hearing is a few weeks away."

"I know, sweets," she says. "Don't worry, I'm sure it will work out fine. But you should probably give him a call today."

"I wonder what's going on?" This can't be good. "I just talked to him the day before yesterday. He didn't say a word about this."

Jules's expression is pained. "Darby, I'm not certain what his reasons are. A friend of Mark's told us last night at the club, and then we heard the same thing from a number of other folks—you know how people in this town talk. The word is he's closing his office and referring all of his clients elsewhere."

"Thanks," I say, giving Jules a quick squeeze before I sprint to the guesthouse. "I'll be back later," I shout over my shoulder. "I've got to find out what the hell is going on with my lawyer."

Ten minutes later I'm dressed and speeding over the bridge to Holt's office. I thought first about calling him, but I want him to look me in the eye when he tells me he's ditching me three weeks before the most important day of my life.

I squeal into the parking deck across from his office and jog across the street, vacillating between being flat-out pissed that he could do this, and completely terrified that I am losing my only chance to get my kids back.

I open the door to his office, and for once, the receptionist is not sitting behind her desk. Not a good sign.

I wait in the lobby for a few seconds, hoping she'll come back, and peek through the hallway to see if I can catch a glimpse of someone. The lobby still looks pretty normal, but I can see stacks of boxes in the hallway that weren't here a few weeks ago. Something is definitely up.

I still don't hear anyone, but I do see a shadow of a figure at the end of the hallway.

"Holt?" I call. No answer.

"Mr. Gregory, are you here?" I yell, a lot louder this time.

Holt comes out of the back office at the sound of my voice, looking surprised. He is carrying an empty file box and is dressed in a T-shirt, blue jeans, and flip-flops. Not exactly the usual attire for a big-time lawyer. Crap. I am so screwed.

"Darby, it's great to see you. I didn't know you were back from Miami," he says, revealing that killer smile.

"Uh, yeah, I'm back. When exactly were you planning on telling me you're closing your law firm?"

"News travels fast," he says, shaking his head. "I should have warned you. I know this town is fueled on gossip. I figured I'd wait to talk to you about this until you got back from Miami."

"What the hell!" I yell. "I don't have a lawyer three weeks before I am supposed to be in court?"

"Darby," he says, his gentle Southern voice still even and calm, "you have a lawyer."

"Well, are you closing your practice or not?"

"No, I am not . . ." he says, setting a box on the floor. "I turned down a prospective client recently, and he was not happy and apparently he's been spreading rumors. I've had calls on it all morning. You didn't, by chance, have dinner at the Oaks Club last night?"

"Jules did," I say. "My friend. That's where she heard it."

"It's not much fun to be the subject of gossip," he says solemnly. Then he cracks a smile when he realizes he's just imparted this little nugget of wisdom on me, gossip victim number one.

"No kidding," I say facetiously. "So why'd you turn down the case?"

"I can't discuss the particulars, but speaking hypothetically, it's very easy in divorce law to get away from the things that are meaningful. Don't get me wrong: I love my job, I love the law. But I never want to get into a situation where I'm not proud of what I do."

I nod, and he continues.

"I love this area of the law because I get to make a difference to people, to families that need me. Family law is messy, it's complicated, but it's the most fulfilling job I can imagine. Because I own my own firm, I won't take a case if it's in direct conflict with my beliefs.

"I don't want to work seventy or eighty hours a week and then wake up one day when I'm sixty and realize my entire existence is helping greedy, angry people duke it out over third cars and airline miles and who gets custody of the family ferret. The stuff doesn't mean anything, it's the people that matter. Sometimes you just look at a case and know you don't want to be involved."

"So, if you're not closing your practice, where's the staff? What's with the boxes?"

"These files are resolved cases we're having moved to storage," he says, looking around at the stacks in the hallway. "I have only two people on my staff, and I believe, at the moment, they're at lunch." He meets my eyes directly. "We're casual today because I don't have any client meetings scheduled."

Holt stands in the hallway, his hands shoved into the pockets of his jeans, looking like he's not quite sure what to say next.

"Okay. Enough about me," he says. "As long as you're here, do you want to get some work done on your case? We really need to go over the timeline of events to make certain we haven't left anything out."

Back to business.

"Sure," I say, nodding. "Might as well." Yep, reconstructing the demise of my marriage sounds like loads of fun. *Way* better than hanging out on the beach.

He disappears into a back office to grab a file folder and then leads me to the conference room.

"Would you like something to drink?" he asks.

"No thanks," I say. I sit near the end of the large conference table, and Holt takes the chair next to mine. Our knees bump accidentally under the table, his jeans against my bare leg, shooting goose bumps traveling up my thigh.

"Here's what I don't understand," Holt says. "Why would Will ruin a perfectly good divorce case by humiliating you in public? It's not rational. People sometimes do this kind of thing when there's a lot of anger and resentment in the marriage for years, but you were under the impression that everything was fine. Will is a PR guy, he obviously had legal counsel before the fact. A short marriage, with no children born as a result . . . what could he gain by sabotaging your career? It basically gives you a claim you wouldn't have had otherwise. It doesn't make any sense to me."

"I don't know," I say. It doesn't make sense to me either.

Holt shows me the timeline he's constructed detailing all of the significant events in my marriage, a color-coded flowchart outlining Will's infidelity in yellow, the damage he and Gigi caused to my career in red, and the events related to custody in blue.

"Wow," I say. "You're the freaking King of PowerPoint."

He laughs. "It helps me stay organized."

We go over the events, one by one, and I feel my gut tighten with every excruciating detail. God, this is just so humiliating. Holt asks questions, and I answer as best I can.

"Darby, I get the feeling you're holding something back here. Are you being dishonest with me? Or are you just not telling me the whole story?" Holt asks, tapping his pen impatiently on his ever-present yellow pad.

"I'm telling you the truth," I say, "and as far as I know, I'm telling you everything." But even as I say the words, I know they're not true. I've never lied to him, but I've held back the messier pieces of myself with every person I've ever met.

People always think I'm so strong, I'm so brave. I'm not—that's just what I want them to think. The instant someone says, "Oh, you poor dear, your parents died when you were a baby?" I just shut down and say something like, "Oh, it was fine, my grandmother raised me. I had a wonderful childhood." There's a part of me that knows for certain that if someone is feeling sorry for you, it means you're weak. Flawed. Prey.

I make things okay for other people, tell them I'm fine, and they don't really make the effort to dig much deeper. I guess it's quite convenient for everyone else if you're strong, if you can handle everything by yourself.

I've found that most people would rather admire a person for their strength than deal with their weaknesses.

And somewhere far below the cool surface I'm sure I'm just a snarled mess of emotions. Fearful. Terrified of being abandoned again. Scared to let anyone see I'm not perfect or, at the very least, damned close to perfect. I can only admit to imperfection in perfectly acceptable ways: I don't snore, but I might occasionally tell jokes in my sleep. I'm a fabulous cook, but I can't make gravy.

I haven't felt completely safe since my grandmother died. I don't trust people until I have about twenty years of history with them, and even then, I'm likely to hold a little something back. I don't even think about it, really; it's just something I do.

"I think we're done for today," he says, meeting my eyes intentionally, "but I want you to think about something—I can't protect you from the things you don't tell me."

"But—" I start to say.

"Darby, sometimes people keep secrets from their lawyers because they don't want to be embarrassed, they don't want to be judged, maybe they think they'll look bad or that no one will ever find out the bad stuff. But somebody always finds out. Let me be straight with you: I don't care what your secrets are. I only care about what's going to win or lose us this case. And you'll make a lot better use of my time if you let me work on how to protect you, and our case, from your secrets, instead of wasting my time while I try to figure out what they are."

"I really don't . . ." I stammer.

"We need every advantage we can get," he says sternly. "The one little thing you keep from me could be the lie that loses your kids."

Oh, God. The thought of that makes my stomach churn, and tears burn my eyes. I'll do anything, *anything*, to get my kids back. Before Lilly and Aidan came into my life, I couldn't imagine anything more terrifying than leaving myself exposed and vulnerable. But losing them, that would be far worse: certain, excruciating anguish—not just my usual constant, nagging terror of some bad thing happening, but a deep cut in my most tender spot. I'm just going to have to force myself to open up. It will probably end up hurting me later, but the risk of losing Lilly and Aidan is too great. I'll tell him anything he wants to know. Even if that means I have to shine a light into every dark corner of my heart.

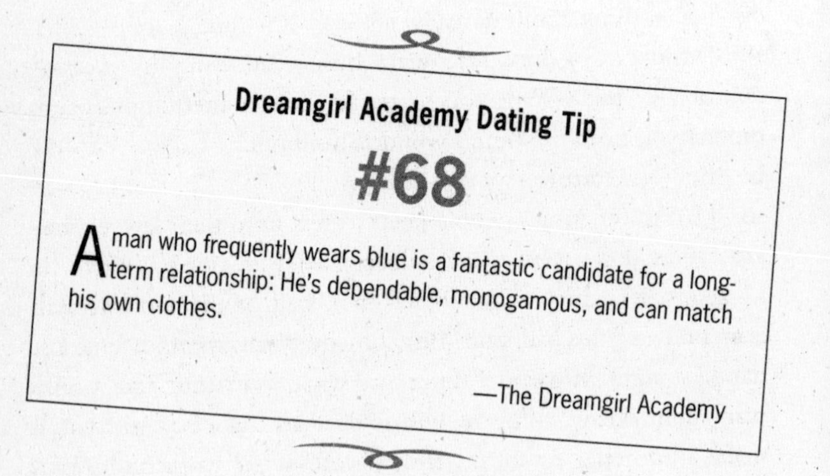
Dreamgirl Academy Dating Tip

#68

A man who frequently wears blue is a fantastic candidate for a long-term relationship: He's dependable, monogamous, and can match his own clothes.

—The Dreamgirl Academy

Chapter 27

The next few weeks are oddly freeing for me, and I find myself in Holt's office nearly every day. Most of our visits begin on the premise that we'll be discussing strategy for the custody hearing, which begins next week, and end with the two of us in some hamburger joint, having the deepest, most personal conversations I have ever experienced in my life.

As terrifying as it has been to open up to Holt, the fact that it is an utter necessity for my custody case makes him a safe confidant for me. The weird thing is, the more I tell him, the more I want to tell him. How crazy is that? There's some part of me that needs someone safe to know me, to really know everything about me, how I feel, what I'm afraid of, why I am the way I am. Holt, unlike anyone else I've ever met, sees right into my soul, and he asks the questions nobody else ever thought to ask. He's seen how desperate I am to be with Lilly and Aidan and how vulnerable I am—things even Will never knew. I've been praised all my life for keeping it together when things were tragically difficult. Holt is the first person to say, "I *know* you lived through it. How did it *affect* you?" Maybe it's because he's a lawyer, he knows how to ask the right questions.

Normally when someone asks me something personal, I shut

myself up as soon as they show a reaction. For me, pity and compassion are the anti-truth serum. But Holt just scribbles away on his legal pad, with no reaction at all, as I spill out every detail about my life.

It is strangely liberating to tell someone my secrets so that they can protect me. Usually, it's just me, trying to protect myself.

One night, after my first excruciating session of soul-baring, I lay in bed awake all night, gripped with panic and freaking out: *Oh my God, I can't believe I actually told him all of those things! I can't believe I told him that I was so humiliated after flunking statistics in college that I almost didn't go back to school the next semester. I felt so alone in the months after my grandmother and aunties were gone, it seemed like the only people I had in the world were my professors—and they only loved me because I was the smart one. After I blew the final exam, I felt like I'd let down the only people in the world who cared anything about me—and if I wasn't the smart one anymore, I was nobody. There was no backup plan, no one who loved me unconditionally.*

Or, God! That I almost said no to Will's marriage proposal because I didn't have a single family member to walk me down the aisle, not one relative to sit on my side of the church. My first thought was, "I can't get married because I can't do it the way you're supposed to do it!" Is that crazy? I barely considered whether I wanted to spend the rest of my life with Will. I was so worried about how it would look, how demeaning it would feel to have the entire right side of the church feeling sorry for the poor little orphan bride with no one to give her away.

It's strange, but Holt has this way of just piercing right through my defenses, sifting through my bullshit and uncovering my deepest fears and sorrows—some I've never acknowledged until now.

"Does losing Lilly feel like losing your mom all over again?" he'd asked.

"How did it affect you when the other girls talked about their mothers?"

"What was it like for you on orientation weekend at college without a parent?"

And I told him. I told him everything, things I've never told anyone, like how I lied when I was at freshman orientation weekend. When people asked where my parents were, I said they were on an extended tour of Europe.

I never intended to lie. It just popped out.

But from the moment that lie left my lips, I realized that people were finally treating me like I was normal. For the first time in my life, I was Darby Vaughn the person, not Darby Vaughn the sad-sack charity case. And it was a relief.

I can't believe I admitted to him that for most of my early twenties, I actually lied to strangers. It was too awful to talk about how my parents had died, not to mention every last relative by the time I was a teenager. I couldn't stand any more of the pity I'd endured all through high school, when no matter what I did, no matter where I went, everyone thought of me as "that poor, poor Darby, the girl who's all alone."

Without the shackles of my depressing family history, the barrier between me and the rest of the world suddenly evaporated. College was a revelation: There wasn't a single person there who knew me as the pathetic little orphan girl. And God, to not have that be the thing that defined me. For once.

I am always horrified by that overtly sympathetic look that people give me when they find out my parents are dead; it colors every impression of me, paints me as a victim, darkens every conversation. They don't know what to say, they feel so sorry for me, and I have to just stand there, graciously accepting their encroaching sympathy, when the last thing I want to do is think about my dead parents again.

And now, Holt knows everything. I have no armor.

As I obsess about the day's confessions in my head, it begins to dawn on me that there is a sort of randomness to the bits and pieces of my history that I have fought to keep hidden from the world. Ninth-grade humiliations and third-grade nothings, the devastating loss of my family: events and failings that would probably seem silly or insignificant to an outsider, mixed with the constant of family tragedy, formed a hard shell around the very core of me.

Every moment of fear or loss or insecurity created an escalating certainty that I would grow up unloved and alone. Every shameful tidbit vehemently contradicts this got-it-all-together persona I've fought so hard to become. My biggest secret is how I covered myself up. And the truth is, I've spent most of my adult life terrified of being found out.

When people ask about my past, I either avoid it, lie, or, most recently, give them an abridged version of the facts with a side of sugar: "I made the best of it, so everything is just peachy." Most people are relieved to talk about anything else, and I get to be the queen of competence and perseverance: Darby "I can handle anything" Vaughn.

Yet when Holt pieces the events of my life together and asks me how it all has affected me, I find myself confessing feelings I've never told anyone. Part of me wonders what any of this has to do with my divorce, or the custody case, but another part of me is so relieved to let it all out, I just keep talking.

Why is it that Will never asked me any of these questions? Was my whole marriage just a sham of superficial emotions? I'm finding myself telling my lawyer far more than I ever revealed to my husband.

As we've gotten closer, and the layers of me are peeled away, I realize that my priorities have been pretty misguided. Vomiting in

Matt Lauer's chrysanthemums is not exactly the worst thing that can happen to a person.

Holt talks, too—I'm a good listener (an extraordinarily helpful skill when you're a person who prefers not to reveal anything emotionally significant about herself). As he talks, I see how he feels torn sometimes: between feeling pride in his legal skills, in making a difference in a family's life, and feeling disappointed when his time and talent are sometimes wasted on dogfights for country club memberships rather than something meaningful. He's inspired by his work, but he worries sometimes that his life has lost its balance. His days are jammed with clients, cases, and conferences; his only relaxation is his daily run on the beach.

"Why don't you date?" I ask.

"What?" He looks surprised.

"You told me once on the phone that you don't date. I was just sitting here, thinking that you're a pretty decent guy, wondering *why* you don't date. Have you had a lot of bad relationships?"

"Do you always ask such personal questions?"

"Yes. I'm a dating expert, remember?" I laugh. "I can't really turn it off. Besides, I've had to confess every detail of my life to you over the last few weeks. The least you can do is answer one simple question. I'm curious."

He squints his eyes, looking serious. "I don't date because I work eighty hours a week. The only people I ever see are clients, lawyers, or judges, and it would be highly unethical to get involved with a colleague or a client." He pauses for a second, deep in thought. "I've spent the last ten years completely focused on building my practice. I guess I get so caught up in my work sometimes that I don't make time for anything else." As he says this, his fingers fiddle with the menu sitting on the table.

He continues, "It's hard, too, to keep my work from tainting my personal life. You find yourself extrapolating all of the horrible experiences you hear all day into your own life. It's tough to balance the part of me that wants what my parents have together—to fall madly, crazy in love—against the experience of spending every single day seeing people at their worst, their relationships in shambles, motivated by greed or money or anger."

"So, no," he says, adjusting his tie, "to answer your question, except for the occasional social function, I don't generally date."

Holt and I are sitting at a downtown pizza shop near his office, waiting out an afternoon thunderstorm. I wonder if the rain will stop soon, or if we'll be trapped here for the rest of the afternoon. Worse things have happened: Holt is good company, and he's nice enough to give me nearly all the black olives from his pizza.

"You'd just steal them anyway," he says with a laugh.

"That is my deep, dark secret," I say. "I'm an olive thief."

"Your deep, dark secret is that you don't have any idea how amazing you are," he pauses, "deep dark secrets and all." He looks at me in a way I haven't seen before, a mix of kindness and something unfamiliar. I wonder if he's just saying that to make me feel better after my weeks of mandatory confessions.

"How do you do it, Darby? How can you pour your heart out to me at the office and always keep yourself so pulled together when anyone else might be watching?"

"Practice," I reply. My whole life has been about putting on a brave face and moving forward. Always moving forward.

"No, I mean, isn't it lonely to live your entire life without ever letting anyone really know you?" he asks, his green eyes penetrating mine.

"Every person I've ever needed has died. My mother, my father, my grandmother, my aunts. Eventually I just stopped needing other people. I learned to depend on myself, take care of myself, shield myself. It's a lot harder for people to hurt you, abandon you, break your heart, if you never let them in." Hearing this, Holt's face darkens.

It hits me that the only reason Lilly and Aidan found their way into my heart is that, for once, I didn't have my guard up. In every other relationship, I've always held a little something back, some fear, some detail, some feeling I kept to myself just in case things went wrong. It seemed prudent to keep myself protected, at least in the most crucial of ways: I think most of us are only one or two truths away from complete and total devastation.

Maybe I played a bigger part in the collapse of my marriage than I'd thought. I wonder if Will sensed that on some level I was keeping him at arm's length? I wonder if he saw how deeply I loved the children, how unprotected I was around them, how quickly I let them in? Maybe he saw what he was missing. I wonder if that might be the very thing that drove him back to Gigi?

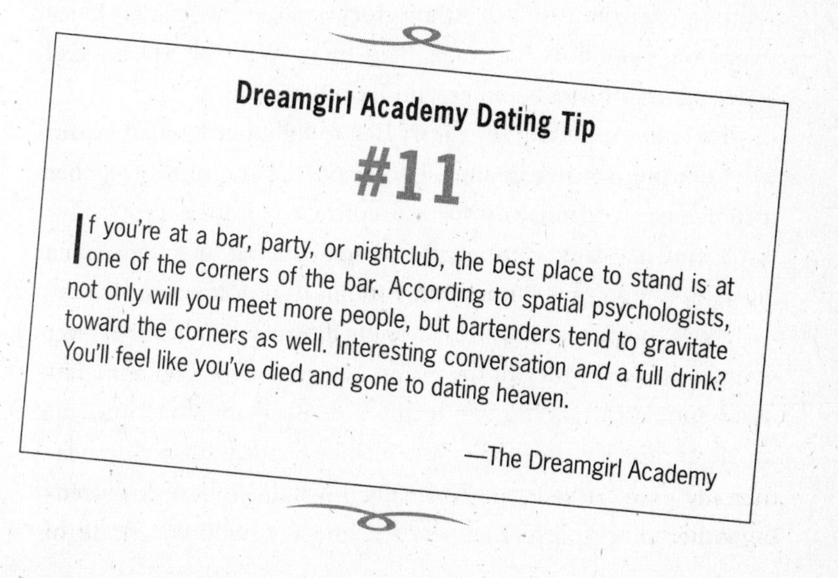

Dreamgirl Academy Dating Tip

#11

If you're at a bar, party, or nightclub, the best place to stand is at one of the corners of the bar. According to spatial psychologists, not only will you meet more people, but bartenders tend to gravitate toward the corners as well. Interesting conversation *and* a full drink? You'll feel like you've died and gone to dating heaven.

—The Dreamgirl Academy

Chapter 28

It's two days before the custody hearing and I'm so nervous I can barely eat or sleep. Which is why I'm not exactly thrilled to be going to a black-tie charity ball that will be attended by practically everyone I know in Sarasota, including almost all of the married couples from my old neighborhood. While I've certainly been subjected to plenty of national humiliation from strangers, my hiding out at Jules's guesthouse, avoiding my old haunts, and going to a different grocery store has helped me to avoid my neighbors (the ones who knew Will was cheating on me long before I did) and certain humiliation.

I'm stuck attending the Heart Ball tonight because last year, in a fit of volunteering insanity, I took on the position of cochair. Attendance is mandatory for the entire committee. Normally I love stuff like this: getting dressed up, dancing all night, sitting down to an elegant dinner. But tonight, I'm going stag in a city where *no one* goes stag—I'm hoping I won't be the first single woman in the history of the event. My *Dating the Dreamgirl* contract stipulates that I can't bring a date to any function, and, frankly, I don't want to take any chances with the custody hearing only two days away. Normally, I wouldn't have a problem with attending an event alone, even one as couple-centric as this one. I'm secure, I'm sociable, you can drop me pretty much anywhere and I'm fine. But tonight, with this crowd, it would be nice to have a little social support. Originally my designated breakup buddy, Jules, was planning to attend with me, but her sitter canceled at the last minute, and Mark is out of town on business. So I'm on my own.

No problem. I can handle this. Just a few quick rounds of mingling, and I'll slip out after they make the announcements, just before they serve dinner.

I sneak into the ballroom through a side door, in an attempt to circumvent a crowd of my former neighbors who are circling society columnist Marjorie North like sharks, angling for a mention—or, even better, a photo—in her prestigious column. Here, as in many society-driven towns, the town slogan might as well be: *I am photographed, therefore I exist.*

I scan the room, looking for a friendly face as the throng of my ex-neighbors bursts through the ballroom doors to my left. Instead I find myself eye-to-eye with the not-so-friendly neighborhood gossip monger, Jeannie Gerbaud. The second she spots me, she speed-walks over as fast as she can manage in her too-tight Prada dress and her too-tall Prada shoes, sloshing the champagne from her glass as she toddles across the room.

"Darby," she gushes, "I never thought you'd have the nerve to show up here! Brave girl! I couldn't do it! To walk around at an event where *every single person* knew my husband *cheated*! I guess that's just me . . . I have such a sense of personal pride . . . but here you are!"

"Yes, here I am," I say. Good grief, is this what I'm in for all night?

"Who are you here with?" Jeannie asks, her eyes scanning the room for better prey, even as she speaks.

"No one," I say. "I'm cochairing the event tonight, so I'm just making a quick appearance."

"Oh!" she says, looking as shocked as though I've just told her the entire state of Rhode Island was flattened by a meteor. "Well," she says, "I must let you get back to your duties. Have a wonderful evening!" She smirks and scurries off, no doubt to disseminate the news of my date-free status. Whatever.

I head over to the table where the rest of the event committee has gathered, to say my hellos and thank-yous.

"Darby," says a blue-haired committee member whose name escapes me, "we can't thank you enough—we have seventy-five more people than last year, and we're on track to raise more than fifty thousand dollars over our goal." She shakes my hand enthusiastically. "You're the reason tonight's gala is such a success."

"Thank you," I say. Now that's a nice surprise. I was feeling sort of worried about letting the ultraefficient committee run itself. "I really can't take any credit," I say with relief, "the committee did most of the work, and they did such a fantastic job. I didn't really need to do much at all."

"No," she says, "I meant, we owe the huge turnout to you. The whole town is here tonight—everyone wanted to see if you'd show up."

"Uh, thanks," I say.

"Don't forget, you need to stop by to see Laura for a photo for the paper."

"Sure," I say, thinking there is no way I'm going anywhere near a photographer tonight.

Making my best effort to smile, I excuse myself to head over to the bar for a glass of white wine. If I'm going to survive the rest of this evening, I'm going to need to be anesthetized.

Glass in hand, I stop to mingle with nearly every familiar person I see. It is strange, really, to feel this alone in a crowd of two hundred people. For once, I'm self-conscious, acutely aware of what people must be thinking about me, and as much as I try not to care, I can feel their stares boring into me from points across the ballroom. I silently repeat my new mantra to myself: *I have nothing to be ashamed of, I have nothing to be ashamed of . . .*

After a few awkward conversations (my small-talk-to-barb ratio is currently 2:1) I make a quick escape to the ladies' lounge for a break from the action. I take my time washing my hands, checking my hair, reapplying lipstick (including gloss and liner, but, hey, I'm killing time), and laughing at myself for having paid $200 for a ticket to an event and then spending all my time in the ladies' room. *I can do this. I can do this. I can do this.*

After fortifying myself with an extra squirt of rose-scented hand lotion, I gather up my courage and head back into the fray. As I return to the ballroom, I can instantly feel the buzz in the room grow louder, and a second later I see why: Ten feet in front of me are Gigi and Will, all smiles as they pose together for a party photographer. The plastic perfect couple. Crap. What the hell are they doing here?

I try to take a breath, but the air lodges in my lungs, and I start to feel as though I might implode. I back up slowly, a smile pasted on my face to avoid drawing any attention to myself, and sneak swiftly along the perimeter of the wall. Crap. Crap. Crap. How am I going to get out of here without being spotted, or worse, photographed? What is he doing here? With her! I'm sure Gigi would love to have the opportunity to torture me in public. Again. The exit is *waaayyyyy* on the other side of the ballroom, and if I go back to the ladies' room it will only be about two minutes before somebody puts it together that I'm hiding out. If I try to cross the ballroom, I'm screwed—aside from the fact that there are six or seven photographers sprinkled throughout the room (Jeez, what is this, the freakin' Oscars?), gossip columnist Marjorie North is blocking the entrance, scouting for interesting angles. No way I'll get past her. I glance around for alternative escape routes and see only one: As nonchalantly as I can, I tail a waiter into the kitchen. The staffers look sort of surprised to see someone dressed in an evening gown appear in the kitchen, but they get over it within thirty seconds and go back to their business.

Now what do I do?

I stand hunched behind a pastry cart, trying to figure out my next move. Obviously, I don't want to be photographed in this situation and land myself back in the tabloids. I'd like to stay far enough from Will and Gigi to avoid a showdown. I pull my cell phone out of my purse to call for help, but I can't get a signal from any part of the kitchen. Not even one bar. Damn. What is this, a prison? Apparently so, and the jailers are all wearing Prada.

I walk the perimeter of the kitchen, searching for an exit, but there doesn't seem to be one, so I resume my post at the cart and try to figure out what to do next.

Twenty-five minutes later, I'm starving to death and the contents of that dessert cart are looking pretty darned good. I've also concluded that the kitchen is a horrible place to stake out an escape route.

First, I can't really scope out the ballroom from the doorway without risking a head injury or other bodily collision. The door swings open every three seconds, thanks to an army of tray-wielding servers bearing glassware, dirty plates, and used shrimp cocktail. Second, I have yet to locate a single person who speaks English. The staffers all seem to speak Spanish or Portuguese, which is unfortunate for me, as I took six years of French in high school and college and only know enough Spanish to obtain a margarita, a chicken, or directions to a bathroom in Mazatlán.

I already know my way to the ladies' room. A margarita might be helpful here, but a chicken isn't going to do me any good at all.

I'm trapped. At least until this shindig is over.

I'm just about to dig in to level three on the pastry cart (What? I'm a stress eater!) when I see Holt poke his head into the kitchen.

Thank God.

Hello, knight in shining armor. Or in Holt's case, knight in spectacularly well-fitting tuxedo. His curly hair is gently slicked into partial submission, and the black fabric of his tux brings his green eyes afire. What is it about formal wear that makes men look so elegant, so dapper? Holt looks positively rakish and undeniably yummy.

I indulge myself with a superquick fantasy involving a tango on the dance floor and a very dramatic dip before I fill him in on the situation at hand. God, I'm such a sucker for a man in a tuxedo. *Down, Darby!*

Holt smiles at me, all dimples and charm, as he strides through the swinging door. Wow, he really does clean up nicely. I think the image of him in that tux is going to be burned into my brain until I'm ninety.

"Having fun?" he asks.

"I'm stuck," I say, rolling my eyes at the absurdity of the situation. "How did you know to find me here?" And how, in the name of all that is chocolate, do I keep getting myself into these jams?

"I saw Gigi and Will posing for pictures, your name was on

the program. Everybody at my table was talking about you showing up tonight. I sort of put one and two together."

"I didn't want another commotion."

"Then you shouldn't have worn that dress," he says, grinning at me wickedly. "Darby, you look absolutely gorgeous."

"Thanks." I smile and a blush warms my cheeks. Hello? What's this? "You look pretty amazing yourself."

"Did you want to leave now? Or did you want to spend a little more quality time with the tower of cheesecake?"

Eyeing the cheesecake, I say, "I think I'm ready to go."

Holt waves at a passing waiter and asks him something in Spanish. The disparity in their speech patterns is hilarious: The waiter is talking a mile a minute, and Holt, in his typical Southern cadence, forms his sentences slowly and melodically. Anyone watching would think that the two were speaking entirely different languages, but Holt must be reasonably fluent, because they seem to understand each other.

The waiter leads us to a small office behind the walk-in freezer and flips on the light.

"*Salida,*" he says, pointing to a narrow hallway.

"*Gracias,*" Holt says as he takes my hand and leads me through the doorway. I feel a little tingle when our fingers touch, which sort of surprises me. I didn't realize I'd been thinking about Holt in that way. Well, except for five minutes ago when I first saw him in his tuxedo. Maybe it's some sort of rescue syndrome, like when injured soldiers fall for the nurses who take care of them.

We follow the dark hallway around what feels like the entire length of the hotel before finally reaching a metal door marked EXIT.

We push our way into the night air, and I am instantly sorry that I left my wrap on my chair back in the ballroom. The waft of evening breeze sends a shiver of goose bumps all over my body.

"Mmm, there's a chill tonight," he says. "Let me give you my coat, Miss Darby." He gallantly removes his tuxedo jacket and places it gently over my shoulders. Sweet, isn't he? You've got to love the manners on these Southern boys.

"Thanks," I say. It's silly, I know, but I adore it when a man offers me his jacket. There's just something so gentlemanly, so wonderfully old-fashioned about it.

The kitchen exit has put us reasonably close to where Holt's car is parked. He offers to drive me home since my car is checked with the valet, and I don't exactly want to put myself back in the thick of the ballroom crowd after my stint hiding out in the kitchen. I guess I can always pick it up tomorrow.

"Do you want to wait here while I go get my car? Or would you rather walk with me?"

"I'll walk with you," I say. He is parked close by; it takes us less than a minute to reach his car. As he opens my door, his hand lingers over mine as I slide into the passenger seat. He walks around in front of the car, and as he passes by me, I feel a little twinge of unfamiliar territory. Is it my imagination, or is something happening here?

I lean over to make sure his door is unlocked, and it is. He gets inside the car and starts the engine as he turns up the heater.

"It'll warm up in a flash," he says, giving me a little wink. I thank him, remembering how often I was practically frozen while riding in the car with Will. He was always hot, I was always cold. He always drove, which meant the air conditioner was always locked in at a bone-chilling 64 degrees. As heat begins to blow through the vents, I realize how nice it is to be warm.

"Are you okay about seeing Will tonight? And her?" he asks softly.

"Yeah, I'm okay. I can't figure out why they would be here. I guess maybe they came in early for the court hearing. Gigi has never been one to miss a party.

The guesthouse is only about ten minutes away, but neither of us says much more during the drive home. I stare out the window and replay the moment of seeing Will for the first time in two months. It was nauseatingly startling to see them together. I have this horrible sensation of having been replaced. And never even missed. Or maybe I was the replacement for Gigi all along.

Seeing them together in a crowd is one of the most horrible, humiliating things I could imagine, so the fact that I'm still alive at the end of the evening is probably a good sign. Running into them makes all of this more real, if that were possible. It burns to see Will with someone else, especially Gigi. What's odd is that after I saw them I felt sort of removed from the situation—how did they become the couple and make me the spinster? It almost felt like it was happening to someone else. Maybe I'm finally coming to terms with Will leaving me. Or, who knows, maybe I'm suffering a psychotic break from reality. If I wake up in the morning slobbering in a straitjacket, I'll know for certain. Seeing them was a shock to my system. I've survived the worst part, right? It still hurts so much.

The drive goes quickly, and Holt pulls in to the driveway of the guesthouse. He turns off the engine and hops out to open my door.

"Thanks for helping me break out of the kitchen," I tell him. He looks at me with a little glimmer in his eyes.

"Anytime, Darby."

"Do you want a drink?" It just sort of pops out, and simultaneously it occurs to me that Holt may have inadvertently ditched a date back at the Heart Ball during his big rescue operation.

"That'd be nice," he drawls.

"Holt," I ask, "did you leave someone at the ball tonight?"

"That," he answers, smiling, "would not be very gentlemanly. No, Miss Darby, I did not leave a young lady all alone at the Heart Ball. I came by myself."

"I just thought . . ." I start to say, but I'm not really sure what I thought.

"I go every year," he says, closing the car door behind me. "My folks are on the board of the Heart Association. Had you not spent the evening hiding in the kitchen, I would have been delighted to introduce you." I roll my eyes at him for giving me a hard time about my hideout as we walk inside the house. Then I slip his jacket from my shoulders and hand it to him once we're inside the front door.

"Thanks for that," I say. "Is wine okay?"

"Great." He puts his jacket on a chair by the door. "Can I help you?"

"I've got it, thanks." I head into the kitchen and pull a nice bottle of wine from the fridge, grabbing a couple of glasses and a corkscrew on my way back to the living room.

We take the bottle out to the wicker settee on the deck, and Holt mans the corkscrew and pours our drinks while I fire up the patio heaters and kick off my shoes.

"Are you warm enough here?" he asks. I nod and toast my glass to the patio heater, which is now giving off a lovely heat. He brings the wineglass to his lips and takes a sip before setting it down on the table in front of him. I stare out into the gulf, watching the waves crash into the shore, one after another.

"Do you see that?" he asks, pointing to something in the darkness on the beach.

"What?" I don't see anything.

"Loggerhead turtle, it looks like. That's odd. You don't usually see them on the beach this time of year." He grabs my hand, setting my glass on the table next to his, and says, "C'mon," pulling me down the steps toward the beach. We tiptoe up to the turtle, which seems to be moving in circles on the sand. When we get closer we can see that although it is a very large turtle, it is not a loggerhead but one of the more common varieties that populate the man-made lakes in Sarasota's gated communities.

"He looks lost," I say.

"I know the feeling," Holt murmurs, his fingers still lingering near mine. I get that tingle again, and suddenly I'm acutely aware of every draw of breath between us. Holt stops speaking and turns to look at me. There is a palpable shift in the energy around us as he takes a step toward me, his eyes stormy with things unsaid. We stare at each other with tacit intensity, neither of us moving to take the next step forward or back. Then, without a word, he pulls me into his arms, his face moving close to mine until our lips are just millimeters apart. Our eyes meet again for a heartbeat, one last chance to retreat before he brings my body to his. He presses one hand against the sweet spot in the small of my back, and the other is entwined in my hair as he leans in to kiss me. His mouth is soft, incredibly soft, and when our lips finally touch his first kiss is so tender and light I'm almost uncertain it actually happened. He kisses me again, more intensely this time. I close my eyes and experience a feeling of being pulled under, like a riptide—as though, if I don't keep my head about me, I'll be transported out to sea. Wrapped in his arms under the full moon,

I have the oddest sensation of wanting to let go, and float away with him.

He pulls back slowly, both of us breathless.

"Darby, I think I could love you," he says softly, his eyes searching mine for a response.

"What?" Did I just hear him right? I think I might still be in shock.

"I know this is probably the worst possible timing," he continues. "I know you're still reeling from everything that's happened. I know there are a million reasons why we shouldn't do this—I'm your attorney, you're going through a difficult divorce, you're vulnerable. It would be definitely unethical for me to get involved with you now. Hell, I could probably get disbarred, but I don't care . . . I've never felt like this before. And no matter how hard I've tried, I can't . . . keep myself . . . from telling you how I feel."

"You said you'd never get involved with a client," I say, stalling for time.

"It's too late, I already am. I've held back all my life, done the right thing, done the smart thing. I've always done exactly what I'm supposed to do. But since I met you, I want more. Remember how I said that seeing people at their worst, going through a divorce, gave me pause about getting into a relationship? You, just you, make me believe in the real thing. For once, I don't care if it's the right thing to do or not. I don't care! Do you understand? Throughout my whole life, my honor, my ethics, and doing the right thing have defined me as a man. But I can't keep a lid on this any longer, I'm going to have to find some other way to solve it. I think you and I could have something I never even believed existed. We should be together. We're *meant* to be together."

My breath catches in my chest. He's right, there is something between us—a sort of short-circuit to raw emotions. I'm surprised and overwhelmed, and flooded with recognition at what he's describing: I've spent my whole life doing the safe thing, the smart thing, too. I don't know how to respond.

"I've been thinking about this for a while," he says. "As your lawyer, the ethical thing to do would have been to wait until your case was finished to tell you how I felt. But, honestly, we could be tied up in court for years. In my head, I just keep going back to watching your show that night, seeing you with those other guys. Truthfully, I worried that if I waited so long to tell you, until the case was over, that you might get involved with someone else. And then, I realized that I had a far bigger ethical dilemma than whether or not to get involved with a client."

"What's that?"

"Just the fact that I *have* these feelings for you is a conflict of interest. It compromises my ability to try your case. From that view, it seems unethical—dishonest, even—*not* to tell you, and continue working on your case."

I get this odd feeling in the pit of my stomach. After the last few weeks, Holt knows practically everything about me and he thinks he could *love* me. Jesus, did he really say that? I was a mess when I met him; I haven't held anything back or packaged up events in my life to make them more presentable—I've just let it all out, every emotion, every fear, every everything. And he wants to be with me. Completely turned inside out, nothing kept back, me. I mean, the real me.

"I had resigned myself to being without someone"—he pauses—"but I realized that I'm cheating us both if I don't at least offer you my heart. I know what your life has been like, and

I understand if you don't want to risk it. But I can't go on acting as though it's business as usual."

Tears sting my eyes and I hold his face in my hands, bringing it down to mine as I kiss him softly on the mouth. The kiss is bittersweet; I'm overcome by the strength of my feelings for him.

"I know it's unfair to ask you to risk your heart again so soon, but life's too short to have any regrets," he says, taking a deep breath.

My brain is on overload: a chaotic gestalt of emotions and rationality spun in a thousand different directions.

"And since my little confession on the beach tonight could kill my career," he cracks, "my love life is pretty much all I've got left."

I smile with him, relieved at the break in intensity, and we stand there, locked in our embrace on the beach. My heart swells with the giddy realization that he's crazy about me, and then, in an instant, it's punctured by reality.

"It's late," I say, smiling purposefully at him. I need time to think this through. Before it goes any further.

Holt walks me back to the guesthouse and helps me to gather the wineglasses from the patio and turn off the heaters. He pulls me close one last time on the doorstep before I go in, a kiss of sweet longing and infinite possibilities.

"Consider us," he says tenderly, that sweet Southern drawl working its magic. Then, he gives me a smile that makes me go weak in the knees.

I take a step back, our fingers still lingering in touch, and then wave good-bye as I slip inside the door. What am I doing? God, this man is just so, well, breathtaking.

Dreamgirl Academy Dating Tip

#94

It's always a good idea to wait at least a month before you sleep with someone new. The reason? There's a hormone that is released in women's bodies during sex called oxytocin (scientists refer to it as "the cuddle hormone"). Suddenly, the guy we think is just so-so *before* we have sex becomes the man of our dreams once the deed is done. It's important to give yourself the opportunity to evaluate the relationship with a clear head, before all those googly-moogly chemicals turn your brain to mush.

—The Dreamgirl Academy

Chapter 29

My cell phone starts ringing less than a minute after I walk in the door.

"Hey, it's Holt."

"Miss me already?" I say flirtatiously. God, what am I doing?

"Actually, I do. I just wanted to tell you, I know the whole 'trapped in the kitchen' thing wasn't so great for you, but I'm really glad that tonight happened. It felt like, I don't know . . . serendipity."

I laugh, and my heart begins to bubble a little before I stop it in its tracks. There are so many reasons why this is a bad idea. I can see myself falling for Holt in a major way, but that voice inside my head keeps screaming, *Are you insane?*

This is a mess. He's my lawyer, I'm getting a divorce, I'm under a contract that says I can't date anyone anyway. This is like a bad movie of the week. But . . . he's so honest and unguarded and wonderful. He sees me. I don't have to filter all of my emotions so he can understand them. He just gets me. Exactly as I am, he gets me. Why is it that when the someone who could be the right guy finally shows up, the one man I'm compelled to open my heart to, he picks *now* to do it? It's so unfair! I just don't know if I can deal with one more complication in my life. And Holt, well that's just about as complicated as it gets, isn't it?

"I'll see you tomorrow," he says softly, his sweet Southern lilt swirling all around my brain. "Good night, Darby." My name still sounds like *Dar-lin'* every time he says it. *Dar-by.* I love that.

"Good night, Holt," I say, as I hang up the phone.

A minute later it rings again. I pick up, giggling in anticipation. What a goofball.

"How am I supposed to get my beauty sleep if you keep calling me?" I say, laughing.

"You never needed much. Beauty sleep," the voice says. And it's not Holt's voice. It's Will's. Could this night possibly get any freakier?

"Why are you calling me?" I ask. "Are the kids okay?" And, *weird*. Is it my imagination, or was he just *flirting* with me?

"The kids are fine. We need to talk."

"What about?" My stomach lurches at the sound of his voice, and I realize that every time I've thought of him during the last three months I've thrown up, or at least come close: when I saw him the day he lied about being out of town, when I found out he cheated, when I realized he'd gone back to Gigi. Apparently, I'm Will-limic. I giggle a little at my own joke. Coping mechanism, I think.

"I was wrong, I made a stupid, horrible mistake, I love you, and seeing you tonight made me realize I want you back," Will says, in one rushed draw of breath, "I made a mistake . . ."

I cannot believe what I'm hearing. "You saw me?" I ask.

"I saw you go into the kitchen," he says. "Thank God Gigi didn't see you, she would have caused a huge scene."

"Will, you pretended everything was great, that we were this big happy family! And then you dumped me and cheated on me and humiliated me on national television," I yell.

"I know, I know, I'm so sorry," he whimpers. "I never meant for it to happen that way . . . I'm so sorry."

"You never meant for this to happen?" I ask. Now I'm seeing red. "How do you accidentally place an item in *USA Today*? How do you accidentally dump me on national TV, while simultaneously clearing out our house, yanking our kids out of school, and moving them across the country in the space of a few days?" I scream, "How is that a fucking accident, Will?"

"Darby, please," he says, "listen to me . . ."

"Fine," I say. "Speak."

"I never meant to hurt you," he begins. "Yes, I was having an affair with Gigi, and I'm sorry, it was wrong. I never should have done it."

Well, *there's* a big revelation. "When did you start sleeping with her? Or did you ever stop? Did you just bang her through our entire marriage?"

"No, no," he says. "I swear. It happened after the *Castaway* wrap party. We were both drunk, we wound up in bed together. The next morning, I felt horrible, I wanted to tell you, but I thought you might leave me. And Gigi said it would hurt you too much if you knew, and that I shouldn't tell."

"So you're taking marriage advice from your ex-wife," I snap.

"Yes, I know it was stupid. I was terrified that I'd get home, and that you'd just *know* somehow. I didn't want to lose you. I didn't tell, you didn't figure it out, and I started feeling like I could just get past it. It was a one-time thing."

"Clearly it wasn't," I say bitterly, "a one-time thing."

"No," he admits. "I saw Gigi a few weeks later. You and I had just had that argument about replacing the carpet in the den. It made me feel good that she wanted me so much. It was a real blow to me when she just left the first time, you know?"

"How long?" I demand.

"Four or five months," he admits.

"Were you with her all those times you were supposed to be in Atlanta?"

"How did you know?"

"I saw you, Will. I saw you at the fucking gas station and then five minutes later you're whining to me on the phone about your terrible flight. You tried to make out like *I* was crazy because I asked you where you were!"

"I'm sorry, I shouldn't have—"

"What about all the dinners at the Ritz? Where were you sleeping on all of those nights when you were supposed to be in Atlanta?"

"Gigi had a suite . . ." His voice trails off.

"Why, Will? Just tell me *why* you did this to me. To us."

"I felt like you didn't need me. You and I were sort of in parenting mode all the time, and Gigi just kept flirting with me, and telling me how great I was—"

"Um, hello, I was in 'parenting mode' with her children! *Your* children!" I say angrily.

"Gigi kept saying you'd never find out, it was just 'our little secret,' and then it happened again."

"And again."

"Well," he adds quietly, "that was about the time she got pregnant."

"Pregnant?" I yell. What the hell?

"Yes, well, it was a surprise to me, too." The line is silent for a minute and then he begins to speak again. "You know how much

I love Lilly and Aidan, and Gigi started pressuring me to leave you, telling me that if I didn't get back together with her that she would never allow me to see the baby. My baby. I didn't know what to do. Lilly and Aidan mean everything—I couldn't stand the thought of not being a father to this unborn child. And I couldn't stand the thought of losing you. My heart was completely torn in half. What was I supposed to do?"

"What were you supposed to do? You were supposed to not screw your ex-wife. You were definitely not supposed to knock her up. And you were abso-fucking-lutely not supposed to blindside me in public, ruin my career, take everything that was important to me." Tears stream silently over my cheeks. Damn Will for creating this fucking mess. "You didn't even give me a chance to say good-bye to Lilly and Aidan. You just stole my life away from me. How could you be so horrible to me?"

"I know, I know, I'm so sorry, Dar. I never meant for any of that to happen. Gigi kept pressuring me to leave you, and I kept wavering back and forth. How was I supposed to choose between my unborn child, and you, the woman I love? I didn't want a divorce! The more I thought about it, the more confused and torn I was."

"Jesus, Will," is all I can say. I cannot believe all of this was happening right under my nose. How could I have been so blind? And oblivious?

He continues, "Then, while you were on tour, Gigi asked me to bring the kids and meet her for a press conference in LA. I thought it was just the usual meet-and-greet for *Castaway*—I had no idea that Gigi was planning on making a statement that we'd gotten back together. When she made the announcement, I stood there in shock. I didn't know what to do, it was live television, for fuck's sake. Then, after the conference, I was trying to figure out how to tell you what had happened before you saw Gigi's press conference, and then I saw the clip of you on *Today*. Everything happened so fast, I was sure you'd never forgive me, I just didn't know what to do. Gigi told me that if I talked to you, or left her after the announcement, I'd never see the child again. She said it would be better for the baby, better for Lilly and Aidan to be with their own mother and father, and that you would never take me back after what we'd done to you."

"She's right."

"I believed her. She'd made arrangements to move the kids and me out of the Sarasota house without my knowledge. By the time we got back from the TV studio that day, the moving trucks were apparently already on their way to California. A week later they showed up at Gigi's house with everything we owned. I didn't know what to do, my life was completely out of control, a hundred and eighty miles an hour in a direction I didn't choose. It was a mess."

I'm silent, completely dumbfounded. Could Gigi really have masterminded this whole nightmare? The *USA Today* article, clearing out our house, and sneaking the kids to California, all of it a plan to practically guarantee I'd never take Will back? And Will, the quintessential people-pleaser, too weak-spined to stand up for our marriage, merely went along with the tide.

"Anytime you called to talk to the kids or me, she'd get so angry. I thought maybe I should stay with her, that it would be best for the family. The kids seemed so happy that we were all together. There were a couple of times we saw you on the cover of a magazine—there was that *People* cover with Tony Kullen, and Gigi was so pissed. I was jealous as hell, I hated to see you with another guy. Gigi kept trying to come up with more ways to get media attention. I think that after *Castaway* ended, she thought it would help her land another job."

"I wondered why she kept on," I say. "She had my husband, the kids, and my career was essentially over. I couldn't figure out why she kept going after me. What more could she want?"

Will sighs. "I knew I'd fucked up, but I just didn't know how to fix it. Darby," he begs, "please let me make things right."

"You can't," I say. "You broke my heart, you made me a joke."

"We could be a family again," he pleads. "Please. You and me, and Lilly and Aidan, in our own house. Just like we were before. We can start over. Please, Darby. I love you, and I swear I'll never hurt you again. Tell me what to do to help you forgive me. I'll go to counseling! I'll never look at another woman again! I'll get Gigi another publicist. Anything you say! Give me another chance. Please." He is sobbing now, snorting and slobbering into the phone, "Please . . . Darby . . . I'm so sorry . . ."

I don't know what to say. The idea of having my life, my family, back makes my heart ache. And as evil as it seems, there's a tiny part of me that wouldn't mind seeing Gigi get a little of what's coming to her. I can't begin to reconcile in my mind how Will could have ever loved me at all and then treated me the way he did. Even if Gigi engineered the whole thing. Just because it wasn't his idea doesn't mean he's not equally culpable. More so, in fact. He was supposed to be my fucking husband. Where was his loyalty to me?! He didn't protect me! He didn't even explain what happened! He let me fry in the media hot plate and cry my eyes out wondering how our perfect life got so far off track.

I loved Will, I did. And Lilly and Aidan mean everything to me. And, God, to rewind the clock a few months and start back fresh, like none of this nightmare ever happened . . . I'd give anything to have my family back. My chances in court are pretty shitty, and letting Will back into my life could solve that in one quick move.

Do Not Pass Go. I could be snuggling Lilly and Aidan by tomorrow night.

I miss what we had together. I miss my old life. I miss my kids. I even miss Will; I just don't know if I could ever, in a million years, forgive him. How could I possibly live with him and myself at the same time? Can I really keep myself from running over Gigi in my giant mommymobile the next time she's in town for visitation? Not likely. Those poor kids. What a messed up situation. How could kids so sweet possibly deserve such screwy parents?

"What are you going to do about the baby?" I ask. I cannot handle one more thing.

"I'm not sure," he says. "I love you. I'll do anything you want. If I can't be with you, none of this means anything." Gawd, Will. Leave it to him to close with something straight out of a Hallmark Channel movie of the week.

"I have to go. I can't do this right now," I say, exhausted. My head hurts and my soul feels like it's been turned inside out.

"Will you at least think about it?" he pleads.

"Yes, Will, I'll think about it." Fuck. I can't imagine how I'm going to be able to think about anything else.

Dreamgirl Academy Dating Tip

#109

There are some times in a relationship when you have to make a decision to forgive someone or move on. But before you can ever do that, you'll need to feel that he truly understands the pain he's caused you.

Don't allow yourself to stay in love-life limbo: If you can't forgive him for what he's done, it's time to cut your losses and end the relationship. But if you do believe the relationship is worth keeping and that he's truly sorry, forgive him, move forward together, and make a point to stop living in the mistakes of the past.

—The Dreamgirl Academy

Chapter 30

I know three couples whose marriages have survived infidelity. But *survive* is the operative word. Usually, the cheating husband goes back to business as usual, pretending that everything is great, while the wife wanders around shell-shocked, an empty smile fixed on her face, numbly digging through the offender's laundry in fear that he's on the prowl again.

I spend all of Sunday trying to figure things out, sort of expecting a last-minute reprieve call from Holt telling me that Will has called off the lawsuit. I'm not certain exactly how that scenario would play out, but in my *Fantasy Island* version, I get to be with my kids and my love life doesn't end with a compulsive cheater or my career in shambles.

I don't know what to do about Will. I don't think I could ever truly forgive him for what he's done. If I take him back, I would be a complete hypocrite, and probably a complete idiot as well. How many times have I told women *Never stay with a cheater! Never!*

Even if there weren't 412 other factors in play here, I can't bear the idea of letting down the millions of women who have followed my advice to the letter—you ladies should hold out for a man who treats you well, but not me; I'll be staying with my piece-of-crap, cheating husband. Thankyouverymuch.

I do a conference call with the Dreamgirls to let them weigh in with advice and opinions. For once, the panel is split: Jules and Sarah think I should take Will back and try to put my family back together (with counseling, and possibly one of those ankle cuffs they use on prisoners), while Tia and Kimberly are firmly planted in the no-effing-way camp.

Tia interrupts the enthusiastic bantering between the girls and asks, "What does Holt think about this? This little development should certainly help your case."

"What do you mean?" I ask.

"Will is clearly waffling between you and Gigi," Tia says. "I'd think that would make him seem less of a stable father figure in the eyes of the court, and Gigi and Will would appear less cohesive as a family."

"I hadn't thought about that," I confess.

"You need to call Holt with this right away," says Tia.

"Oh no," I moan, "I can't tell him this."

"Why the hell not?" asks Tia. Sarah, Kimberly, and Jules all pipe in, wondering why I would withhold such information from my attorney.

I take a deep breath and let it all out. "He kissed me last night, and told me he wants to be with me."

"Who? Will?" asks Tia.

"No, Holt. My attorney."

"Well!" exclaims Sarah. "And what did *you* say?"

"I didn't say anything. I'm pretty sure I'm not ready to start something with him right now. It's complicated, you know?"

"Jules," says Tia matter-of-factly, "you owe me twenty bucks."

"What for?"

"I told Jules you two would be locking lips inside of three months. He's gorgeous, why wouldn't you kiss him?"

"Great. Thanks."

"How do you feel about him?" asks Jules gently.

"I don't know," I say, as an ache creeps into my chest. "Holt is extraordinary, I think he might be the kind of man I was always too afraid to hope for."

Jules sighs. "Oh, honey, what are you gonna do?"

"I think we just met at the wrong time," I say, as tears begin to form. "I can't deal with this now." I pause and take a breath. "There's a lot to think about. Will showing up now is so confusing. I miss being part of a family, and I don't know if I can ever forgive Will, but I do know that before any of this happened, our life together was pretty damned good."

"On what planet does cheating and public torture fall into the category of pretty damned good?" demands Tia.

"Tia," says Jules softly, "let Darby be. This is her decision."

My head is pounding from trying to untangle the mess with Will and the kids. "I really need to think through this situation with Will first, before I even consider anything else. If Will and I get back together, it's a moot point anyway."

"Sleep with Holt and have your own kids. Problem solved," says Tia.

"Tia, stop!" hisses Jules. "Darby, whatever your decision, we will love you and we're here for you. It's your life, sweetie. Focus on what's really important to you. If you do that, you'll know what to do."

"Lilly and Aidan are the most important," I point out.

The rest of my friends echo their support and promise to keep me in their thoughts and prayers.

"Call Holt now," instructs Tia. "He needs to know what Will said. If you decide not to take Will back, this might have some bearing on your case. This is big. You can't keep him out of the loop."

"I don't want to hurt him," I say.

"He's your attorney, Darby," Tia says. "He needs to know all of the facts."

She's right. Crap, I know she's right.

I hang up with the girls and call Holt, completely dreading having this discussion with him. If he were just my attorney, and not the guy who kissed me so tenderly my knees buckled on the beach last night, this would not be a big deal at all. But he did. And it is.

"Holt, it's Darby," I say, taking a deep breath, surprised to hear him answer so quickly—the phone only rang once. Okay, it's better just to come straight out with it, right?

"Sweet Darby," he drawls, "boy am I glad to hear your voice." He sounds so happy, so light. Jesus, this is going to be harder than I'd thought.

"We need to talk about your case," he says. "After what happened last night, I'm going to resign as your attorney. As I said, the fact that I have feelings for you could compromise my ability to try your case. I want to make sure you have the best representation, both personally and professionally. It would be unethical for me to continue on as your lawyer, feeling the way that I do."

"What?" I say, dumbfounded.

"Don't worry," he says, attempting to soothe me. "I have a colleague, John Mayoue, who's a good friend. He's the preeminent family law attorney in the country, a real powerhouse. Mayoue's a pioneer in the field in stepparents' rights. I spoke with him last night, and it shouldn't take more than a few days to get him up to speed on your case."

I panic. I just spent two weeks in a soul-searching nightmare with Holt, and now he wants to bring some stranger into the deal? I'm supposed to go through all of this again with some new person? Just because he has feelings for me? I don't think so.

"You're the best attorney in your field. I don't *want* another lawyer. You're just going to have to bury those feelings and do your job."

Holt is silent for a few seconds, and then begins to speak. "I can understand your ambivalence about bringing someone else in at this point, I really can—"

"I have something to say," I interrupt. "I . . . I . . . really don't want to hurt you."

"Darby," says Holt, his voice suddenly solemn, "I'm a grown man. I can fend for myself. Let's have it."

Good gracious, a grown man. Have I ever in my life met a man who considered himself to be a *grown man*? They think of themselves as guys, sure, and more accurately, big boys. But a *grown man*? I thought grown men had gone the way of the dinosaur, long gone since the days of Cary Grant. My heart skips another beat, but I take him at his word.

"Holt," I say carefully, "I want you to know last night was amazing."

"Yes, it was," he drawls, in that measured lawyer's tone, "and—"

"And there's been a development," I say, shifting uncomfortably in my seat. God, this is horrible; I don't want to tell him.

"What kind of development?"

"Will called me last night after you dropped me off. He wants us to get back together . . . to be a family again . . . live in our old house . . . me and Will and the kids."

"And, what did you tell him?" he asks, his usually smooth voice full of gravel.

"I told him I'd have to think about it."

"Think about it?" he says incredulously. "What the hell, Darby?"

"If I get back together with him, this custody case goes away. I get my family back, my *life* back. You said yourself that I don't stand a chance of winning this thing. This might be the only way."

"And you'd spend the rest of your life with someone who treats you as . . . as *disposable*?" he says, his voice tense with emotion. "What kind of lesson are you giving those kids, Darby? Do you really want to let them see you this way? Are you willing to sell your soul to be with them? Your dignity? What kind of mother can you be without that?"

"Is that the advice you're giving me as my lawyer?"

"No," he says, "it's the advice I'm giving you as someone who cares about you."

"You're not exactly unbiased. Is this my best chance to be with my children? I mean, if I don't go back to Will, can you guarantee me you'll get my kids back today? This week? This month even?"

"I promised you I would fight this through to the end."

"That's not really a promise you're planning to keep, is it? Two minutes ago you were suggesting we dump my case on some law buddy of yours." Instantly I regret saying that. I know that honor is something Holt takes very seriously, and I've just informed him in no uncertain terms that I don't take him at his word.

"You want unbiased?" he says angrily. "I'll give you unbiased. I will keep fighting this as long as it takes. But I can't guarantee you'll get custody of your kids today. Darby, I can't even guarantee you'll get visitation. But I do guarantee that if you take Will back, you'll be back in my office in two years, tops. At the rate he's going, you could be back here in a couple of months." He pauses and takes a breath. "As your attorney, I would advise you not to let this bastard back into your life. Or your bed. Period."

"I don't know what I'm going to do," I say. I'm exhausted with my miserable options.

"You deserve better, Darby," his frustration buzzing through the phone lines.

"I deserve to have my family," I reply. And that is the end of our conversation.

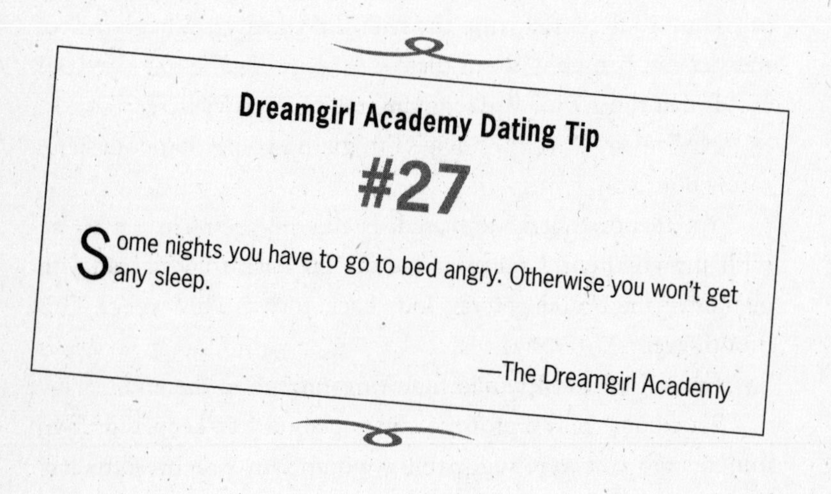

Chapter 31

Monday morning comes and I still don't know what I'm going to do about Will. I shower slowly, completely unable to focus as I ready myself to go to the courthouse for our custody hearing—choices bang around my brain like an orangutan on the loose in Tiffany's. I can hear raindrops pounding the roof, and the ocean roars with the swell of the storm. It is dark outside; gray seeps into the house in the scarce morning light, sneaking under the doorjambs and permeating through the window blinds. I wander into the bedroom, hair dripping, wrapped in my favorite bathrobe, to put on a little music, but I can't find a selection depressing enough to suit my mood.

Will called twice yesterday, leaving long, rambling messages on my cell phone, begging for one more chance. I was struck by the fact that both messages had kid and crowd noises clanging in the background, and I wondered where Will snuck off to call me. The background sounds gave me a wave of nausea; where did he make his secret calls to Gigi when he was with me? I can't help but picture Will, the perfect husband, offering to take the kids out for a day at the park, and then conspiring about his next rendezvous while Aidan and Lilly played nearby on the swings; or sneaking off to the men's room to call Gigi while I sat alone in a restaurant, picking at the calamari and wondering why my husband was in the bathroom for twenty-five minutes. If I had to guess, I'd venture that Gigi doesn't have any idea that Will is angling for reconciliation with me now. If I turn him down, will he leave her anyway? Or will he stay with her and pretend nothing ever happened?

If Gigi hadn't forced his hand, would he still be sleeping with her and betraying me?

I honestly don't know what to do. I've been avoiding Will's calls and I haven't spoken with Holt since yesterday. I have no idea what I'm going to say when I see him. In another time, in another situation, Holt and I could have been amazing for each other. He has sort of taken me by surprise, and I found myself won over before I ever had an inkling that I was even under attack. He has such depth, such a spark, it makes me wonder what could be. But winning this custody case is the most important thing in my life: I need an attorney, the best attorney, not some romantic complication. No matter how compelling or charismatic he is.

My mind wanders back to that kiss on the beach; my heart twists just thinking about it. Those soulful green eyes, his wicked sense of humor. He's so smart—nothing gets past him, and that's insanely appealing. He calls me on all my crap, which irritates me to no end, but, frankly, is a huge relief. At last, someone I can be myself with. He's the first person to see who I really am. I feel safe around him, protected, something I can't remember ever feeling before. I do know without a doubt that if I let myself, I could love him, really love him—and that's what terrifies me. Holt already knows all my soft spots, and being so vulnerable scares the crap out of me. Losing Lilly and Aidan has been hard enough. My soul couldn't take another loss that deep. I always knew with Will—with any man, really—that if he was suddenly gone, I'd be okay, I'd move on. Like many smart women, I've always fallen in love with my head. But Holt has somehow managed to get my heart involved without the consent of my brain. And even this early on, I know that losing someone who has reached so far into the depths of me would be devastating. I can't set myself up for that. I just can't.

I feel tears escaping and I wipe them away quickly. How did this guy get so far under my skin? I check my reflection in the mirror one last time before I go out the door, and see puffy eyes and ruddy cheeks. What the hell has happened to me? I want all of this to be over.

The drive over to the courthouse is slow and miserable, as traffic lurches and skids on the rainy streets. I creep from one torrential downpour to the next, and a drive that should take fifteen minutes ends up taking thirty-five.

I rummage around the backseat for my umbrella, and when I open it, I discover that one of the wires has poked through, causing it to spring a leak. Perfect. The rain is coming down in torrents, but I guess a leaky umbrella is better than none at all. I pop it open above my head and sprint across the parking lot, a steady stream of rain sneaking through the skylight in the torn plastic. By the time I make it to the steps of the courthouse, the wind has whipped the compromised umbrella practically inside out and I'm soaked all the way through. Holt is waiting for me outside, and as I approach, he wordlessly holds his umbrella over my head as sheets of rain wet his face and eyelashes, pasting dark brown curls to his forehead.

Our eyes catch, and I bite my lip to keep any tears from escaping. He looks at me intently, and I can't tell if it's sorrow in his eyes or rage, or maybe a mixture of something else.

"It's this way," he says, leading me to a corridor. I follow him down the hallway, until I spot Gigi, Will, their attorney, and the kids. I'd sort of braced myself to see Will and Gigi, but it didn't occur to me that Lilly and Aidan would be here, too. God, how awful to put them through this mess.

"What the hell is Sol thinking?" Holt mutters. "Those kids shouldn't be here."

I feel a squeeze in my chest at seeing them again. It's been almost three months and the hurt of missing them is still as fresh as the first day Will stole them away. Gigi is bent over making silly faces as Aidan and Lilly giggle and shriek with laughter. It's a bittersweet moment—I'm glad to see them so happy, to see Gigi so thoroughly engaged with them. And it breaks my heart to think of everything I've missed in the last few months. Lilly and Aidan look bigger already, Lilly's hair is tied up in braids in a style that's outside my repertoire, and Aidan looks like he's grown at least two inches. How did I get so far away from them in such a short span of time? Will notices me, acknowledges me with a little nod, and sort of raises his eyebrows. Gigi looks up from the children, stares me down for a few seconds, and then resumes playing with the kids, as though I've evaporated.

But Lilly and Aidan spot me and come running over, their shoes squeaking on the wet marble floor, shouting "Darby!" I sink down to my knees to embrace them as they run toward me, and it takes a heartbeat for me to realize they just called me "Darby" and not "Dar-mama."

"Oh my sweethearts," I say, wrapping my arms around both of them, inhaling the scent of their hair and kissing their warm little cheeks.

"We missed you so much!" says Lilly, waving her arms and twirling the skirt of her pretty pink dress.

"I missed you too, Lilly Bean," I say, tears pouring out of me, "I love you so much."

"I love you too, Darby," Lilly says, smiling sweetly. Aidan keeps himself under my arm, grinning at me and nodding, but as usual, he lets his sister do most of the talking. He is missing both front teeth, and I feel a little twinge of sadness, hoping the tooth fairy in California did something special. Lilly launches into a rundown of all of their activities over the last few months, including details of several trips to Disneyland and a cookie-baking experience where Gigi accidentally dropped a bag of flour on the cat.

"You should have been there!" she squeals excitedly.

"I'm sorry I missed it," I say, and I am. I'm relieved that the kids have been so cared for in recent months; they seem genuinely happy. But part of me is incredibly jealous that I wasn't the one to do it. Where have these two superparents been over the last four years?

The kids tell me about their new school in California, new friends and new toys, and Aidan throws his arms around my neck for another hug. As I squeeze him, I notice Holt is watching me. When our eyes meet, he nods a bit and slowly forces a smile.

"Kids, it's time to go now," says Will. A young woman appears in the hallway. She has a backpack slung over her shoulder and she's carrying a juice box. They squeeze me one more time and then break the embrace to go running back to where Will and Gigi are standing. The young woman leads Lilly and Aidan down the hallway, toward the main entrance. I feel a little pang of sadness as the kids walk off with a caretaker I don't know. Did Will and Gigi bring a nanny all the way from California? I'm sidetracked for a second, thinking maybe I should have given Will the numbers of a few of our neighborhood babysitters. It's been so long since Gigi lived here, I doubt she'd have anyone to call, and Will hasn't arranged for a babysitter in four years.

Gigi shoots me a harsh look, and then files into the courtroom after Sol, their attorney. In person, Sol Weinstein looks just as he does on television: like an oil slick in an Armani suit.

Will, Holt, and I are left standing outside in the hallway.

"I thought you might like to see the kids," says Will. I nod in thanks.

"Darby, I can't go on like this," Will whispers. "Have you considered what we talked about?"

I can't believe he's asking me this with Gigi less than ten feet away. I have to say, he looks genuinely distressed. He leans forward a bit as he waits for my response, as though he is attempting to psychically manipulate my answer into the one he wants to hear.

My heart pounds as I scramble to come up with something to say. "Will, I . . . um . . ."

Holt steps quickly to my side.

"Mr. Bradley," Holt says, "please refrain from addressing my client without your attorney present." He gently takes my elbow and leads me into the courtroom, moving with a quiet confidence.

Will purses his lips and quietly follows us.

The room looks different than I imagined. I guess the picture of a courtroom I had in my mind was just a montage of images from television dramas and John Grisham novels, all marble and mahogany, none of it really based on reality. The room is smaller than I expected, and, well, less dramatic. It's sort of beige and bland and feels more like the DMV than the center of justice.

The courtroom buzzes quietly. The judge's bench is empty and a bailiff stands nearby, looking bored. The court reporter pulls supplies from a black case and readies her equipment for the day ahead. Will joins Gigi and their attorney at their table, while Holt leads me to the table on the other side.

The butterflies in my stomach are doing backflips and my shoulders are pinched with stress. I look over to Will's table and see Gigi leaning over the railing, whispering to him. I look around our table and the empty seats behind my side of the railing. I wish I had someone to sit on my side of the courtroom. This is like my wedding all over again. The thought seeps in again that if I just take Will back, this mess will end and I can have my life back.

The judge enters from a door to the left of her bench.

"All rise, the Honorable Judge Margaret McDowell presiding," barks the bailiff.

We rise, then sit after the judge has taken her seat. The attorneys take turns speaking, making motions, approaching the bench, and requesting that various files, papers, and videotapes be admitted into evidence.

Holt inserts the *Today* show tape in a VCR and plays it for the judge. At the moment when Matt Lauer informs me of the *USA Today* article announcing my divorce, Will visibly flinches. And when I throw up, and then pass out on-screen, even Gigi looks surprisingly mortified. I hear a few quiet chuckles around the room as the tape concludes. The male bailiff near the judge's bench is seriously working to suppress a smile, but the female bailiff on the other side of the room looks like she might like to shoot someone.

Holt brings Will up onto the stand first. Will takes the oath and then sits.

"How long were you married to Darby Vaughn?" Holt asks.

"Three years," Will responds.

"During the marriage to Darby, approximately how long were you having sexual relations with your former wife, Gigi Bissanti?"

"About five months," Will admits, "I'm sorry to say . . ." Hurt slices through me, to have him admit it, right there. Humiliating. Holt's eyes penetrate Will's, scanning for chinks in the armor. Holt's usually comforting Southern drawl has given way to precisely controlled contempt. It is obvious to me that Holt is taking Will's treatment of me personally; I can see in his face that he wants to make Will pay.

Holt asks the judge to admit into evidence the airline receipts for the clandestine trips taken to LA, and then demands that Will state his exact purpose for visiting California on each occasion.

"And during the time you were married to Gigi Bissanti, approximately how many months were you having an extramarital affair with Darby Vaughn?" Holt asks.

"None," Will says. "Darby and I didn't even meet until after Gigi and I had been divorced for a year."

"And where did you meet her?" asks Holt.

"I met her on a plane, on tour for her first book," Will replies.

Holt shows documents to Will, one to confirm the date when my book was released, one a copy of Will and Gigi's divorce documents. Will agrees that the dates and documents are accurate.

Holt asks the judge to dismiss Gigi's counterclaim that I interfered with her marriage to Will based on Will's testimony and the evidence he has in hand. Gigi's attorney voices a wobbly objection, but the judge is quick to dismiss.

"Did you love your wife, Darby?" Holt asks. Will shifts uncomfortably in his seat under the pressure of Holt's penetrating gaze.

"Yes," says Will.

I feel a rush of relief to hear him say it in court, in front of a judge and Gigi and everyone. There have been dozens of times in the last few months when I wondered if Will ever loved me at all.

"Do you think it was cruel to allow her to find out on live television that you were divorcing her?"

"Yes," says Will, "I'm truly sorry for what happened. I never meant to hurt her that way."

"You never meant to hurt her *in that way*, you said. In what way *did* you mean to hurt her?" questions Holt, pacing in front of the witness box.

"I never meant to hurt her," Will says.

"Never?" His eyes flash as he goes in for the kill. "Did you think you might have hurt her when you had sex with another woman?"

"Yes," says Will.

"Do you think you might have hurt her when you and your ex-wife Gigi Bissanti publicly sabotaged her career?"

"Yes," says Will.

"Do you think you might have hurt her when you moved the children she had loved and cared for, the children she had been a psychological parent to—and was the primary caretaker for—to another state while she was out of town?"

"Yes," says Will.

"Do you think for one second that you ever deserved this woman?" asks Holt, as he leans on the railing in front of the witness stand.

"Move to strike! Irrelevant," interjects Will's attorney.

The judge sustains the objection as Will very quietly says,

"No." Holt looks embarrassed for a second, and then composes himself to continue the questioning. The judge decides it's time for a break and calls a recess for lunch.

Gigi, Will, and Sol scurry off, presumably to discuss the proceedings so far. Holt and I sit at the table for a few minutes, lingering to create a little space between them and us.

Holt asks me if I'd like to grab a sandwich down the street, and I decline. I'm too stressed out to eat. I'd rather hide out in my car and have a good cry.

When the recess is over, we return to the courtroom. Our hearing resumes and Holt brings Will back onto the stand to bat him around a bit more. Oddly enough, instead of resisting or even defending himself, Will seems genuinely sorry for the pain he's inflicted on me. Maybe he is.

Gigi is up next, and from her testimony and Will's, it's become quite apparent that she was, in fact, the mastermind behind the whole *Today* show fiasco. I keep expecting that she'll be at least a little regretful or ashamed for everything that's happened, as Will seems to be, but she shows no outward signs of remorse.

She holds her head up and stares straight ahead through all of the questioning. Her answers to Holt's questions are arrogant, clipped, and chilly. Holt digs deeper, almost ruthlessly prodding her. Gigi's lack of remorse and sense of entitlement are astounding to me, and from the disdainful expression on Her Honor's face, to the judge as well. As I listen to her justifying her actions, it only confirms to me that Gigi has always and will always see Will and the children as *her* family. She feels no guilt in taking them back, even if it was she who left them in the first place. It seems that from Gigi's perspective, she was merely reclaiming what was rightfully hers. To her, that end justified any means.

Her demeanor makes me angry at first, but the realization hits that in her mind, through her filter of reality, she was simply defending her family, doing whatever she had to do to keep them together. And, for once in my life, I understand where she's coming from. A family is, after all, more important than anything.

The judge ends the proceedings for the day and states that we'll resume tomorrow at nine A.M.

Gigi and Will file out, and Sol Weinstein, the opposing attorney, strides toward our table.

"I'll call you later and we can see where we are," he says to Holt.

"Sure," Holt replies.

"What's that about?" I ask.

"He wants to talk settlement agreement. We poked some major holes in their case today, Will is a noodle on the stand, and Gigi came off as ruthless. That judge looked like she wanted to throttle Will when she saw the *Today* tape. We're in better shape than I'd thought."

I blink, and steady myself for what I'm about to do. I hope I'm making the right decision.

As soon as the courtroom empties, I lean over to Holt and say, "Please drop the custody case. I don't want to go forward."

He looks at me, clearly shocked, and shakes his head in disbelief.

"Darby, don't . . ."

"Holt," I say, "I'm sorry, I can't talk about this now. I'll call you later." I gather my bag and my shredded umbrella. Grabbing my coat from the back of the chair, I walk as fast as I can down the aisle toward the door.

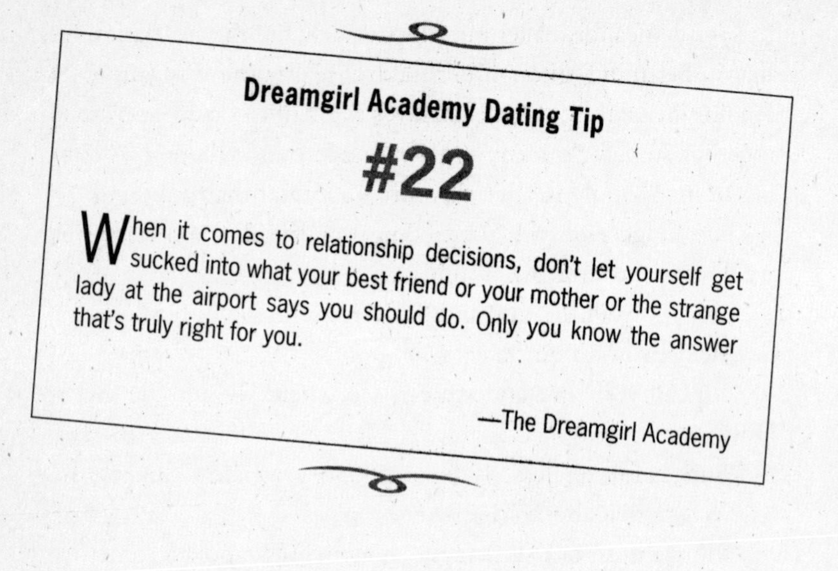
Dreamgirl Academy Dating Tip

#22

When it comes to relationship decisions, don't let yourself get sucked into what your best friend or your mother or the strange lady at the airport says you should do. Only you know the answer that's truly right for you.

—The Dreamgirl Academy

Chapter 32

I wish the rain would let up. I walk quickly to my car, pulling my coat around me and hoping I don't run into anyone on the way out. Finally behind the wheel of the car, I sit, out of breath, my emotions in a flurry.

It would be a lot easier to think of Gigi as evil, or crazy, but swirling around in my mind is the notion that maybe Gigi and I are more alike than I could ever imagine. She loved her family, yes, and when she realized she'd lost them, she did everything in her power to get them back. Can I blame her for that? No, I did, and would do again, the same thing. Gigi is aggressive and ambitious when it comes to her career, for certain, but so am I. And I'll bet that, like me, like so many other mothers I know, she had no idea how having a family is a sacrifice of your ambitions. Can you just put a part of you that big to sleep? And then wake it up some fifteen years later when the kids are grown-up enough not to need you? That's what we're supposed to do, isn't it? Maybe she tried, and she just couldn't do it, and it all sort of exploded out of her in this hugely dysfunctional way. Did Gigi believe, as I did, that Will would share more of the responsibility, make more sacrifices with his time, so that Gigi's tremendous ambition would not be the sole offering to the gods of parenting? Did she enter into motherhood with blinders on, believing she really could have it all, and then learning (like the victim of a twisted reality bait-and-switch scheme) that whether it was her career or her children, someone was going to be getting the short end of the stick? "Having it all" is a big load of crap, at least for the mom. You can't really have it all, can you? When children are in the picture, somebody has to make sure they come before everything else. And that person is almost always the mom.

I can't believe I'm thinking this, but I'm beginning to understand Gigi. I understand her ambition, and I share it, though in a different way. Maybe she left because she thought her family would always be there for her, but then she realized what she'd lost and she decided to come back. I, on the other hand, have lived my entire life in fear that my family would disappear in a flash, and so I was far more willing to forgo my own ambitions for the privilege of having a family. And it *was* a privilege, though I'd be lying if I didn't admit I resented it sometimes. Will's career never seemed to suffer. He never missed an important meeting, never had to give up a big opportunity because one of the kids caught a stomach bug or he couldn't find a suitable babysitter at the last minute. Will always had a suitable babysitter at the last minute: me. And before me, Gigi. And I'd bet my life that neither one of us had any idea what we were getting ourselves into.

Could I ever leave my kids the way Gigi did? No. But I sure can't blame her for doing whatever it took to get them back. I remember hearing a news story a few years back about a mother in a grocery store parking lot. She put her baby in the car seat and walked a few yards away to return the shopping cart. Some nut jumped into her car when the mother was just ten feet away, and drove off with her baby inside. The mother grabbed hold of the bumper and was dragged three-quarters of a mile on the back end of that car. I remember hearing the story on the news, the camera fixed on the mother, her clothing and her face ragged and torn, stained with dirt and oil and determination, holding that baby in her arms. She told the reporter she would never have let go of that car as long as her child was inside. I watched the story with tears in my eyes, and I knew in the very bottom of my soul that I would never have let go, either.

I feel like, on a certain level, I know Gigi. And somehow, with everything she's done to me, I feel myself forgiving her. I don't understand her in many ways, but we're far more alike than I'd thought.

I drive home slowly, plotting out in my head what I'm going to say to Will. What's horrible about this situation is that there is no clear right and wrong. The three of us have conflicting needs, and no matter how this all shakes out, someone is going home broken-hearted. Will did the wrong thing and then tried to do the right thing. Gigi did too, I guess. Or maybe she tried to do the right thing by doing the wrong thing. And now, I'm not sure if what I'm about to do is right, or wrong, or somewhere in the middle.

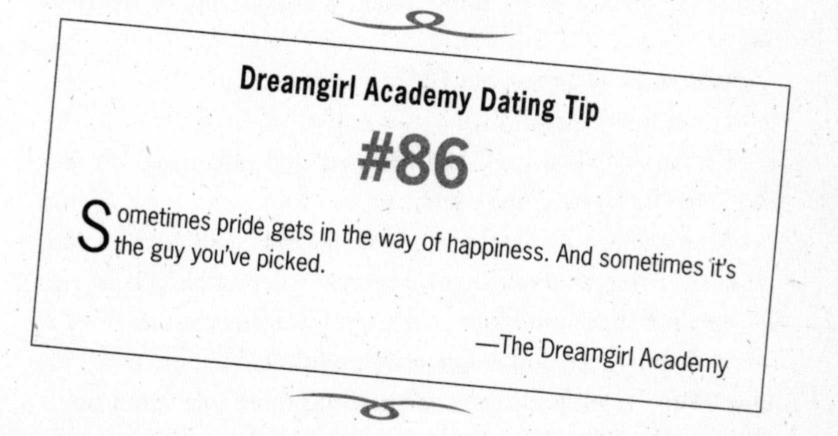

Chapter 33

As soon as I get home, I drop my soggy things by the door, put a little Amos Lee on the CD player, and sink into a hot bath. When the phone starts ringing, I turn up the music and the water to drown it out. I will talk when I'm ready.

An hour or so later, I emerge from the tub, wrapping my favorite pink terry-cloth bathrobe around me. It is thick and comforting—Lilly and Aidan gave it to me two years ago for Mother's Day, and I think of them every time I put it on.

I sit on the sofa and dial the phone before I lose my nerve. This is my chance to set things right. Will picks up on the first ring.

"Where are you?" he says.

"I'm at Jules's guesthouse."

"I'll call you right back," he whispers, and then hangs up the phone before he hears my response.

Great. I check the answering machine and see I have eleven messages. I skip through them as quickly as possible. There are voicemails from Tia and Jules, one from my agent, another from a *Dreamgirl* producer, and a guy calling with an "opportunity" to upgrade my cable package. And there are three each from both Will and Holt, just since five o'clock. Will's messages are progressively more desperate, pleading for me to take him back. Holt's three messages are brief: *Darby, we need to talk. Darby, please don't make any decision before we speak. Darby, I'm on my cell, please call me back immediately.*

I get up to pour myself a glass of wine, and then sit back on the couch to wait for Will's call, remembering how many times I've told women never to waste their lives sitting around waiting around for the phone to ring. I guess I've said a lot of things.

After a few more minutes, the phone rings. A shot of nerves hits my stomach as Will's cell phone number comes up on the caller ID.

"Hello?" I say.

"Darby?"

"I'm here. I need to talk to you."

"Oh God, Darby, please tell me we can work on this. It killed me today to see you, and not be able to hold you. I'm so sorry about today. I'm so sorry for what I've done to you. I hate that I've disappointed you. I swear I'll spend every day of eternity making it up to you."

"No, you won't, Will."

"I promise, I will. I love you, I've always loved you. I've just made a horrible mistake. Please, please let me make it up to you."

"Will, it's over," I say. "I don't want you back. I love Aidan and Lilly, and that's the only reason I considered it."

"We can be a family again. The kids need you! I swear, I'll do whatever it takes to make things right." His comment about the kids hits me right in the ribs, but I resolve to stay strong.

"Please, Darby, I'll leave Gigi tonight. Please reconsider. Meet me tonight and let's talk it over," he begs.

This, I know from experience, is a very bad plan. It's much

harder to turn someone down in person, especially when you have so much history together. It's like the old traveling salesman edict: If they can just get inside your door, they have a 90 percent chance of making the sale. For once, I'm keeping Will on the porch.

"We can make this work," he says. "I promise, I've changed."

This pisses me off. "Will, it seems to me that you're playing the exact same game as before. You've just switched the players. One of these days, you'd better stop jerking around the mothers of your children."

"We can work this out," he insists.

"Will, I'm finished with you. You've betrayed me, it doesn't matter how sorry you are. I owe it to myself to find someone who knows what love really means," I say firmly. "And you are not that guy."

"Darby—"

"I'm done, Will." I hang up the phone and I feel stronger than I have in months. No matter what happens now, I will make it through. Cutting him loose was the hard part, but after what happened in court, I know it was the right thing to do.

Earlier today, right after Gigi's testimony, I had the heart-wrenching realization that I do not mean the same thing to Lilly and Aidan as they mean to me. My soul is heavy with the disillusion. I love them absolutely and think of them as my own children, but I've realized that as much as we love and care for each other, Lilly and Aidan never saw me as their mother. I was the substitute, the one who stepped in while their mother wasn't there for them. And it doesn't really matter if I was better at the job, or if I wanted it more, or, frankly, if I was just the only one to show up to do it. For any child, there's no substitute for your real mother, or your real father.

If anyone knows that, I do.

My grandmother and my aunties were the most loving, caring guardians any person could hope for, and growing up, there was never a day when I didn't feel cherished. But no matter how much my grandmother loved me, the person I really needed in my life was my own mother. And the fact that she was gone left a huge hole. There is no substitute that can fill that need, no matter how wonderful or how loving. I suffered because my parents weren't with me. I can see that taking Lilly and Aidan away from their mother would be cruel. The truth has dawned in the depths of my soul—it doesn't matter that she's not the best mother on the planet, she's *their* mother. Lilly and Aidan will be happier, better off, with Will and Gigi. I can love these amazing children, and I can be here for them throughout their lives. And although it breaks my heart, I know that the most loving thing I can do for them is to stop standing in their way.

Lilly and Aidan are family to me, and even though I am not their mother, they will always be my children. And a real mom knows that whatever your kids need comes first.

Can You Reform a Cheater?

by Darby Vaughn

Should you stay or should you go?

Every week I get about 50 letters from women and men who want to know if they should stay with someone who has cheated on them. Nearly always, the letter is peppered with reasons why the cheater might have been compelled to cheat, and sometimes even includes a rationale why it never would have happened had it not been for the evil home-wrecker who hypnotized the poor, innocent cheater and forced him into actions against his will. The request for help is usually fairly evenly divided between "What should I do?" and "How can I make it stop?"

While I consider myself to be quite the mushball romantic, my feelings on cheating have a much harder edge. Cheating, in my opinion, is a deal-breaker.

If it happens once, it will happen again. Why? When you stay with a person who has cheated on you, you've essentially taught them that they can sleep with somebody else and *you'll take them back*. Wow, that's pretty great news for them!

Even if you manage to get past the lies, the heartache, and the ten pounds you'll put on with comfort food, a cloud will always hang over your relationship. You'll never truly feel cherished or completely loved. Why torture yourself with feelings of self-doubt and insecurity? Tell that cheater to hit the road; lock yourself in your apartment with your closest friends, a stack of sappy movies, and a couple of quarts of your favorite brand of frozen happiness. Move on, and find someone who gives you the love and respect you deserve. Otherwise, you're just cheating yourself.

Chapter 34

I feel so good about sending Will on his way, I crank up the CD player and give myself a little musical revue with the Female National Anthem, "I Will Survive." With the music nice and loud, I sing and dance around in my bathrobe like a maniac until I'm panting, happy and ready to pass out. Which is exactly when the doorbell rings.

I yank it open, trying to catch my breath, and find Holt standing on my front porch with his hands stuffed in the front pockets of his jeans and a loaded messenger bag slung over his shoulder.

Holt takes one look at me, breathing hard with my robe askew, and asks, "Is this a bad time?"

"Hey pal," I say, "get your mind out of the gutter."

"Sorry," he says, looking down at his shoes.

"Come in," I say, opening the door a little wider as I straighten my robe. He ducks through the door and lifts the bag over his head, setting it on the floor next to the couch.

"Are you okay?" he asks, his eyes deep with concern.

"I'm good, actually."

He eyes me warily. "I'm glad to hear that." He pauses for a second, brushing a dark curl away from his ear—a classic Holt move I've come to adore. His expression is so serious, all business. It reminds me of the first time I met him.

"We've got to talk about the case. I need to know how you want me to proceed. We can't just drop the custody case and walk away. You're in the middle of divorce proceedings, too."

I motion for him to sit on the couch, and he takes a seat on the left side of the sofa.

"I know," I say, joining him on the couch. "I'm sorry I ran out today." He looks down, fumbling with some papers in his bag. I watch his face for a few seconds until he feels my stare and turns his head to meet my gaze.

"Are you not going through with the divorce?" he asks. "Is that why you want to drop the case? Because you're going back to him?" He's watching my reaction so intently, I feel like I might forget to breathe.

"I told Will it's over. I'm not going back to him." I see him lose his breath for a fraction of a second, and he reaches out as though he were going to touch my hand, but pulls back just an inch before our fingers make contact.

"Why would you drop the custody case?" he asks, his brow furrowing. "I saw you with Lilly and Aidan today. I know what they mean to you, how much you want to be with them. I know it was tough on you, but we had a strong day in court. I'm starting to think we might be able to actually win this thing."

I explain that I've realized that although being with the kids every day would be the greatest thing in my life, it would likely be the heartbreak of theirs. I love them, and I'll do anything I can to protect them. Even if that means giving them up.

"Maybe you don't have to give them up entirely," he suggests.

"What do you mean?"

"Will's attorney proposed a settlement after court today. We had a very good day on the stand, so they're starting to panic a bit. They're offering half the business assets, which is fair, plus the Sarasota house, and four weekends a year and two weeks every summer with Lilly and Aidan. I know you wanted full custody, so I didn't think you'd go for it, but the offer is still on the table."

"I could still see them, be a part of their lives." Sure, I'd be more like an aunt, but I'd get to see them regularly, without, you know, destroying their lives. I feel a sense of relief wash over me—this seems like a solution that could work out for all of us. And, frankly, now that she's back into the swing of full-time parenting, Gigi will probably be relieved to have a guaranteed babysitter a few times a year.

"Take the deal," I say. "I don't want to drag this out any longer."

"Okay," Holt replies. I head into the kitchen to get us a couple of beers from the icebox to celebrate, and Holt makes the call to Gigi and Will's attorney to accept their offer.

Ten minutes later my case is tentatively settled. Instead of another day of testifying about the sorry state of my (former) marriage, tomorrow we'll be signing papers. My emotions are a blue cocktail of melancholy, relief, and sorrow.

We take our beers outside and sit side by side on the porch swing. The rain has finally stopped, and the ocean is wild with the swell of the storm. We rock gently in the breeze, neither of us saying a word. One of the things I like about Holt is that it's incredibly easy to be with him, even when we're not doing or saying anything at all. Despite the fact that I'm hanging out with my divorce attorney in a fluffy pink bathrobe, I am remarkably at ease.

"Thank you for everything you've done," I say.

"It's been my pleasure, Darby, really," he says, his eyes picking up little bits of light reflected off the water. "I'm glad I could help."

We stare off at the beach in silence again, watching the waves crash on the shore. The breeze is starting to get chilly, and a tiny gust sends a shiver through my entire body.

"Are you cold?" Holt asks.

"Maybe I should put something else on."

"Stay where you are. Let me get you a blanket." He disappears into the house and returns with a quilt. It's funny that he picked that one. Jules has half a dozen chenille throws scattered throughout the guesthouse. But he chose the quilt. It is a favorite of mine, actually, the one my grandmother made for me when I was a kid. The squares are made from the fabric of old dresses of my mother and my aunts. There's even a piece of the fabric from my father's best-loved suit.

He wraps the quilt around me, tucking it under me. He sits right next to me and puts his arm around my shoulders.

"Better?" he asks.

"Much," I say. His arm around me feels, oddly, almost chaste. His other hand rests on the swing, and it becomes clear after a few minutes that he has no intention of putting the moves on me. Which is probably why I can't stop thinking about putting the moves on him.

Sitting here in the dark with him, snuggled under his arm, listening to him breathe, I can't stop thinking about the things he said to me the other night. And that kiss. He's such a gentleman; he's probably trying to give me the space I need after quite possibly the most stressful day on record, but my mind keeps wandering back to the other night on the beach.

Every part of me wants to kiss him right now—except my

brain, which is screaming that I should run in the other direction, or face certain doom.

My brain loses. I tilt my head back and rest it on the back of the porch swing, angling my face toward his. He is looking out at the ocean, but he moves his head down when he feels my breath against his throat.

"Darby," he says softly.

I free my hand from the blanket and press my finger against his bottom lip.

"I don't want to talk . . ." I say. For once, I don't want to think. I don't want to worry about tomorrow. I don't want to do anything but just be. My emotions are so raw; I'm weary and vulnerable from being strung out emotionally for so long. I'm just lonely and sad and relieved that this is all over, and I just want someone to hold me tonight.

He moves his face toward mine slowly, his eyes brimming with uncertainty. I grab the collar of his shirt gently and pull him toward me, bringing his mouth to mine. He kisses me hard, taking my breath away in the most delicious way. He plants kisses on my cheeks, my eyelids, my throat before pulling me into his lap, quilt and all. Our lips meet again, and we hungrily tear at each other's clothes. I slide my hands up under his T-shirt and they glide across his smooth, firmly muscled stomach and up his chest. The quilt drops to the ground, and despite the heat we are generating between the two of us, I begin to shiver in the chilly evening breeze. Holt scoops me up in his arms and carries me through the doorway and into the house.

"Bedroom is to the left," I say breathlessly, nuzzling his neck as he carries me through the house and sets me gently on the bed. We kiss for hours, making love. God, I'd almost forgotten what that was like; the marathon of newness, the thrill of exploring someone new for the first time. It is a first time like I've never experienced: Holt is tender and deeply passionate, and it's sweetly comfortable between us, without any of the usual first-time weirdness.

By three A.M., we are spent, finally, giggly and starving. Holt pulls on his jeans, digs through the refrigerator, and comes up with ingredients for omelets. We have just enough eggs, ham, tomatoes, and cheese to make a feast. As Holt cooks the eggs, I pour juice and take out silverware. I watch him fluffing the omelet with the spatula, looking pretty yummy himself, shirtless and barefoot, with the top of his jeans still unbuttoned. He catches me staring and smiles back; his dark curls are mussed and sexy. Wrapped in a sheet, I stand behind him while he finishes with the eggs, snaking my arms around his waist and tracing circles in the taut muscles on his stomach.

Later we're sitting cross-legged in bed, eating eggs and talking about everything under the moon, when Holt looks me directly in the eye, his face serious and contemplative. He pushes a strand of hair out of my face, wrapping the curl around his little finger.

"I'm going to ask the lawyer I mentioned earlier, John Mayoue, to sit in on the settlement conference tomorrow afternoon," he says. "And in the unlikely event the settlement deal falls through, he'll take over the case."

"What?" I sit up in the bed and pull the covers around me protectively.

"Darby, I thought I'd made it clear. I can't try this case if we're emotionally involved. And after tonight, we definitely are. Emotionally involved."

"And I thought I'd made it perfectly clear that I didn't want another attorney on this case. I don't even know this person!"

There's no way I can go through this whole nightmarish, soul-baring process again with somebody new. "I can't even think about this now."

The blood drains from his face. Clearly this was not the response he was expecting.

"What do you mean you can't think about this now? Didn't you give this any thought before we started? I mean, I'm crazy about you, Darby, the last thing I want to do is hurt you. But it's my job to protect your interests, and I can't do that if I have an emotional stake in the outcome of your case. Why are we even doing this if you're not sure?" Hurt is radiating from his face.

"I think you're so . . . great, it felt right, I'm sorry," I say quietly. *Damn it! I shouldn't have let myself jump into this without thinking it through to the end.* "Maybe it was a mistake to do this now. I don't know, I wondered if this thing between us would be as amazing as I thought it would be. I don't want to hurt you. I just—"

"You're sorry?" he says, sitting straight up in bed. "And now that you know, you're going to what? Run in the other direction?"

This was a mistake. He's my attorney and we're friends and I'm not ready and I never should have let myself get swept away like this.

"Holt, the more I'm with you, the more I want to be with you. I keep telling myself I can stop before I'm in too far over my head. The problem is, I don't know, maybe I'm already in over my head."

Holt stands up and begins to pace. "Darby, I want you to go into this with your eyes open. I don't want to be some habit you're trying to break. I think I'm falling in love with you."

"Holt, if I let myself fall in love with you, and something happens, I'll be alone again. You don't know what it's been like for me. I have to protect myself."

"If you *let* yourself fall in love with me? Darby, I didn't know that falling in love was something you could control," he says grimly. "But, I guess, if anybody can, it's you. Just give this some thought: You can run away from this amazing thing between us, and be with some safe, shallow guy instead. But remember that there's not a guarantee in the world that he won't sleep with your next-door neighbor or get mowed down by a crosstown bus on some random Tuesday. You can't protect yourself from everything. You simply can't."

"That's not fair. You know my history."

"Yes, I do, and I don't see how living in fear and trying to control everything so you can avoid getting hurt has helped you one little bit. Sometimes the best parts of life are the messiest, Darby. Maybe it's time to try something new. You *hand-picked* Will using your heartbreak-free system, and look where that got you." With that, he gathers up his things and pulls his shirt over his head. "I can promise you, I'll never break your heart like that."

I choke out, "No you can't." I can't protect myself with Holt, there's nothing I've held back. I'm terrified of letting myself go down this path, of losing control.

"I know this is a risk for you, but I'm asking you to take a chance."

"You just don't know—"

"I don't know about risk?" he says angrily. "How about this: I just risked the career I love, my ethics, my entire reputation to be with you. How's that for risk?"

"I'm sorry . . . I didn't think about it before we . . ."

My eyes sting with tears, and Holt looks exasperated. "I'm sorry, Darby."

I can't think how to respond, and a minute later he's quietly dressed and gone. I don't know how to solve this. After he's left, I sit in bed thinking about everything he said to me, inhaling his scent that lingers on my pillows. This is what happens the one time in my life when I don't analyze every possibility to death.

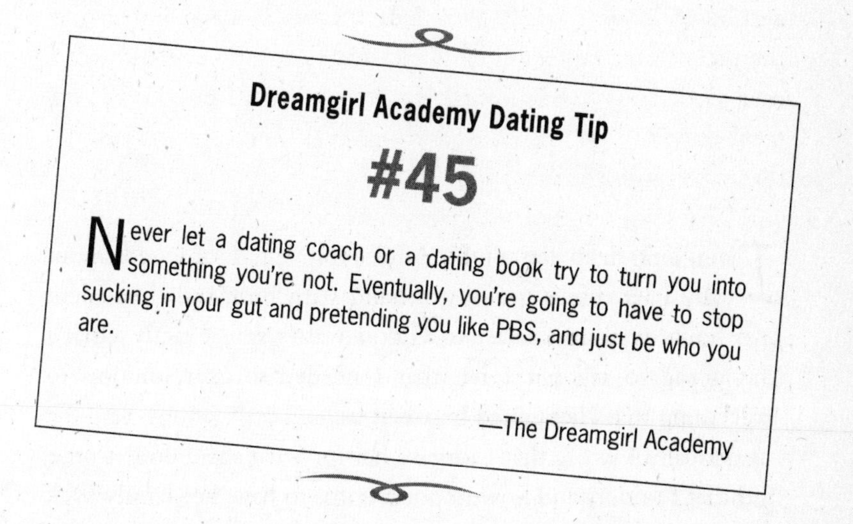

Dreamgirl Academy Dating Tip

#45

Never let a dating coach or a dating book try to turn you into something you're not. Eventually, you're going to have to stop sucking in your gut and pretending you like PBS, and just be who you are.

—The Dreamgirl Academy

Chapter 35

I couldn't sleep last night. After Holt left, I obsessed about why I let things get out of hand with him, and then spent two hours writing a letter to Gigi. I wasn't sure exactly what I was going to say, but I felt that I needed some resolution to everything that's happened between us.

Basically, I wrote that I forgave her for what she'd done to me, and that I understand how important it is to have her family back together, especially with a new baby on the way. Yes, she was awful to me, but there's something really healing for me about letting go of my anger and hurt feelings for her. If I look hard enough, I can find some empathy for her, some understanding of her choices. The letter was short; I wished Gigi, Will, and the children the best, and told her I harbored no ill feelings, and that I would do my best to make my visitation with the kids as stress-free and pleasant for everyone as possible.

This morning we signed the divorce settlement papers with little fanfare. Holt was all business, strangely distant, except for the odd nod or raised eyebrow in my direction. There was a brief moment in the middle of the meeting when our knees bumped under the table, and instead of pulling back, neither of us moved a muscle. Holt glanced at me across the table, the slightest hint of intrigue in his eyes. We stayed as we were, knees touching until I had to shift position to answer a question from the other attorney. I spent the rest of the meeting trying to orchestrate another accidental knee bump. No luck.

Gigi caught up to me after the settlement meeting, and we had the first real conversation we've ever had. I guess my letter to her really opened a door for us. She apologized for hurting me, and she thanked me for not pursuing full custody of Lilly and Aidan. She told me that I'm welcome to visit the kids anytime I'm in California, and that we can make whatever arrangements we need to for summer break. Gigi is a mother, too, and even though I've been harsh about that particular skill set of hers, she said something to me that was quite remarkable: She realized that the kids were missing me, probably in the way they missed her when she was gone, and to keep Lilly and Aidan away from me would only hurt them. She said she couldn't bear to break their hearts.

"I can't thank you enough for being there for Lilly and Aidan," said Gigi. "I know it cost you, but thank you for loving them."

I'd like to have come up with something snappy like "anytime," but, in all honesty, I just stood there smiling with tears streaming down my face. We set a date for me to come visit the kids next month.

I debated about whether to tell Gigi about Will's failed reconciliation attempt, and decided to keep my mouth closed. I'm sure Will really was torn between the two of us, and maybe now that I'm out of the picture he'll get himself together. I can't help but think there's a reason Will and Gigi keep connecting. I gave her a business card for a marriage workshop that I've heard is particularly effective in helping couples get past infidelity. I hope, for Lilly and Aidan's sake, that the two of them manage to pull it together.

There were half a dozen TV crews on the steps of the courthouse when I finally left, and they asked me for my comments on the proceedings, and how Will and Gigi have wrecked my life and killed my career (their words).

I looked smack into the camera lens and said, "I hope they find their way. I wish them all happiness, especially the kids. They're the greatest kids, and what's most important is that they have a lot of people who truly love them. I love you monkeys!"

Later in the afternoon Holland sent over my contract for *Dating the Dreamgirl.* The network wants to pick up the show for a full twenty-six episodes. Holland is, of course, anxious for me to sign, but I've decided to pass. My career is already back on track (sort of), and, frankly, there has to be a better way to revive my reputation. I don't want to waste another six months of my life on reality TV. I'd rather take my chances with plain old reality.

The one thing that the show has helped me to realize is that my reasons for becoming a dating coach had nothing to do with becoming famous. My goal has always been to help other women, and, somehow, I managed to get off track.

I don't need to be famous to help other women. I don't need a TV series or a radio show. I can accomplish something more important by speaking to women directly, the way I used to before all of this craziness started, at Dreamgirl Academies across the country. I can do what I love again; I can actually take the time to help women, and not just slap on an emotional Band-Aid in the ninety seconds before the commercial break. From now on, I'm thinking smaller, with truer intentions.

So, no more spin dating for me. No more celebrity fauxmances. No more staged first-date kisses in front of a cardboard door. From here on out, I'm only looking for the real thing.

That one little on-camera comment on the steps of the courthouse created an avalanche of supportive fan letters and Web postings, and all of a sudden I've become the icon for spurned wives, stepmothers, and humiliated, heartbroken women everywhere. Kendall tells me that media requests have been flooding her office, but now, instead of the "how-to" of happily every after, the topics everyone wants to talk to me about are empowerment, survival, and enduring public humiliation with grace.

I realize that what Holt said was right. I have lived my entire life in fear. It's understandable, of course, given my background. But everything I've done in my life to this point has been about controlling every foreseeable event in my relationships, always letting my brain pull rank on my emotions, and hedging my bets to ensure I wouldn't ever be hurt or abandoned again. As long as I can remember, I've put a lid on my emotions and thought my way through heartache. And it worked. Just not in the way I'd hoped.

But I've come to realize that playing it safe isn't really any safer at all. I kept thinking that if I could just make my life look perfect on the outside, the rest of it would fall into line; that if I could make myself *look* happy, I wouldn't be so lonely.

Holt was right, all my efforts didn't protect me from Will, and they didn't keep my heart from breaking over Lilly and Aidan. What have I been missing? I've always believed that if I followed a plan and picked the right person to marry, I would never have problems. Now, I realize everybody has problems. You can't script your whole life. You can't keep other people from getting sick, or dying in a freak accident, or falling in love with someone who isn't you.

Following relationship rules is like wearing a life vest in the water: They can help you to survive, and they can keep you from drowning if you have a tendency to panic or get yourself in too deep, too fast. But if you don't trust yourself to take it off sometimes and dive in without it, you'll never learn to swim in the deep end.

I've spent my whole life wearing a safety vest, and consequently, I think I may have sacrificed my every chance to experience the deepest depths of love.

You can't manufacture love by adhering to a plan. And I've missed out on a lot because it didn't fit within the context of the life I was trying so desperately to create.

I've learned that no amount of competence can make other people do what you want or need them to do, and that when it comes to matters of the heart, none of us are in complete control.

Chapter 36

Holt and I are back on the porch swing, sharing a bottle of pinot and listening to the waves. I asked him to stop by tonight, but I'm not sure I have the nerve to say what's been on my mind. I know what I need to do, and I've never been so nervous in my life. The connection between us is worth too much to throw away, but despite my better efforts, I cannot stop my brain from reminding me every minute: *I'm too vulnerable. It's too soon.*

My heart and brain are pulling me in two different directions: a tug-of-war between everything my soul wants and an overwhelming compulsion to do what I've always done—protect myself the best I can.

"I've been thinking about what you said the other night," I tell him.

For the past few days, I've been going back and forth in my mind: If I let things end between us the way they are now, I'll be heartbroken. And if I let myself love him, I'm terrified about leaving myself exposed. It hurt so much to lose Lilly and Aidan, my grandmother, my parents. I'm afraid to open myself up again.

I take a deep breath before I continue. *This is harder than I ever thought it would be.* "I just wanted to apologize. The other night, I didn't consider how what happened between us would put you in such a precarious professional position. I'm truly sorry. You're the best lawyer I've ever known, and I'd be a fool not to want you to represent me."

"It's fine, Darby," he says brusquely, as his face takes on a solemn cast.

"Holt," I say, exhaling nervous energy. "You're fired."

It takes a second for him to register what I've just said.

He rolls his eyes at me, and a quirky smile spreads slowly across his face. "Thanks. And after all I've done for you, too."

Our eyes meet and I smile at him. "I didn't know my heart ran this deep until I met you. If it weren't for Lilly and Aidan, I never would have allowed you to dig so far into my soul. Letting you see me for who I really am has been one of the scariest experiences of my life, but it's also been the most liberating. I don't want to go back to what I was before. I can't keep living in fear, or I'll never be part of anything real again."

Holt smiles back at me, his eyes warm and melting.

Pausing to take another breath, I gather up my courage. "I think I could love you, too."

For the first time in my life, I'm letting my heart overrule my head—including every terrifying, heart-crushing, run-the-other-direction scenario it can expel.

I've decided to take the risk with Holt—not for the manufactured chick-flick version of "happily ever after" I've been scripting all my life, but for real love, right now. If I'm ever going to experience the depths of all-out, hold-nothing-back love, I have to be brave enough to let it in.

"Really?" he asks.

"Really," I say.

I gently touch the dimple on his cheek, then burrow my way under his arm.

I tilt my face up to meet his and he leans down slowly until our lips touch, just barely, sending shivers all the way down to my toes. His kiss is tentative at first, and then he sweeps me into his arms and kisses me longingly.

"Do what you will with my heart, darlin', it's all yours," he says with a laugh, warming me with that sweet Southern drawl.

"All mine? What kind of divorce attorney says stuff like that?" I tease. He smiles and traces my cheek with his finger.

"What if you're wrong?" I ask.

His expression turns serious.

"I'm not wrong," he whispers, his kiss lingering on my forehead. "We both know I'm not."

With that, I can feel the last piece of the dam in my heart break free, sending a torrent of emotions, fears, hopes, and love flowing over me. And instead of the terror of being carried away, I can finally feel myself floating.

In the past, I would have talked myself out of this relationship before it ever started, knowing how vulnerable I am, how much I stand to lose. But when I let go of the fear that has driven me all of my life, I can feel in every cell of my body that Holt and I were meant to be. And sometimes, letting your heart lead the way can be the smartest decision you ever make.

Acknowledgments

My Fifteen Minutes in Print

I am so thankful to all of the people who made *Fifteen Minutes of Shame* into a year of near bliss.

As much as we authors claim otherwise, books are rarely created by some lone wordsmith, hacking away at the computer at three in the morning. There are so many people who have contributed to this book in some way. (And hopefully, I won't forget to mention any of them.) So at the risk of sounding like an overenthusiastic soap opera actress who's just won her first Emmy, I'd like to say thank you to my friends, idols, and colleagues:

My sweet, charming, and insightful husband, Tom, the love of my life. And to my babies, Quinn and Elle, for being hilarious and inspiring, and, most of all, mine; for being patient and not complaining about another night of spaghetti (okay, who doesn't love spaghetti) when I was on deadline. My mom for her unwavering support and enthusiasm, even when I called her up and said, "I love you dearly, but I'm going to have to kill off the mom."

Our family, the original Dreamgirls, and to the women who inspire me, make me laugh, and mix a mean batch of guacamole: my aunt Jerry and Mary, Steph, Lizzy, and Cassie, all of the Parks Women past, present, and future.

The John Grisham Coffee Club (otherwise known as Mid-listers Anonymous) for making life as an author possible for extreme extroverts:

Lisa Earle (or not to Earle) McLeod, my dearest friend, my frequent and favorite writing partner, and author of *Forget Perfect, Finding Grace When You Can't Even Find Clean Underwear,* and the book that will change the world, *Triangle of Truth*. I take full credit for all of her best work, as she, rightfully, takes full credit for mine. Thanks to our husbands (and children) for being so patient with our nine-calls-a-day phone habit.

The hilarious Michael Alvear, my favorite TV star, and Susan Harrow, media coaching genius who's turned me into a sound-bite maven and has me prepped and ready to roll for *Oprah*. (Just in case they were wondering.)

Many, many thanks to celebrity family attorney John C. Mayoue, of Warner, Mayoue, Bates & Nolen in Atlanta, author of *Balancing Competing Interests in Family* and *Stepping in the Parent—The Legal Rights of Stepparents* for his endless patience in explaining legal and ethical issues, and for giving me a living, breathing example of Southern charm and legal prowess.

The legal issues I managed to get right are entirely to his credit, but any errors are all mine.

Real-life Sarasota society photographer Laura North. And the reigning queen of Sarasota gossip, society columnist Marjorie North. Anyone who's ever met either of you would know you'd have sprung Darby from the kitchen yourselves.

My fabulous agent, Lorraine Kisly, for being such an extraordinary supporter. My publisher and former editor, the brilliant Trena Keating, who gets it. A million thanks to my wonderful editor, Allison Dickens, whose passion for her work made mine infinitely better. (Hey, that's not a spatula.) And thanks to a woman with vision, Cherise Davis.

Marie Coolman for her big thinking, Nadia Kashper and the rest of the Plume team for their enthusiasm and hard work. Thanks to my TV family at *Daytime*—Cyndi, Dave, Lindsay, Coleen, Marci, Jen, April, Rob, the other Rob, Jill, EJ, Ben, PJ, Chip, Larry, Sam, and resident mystery man, Steve—you guys are great. Big thanks to the crew, you're the best! And thanks to Kim Hughes for her support, talent, and vision.

Matt Lauer (who's never met me and probably doesn't have a clue I exist), whose eye-crinkle during the "you don't know the history of psychiatry" segment inspired the entire *Today* show scene.

Andrea Smith for her invaluable help and her producer's-eye view into news shows vs. entertainment shows.

The brilliant Eric Straus and the whole PreDating team. Thanks to the TR girls: Susan, Heidi, Seanna, Angela, Rebecca, Jennifer, Tessa, Laura, Iris, and all the rest, the biggest reason why Sarasota is the most fabulous place we've ever lived. Thanks to Teresa Tapp, who got me in shape for my book tour after four months of M&M's and Cheetos. Thanks to Miss Patty, who feels like a member of the family and made it possible for me to write and be a mom at the same time. Thanks to Melanie, bestselling author-to-be, for answering my calls and taking care of the details.

And last, thanks to my readers, and the thousands of self-made Dreamgirls and Dreamgirls-in-training who have written or shown up to Dreamgirl Academy events—I thank you from the bottom of my heart. You are the reason I do what I do, and I'm pulling for each and every one of you.

Don't Miss Dating Tips from
Lisa Daily

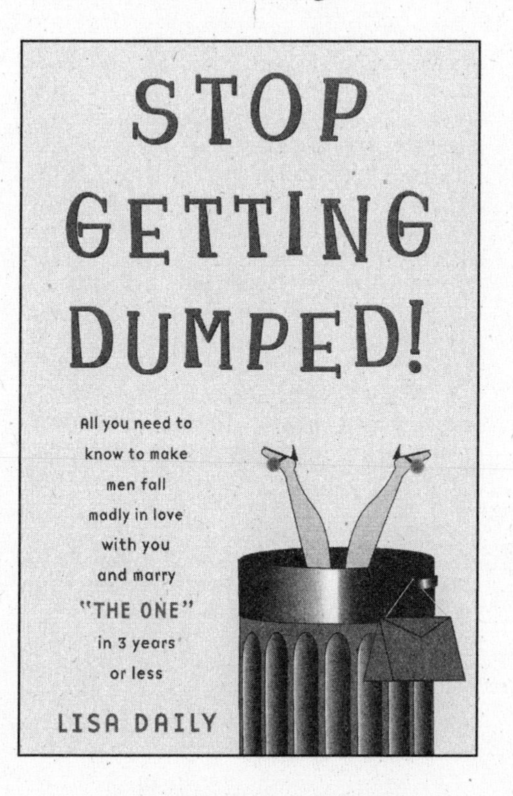

ISBN 978-0-452-28383-1

www.lisadaily.com

Available wherever books are sold.

Plume
A member of Penguin Group (USA) Inc.
www.penguin.com